Next Year I'll Be Perfect

Laura Kilmartin

Laura Kilmartin (signature)

booktrope

Booktrope Editions
Seattle WA 2012

Cover Design by Greg Simanson

Edited by Nikki Van De Car

*This is a work of fiction. Names, characters, places, brands, media, and
incidents are either the product of the author's imagination or are used
fictitiously. Any resemblance to similarly named places or to persons living
or deceased is unintentional.*

PRINT ISBN 978-1-935961-72-7
EPUB ISBN 978-1-62015-076-4

For further information regarding permissions, please contact
info@booktrope.com.

Library of Congress Control Number: 2012948692

Acknowledgments

As is true for most of my successes in life, this book would not have been possible without the love and support of my family: My parents Michael and Anne Kilmartin and my sister Catherine Krusiec. "Thank you" does not begin to cover the encouragement I drew from their unyielding belief that I would someday be a published novelist.

I am also fortunate to have a life full of people who inspire me and make me laugh on a daily basis: The Nantucket Girls; The Boston Girls; my close friends from Westbrook High School, St. Michael's College and The University of Maine School of Law; my Stonecoast pals; and my work family.

Thank you to Tess Hardwick and Tracey Hansen for their book, Write for the Fight: A Collection of Seasonal Essays that introduced me to the incredible world of Booktrope Publishing and all of the wonderful people I've met there including Kenneth Shear, Katherine Sears and Heather Ludviksson.

I owe special thanks to Nikki Van De Car who edited my book and in doing so made it so much better. She was able to say in a very nice way, "I think your characters are probably doing something during the seven pages of dialogue without any action. You might want to share what's going on in your head with the rest of the class…" Thanks also go to Cathy Shaw who proofread the final version and Greg Simanson who designed the book cover of my dreams.

Finally, a gigantic thank-you goes out to Kara Mann who managed the entire book publication process. She shared my vision, spoke my language and - most of all - kept me from going off the deep end.

—Laura Kilmartin

September

I SCRAPED THE LAST BARNACLES of peanut butter frosting from the edge of the cake pan and surveyed the disaster that had once been my kitchen. Plates drowned in messy blobs of ice cream, loosely crumpled wrapping paper strewn about the room, and two absurd lumps of wax shaped loosely like a "2" and a "9" were all that remained of the night's celebration.

My twenty-ninth birthday.

Reeling from the frightening fact this would be the last birthday I would celebrate in my twenties – and perhaps just a bit from the vodka tonics – I picked up the candles that had been set aflame just a few hours earlier and flung them one after the other into the sink where they landed with a satisfying "plunk".

My hand poised ready at the garbage disposal switch, I wondered when I had graduated from a package of cute little pastel candles to these chunky monstrosities. At what age did society decide that the sheer volume of my years on earth became a violation of the fire code?

"Twenty-one."

Startled, I turned toward my friend Livvie, so silent in her inspection of my birthday loot that I'd forgotten she was still in the room. "What?"

"I'm answering your question. Twenty-one."

Whoops. I hadn't realized I'd asked it aloud.

But since I had…

"Okay, I'll bite. Why 'twenty-one'?"

Livvie rose, and knowing she had my attention, took her time fishing a bottle of Sam Adams out of the fridge and taking a long pull before explaining, "There are twenty little pastel candles in every box. No one buys more than one box at a time, so by the time you hit twenty-one, you've got to figure out another way of lighting up your cake."

Oh.

"And take those candles out of the sink," she demanded. "You'll clog up the disposal."

Livvie DiMarco. The person in my life responsible for holding my hair back after a rough night out on the town, for making sure my shoes matched my purse, for knowing just when to bring over a pint of ice cream, was now apparently also responsible for keeping my plumbing bills to a minimum.

Livvie had accepted these roles of questionable distinction along with the title of "Sarah Bennett's Best Friend" shortly after we met six years ago at Maine Law School's new-student reception. I had been twenty-three years old, lingering near the entrance to the classroom in my floral Laura Ashley skirt and powder-blue twin set, not quite ready to join the other young professional wannabes milling about when she spotted me.

For reasons still unknown, but to my eternal gratitude, Livvie trotted her five-foot Mary Lou Retton frame over, thrust out her hand and said, "Olivia DiMarco. My friends call me Livvie." Then, thrusting a hip against the door frame and crossing her arms across her chest, she studied the room and muttered, "Jesus, why would anyone in their right mind want to be a lawyer, anyway? What the hell were we thinking?"

Voicing the very question that had been churning through my thoughts, I handed my new friend a cup of warm punch and responded, "No idea."

A bond of friendship was forever sealed over bad punch and expletives, thus explaining why Livvie was the last soul remaining at my birthday party, stealthily trying to clean up the place without my noticing.

"Hey," I blurted, trying to draw my friend's attention away from the plates and cups she was beginning to clear. "I was just thinking about the day we met. Can you imagine if you'd struck up a conversation with someone else? Like Ellie Stanton or Donna Cross? You might be best friends with one of them right now and eating their birthday cake."

"Couldn't happen." Livvie sat, picking at the remnants of her own slice of cake. "First: I'm convinced that Ellie doesn't actually eat. Can't have that body and still consume food."

She had a point. In the three years of law school and four years since graduation, I'd never actually seen Ellie eat. Whenever I envied how amazing she looked in a pair of tight jeans, I thought of peanut butter cake frosting, and how I could have it, and she never could. My roomy, size twelve jeans seemed a small price to pay for that kind of happiness.

"Donna probably does eat," Livvie allowed, "but only sandwiches. She's too dumb to figure out which end of the fork to pick up. Nope. For better or worse, you're it."

Aww. That was the sweetest thing Livvie ever said to me.

"Of course, when you were standing there on the first day of classes looking like Miss Beedle, the Walnut Grove school marm, I didn't realize what a pain in my ass you were going to be."

Now *that* was the affection I was used to.

"Speaking of which…" My friend leapt from the kitchen stool which, along with its twin and a low counter composed my apartment's tiny dining space, and reached for her purse. "I almost forgot. I have a present for you."

"You already gave me my present." I protested, pointing to the DVD sets for the final two seasons of Gilmore Girls, completing my collection of the entire television series.

"Yeah, well, this isn't really a present from me," she said, thrusting an envelope toward me. "I'm just the messenger."

"Who is it from?" I asked, taking the well-worn paper from her hand. I exchanged birthday presents with a very small circle of friends, and they had already all been accounted for. Looking closer, I startled slightly. My name was written in a very familiar handwriting.

My own.

"What is this, Livvie?"

I actually flinched at the wicked grin I received, knowing from experience that the events it heralded could range from drunk-dialing ex-boyfriends to Class E misdemeanors.

"Do you remember your twenty-fifth birthday?"

"Some of it," I answered honestly, as what I did remember was wrapped in a haze of tequila, limes, salt, and an unfortunate chaser of chocolate milkshake. We had been a month into our third and final year of law school when I hit that milestone, and a bunch of us went out for a huge Mexican dinner. At that time most of my friends were law students, and we were all either living on student loan checks or handouts from Daddy, so most social events revolved around Pay-per-view movies, frozen pizza, and a box of wine. An actual sit-down dinner made an impression. "But what does this letter have to do with my twenty-fifth birthday—"

Uh oh.

Just as the question left my lips, a memory flashed, revealing the contents of the benign-looking envelope and filling me with a certain dread. After my birthday dinner, the evening had ended as most parties did back then: in the living room of my apartment where my friends and I would talk, drink, and dream about the future.

"This isn't…"

"Oh yes it is." Livvie sing-songed back at me.

I dropped the envelope on the counter and scooted my stool backward, as if the slight physical distance might protect me.

"Oh, come on, Sarah. It's funny."

"If this is the letter I think it is, there's nothing funny about it at all." I snagged a spoon from one of the dirty plates littering my kitchen and ignored Livvie's wrinkled nose of disgust as I staggered to the freezer. Just as I'd hoped, a full pint of Chunky Monkey was wedged behind several freezer bags of broccoli and a large box of vegetarian breakfast sausage.

I briefly toyed with the idea of pulling out the ice cream scoop and a bowl to measure out my portion, but discarded the idea almost immediately. Nope. This letter Livvie had handed me, and the implications of its contents, called for diving in face first.

Which I did.

"Get over here, Sarah."

"Mmmmph mmmanaaa."

"I don't care that you 'don't wanna.'" Livvie rolled her eyes. "For God's sake, get your ass over here."

Never one to react well to a direct order, I instead planted my feet more firmly and took another enormous spoonful of ice cream.

Ow. Brain freeze.

Recognizing her mistake immediately, my friend sighed and held her hands in surrender. "You are a lot of work, kid. Fine. Please sit down. Please read the letter. Please let me out of this stupid obligation I've had hanging over my head for the last four years."

Direct orders may not work on me, but I rarely ignored the frustrated plea of my best friend. Putting Ben & Jerry back in the freezer, I slunk over to the counter and again picked up my dreaded "present." Flipping over the envelope, I read the words, "To be delivered by Olivia Margaret DiMarco at her discretion" written in my friend's large, loopy script over the seal.

"So, why did you decide to give me this now? Why not wait until next year?"

"Please." Livvie dismissed my question with a derisive snort. "Next year, when you actually turn thirty, I'm going to have you on suicide watch. Do you really think it's a good idea to hand you this letter then?"

"Probably not." I admitted. Hoping to stall another minute or two, I tapped the envelope on the table. "Hey, Livvie, remember that time when…"

"For the love of God, Sarah. Please just open it already so we can finish cleaning up." She nodded her chin toward the envelope.

Unable to stall further, I ripped open the envelope. It, and the paper it contained were both a cream-colored, heavy bond. Resume-quality. I vividly remembered the trip to Staples the spring of my first year of law school when I'd purchased the paper, envelopes and even a new ink cartridge for my printer. Competition for summer internships had been fierce, so I pulled out all the stops to make a favorable first impression on potential employers.

I was thrilled when my efforts paid off and I was offered a summer job at the largest law firm in Portland. I was less than thrilled, though, when I realized the job entailed copying files, scheduling meetings and fetching coffee.

As much as I tried to convince myself, I'd found it difficult to believe that Atticus Finch had started his career picking up his boss' daughter at day care when a deposition ran late.

Months later, when the job had ended and my birthday rolled around again, I knew a few sheets remained from my stash of good paper. After dinner, while my friends waited patiently, I ransacked my bedroom closet to find it. I had set in my mind that an important letter must be written on important paper.

And an important letter it was. Finally finding the courage to smooth out its folds, I read its contents for the first time in four years while Livvie stood over my shoulder, doing the same.

> I, Sarah Jackson Bennett, being of mildly inebriated (but sound) mind and body do hereby swear before God and these witnesses that by the time I reach thirty years of age, I will have accomplished the following:
>
> 1. Be happily married
> 2. Fit into a size six purple suede miniskirt
> 3. Be partner at a law firm
> 4. See Bruce Springsteen in concert
> 5. Sleep with George Clooney (preferably before #1, but if not, make it a condition of the pre-nup)
> 6. Own my own home
> 7. Visit Jimmy Stewart's star on the Hollywood Walk of Fame
> 8. Climb Mt. Katahdin
>
> *Sarah Jackson Bennett, aged 25*
> Witness: *Ryan James Corruchi, aged 27*
> Witness: *Olivia Margaret DiMarco (age withheld)*

"A purple suede miniskirt?" Livvie grabbed the paper and feigned inspection of the date. "I'm sorry, did you make this list in 1987?"

"Hey, we live in Maine, not Milan. Excuse me if fashion comes a little late to some parts of the world." I joked, searching for a reason for such a ridiculous goal. "Wait! Don't you remember?

"PATTY KELSNIK!!!" We shouted simultaneously, collapsing into laughter.

"Oh, that terrible purple suede miniskirt she used to wear when we went dancing on Fore Street," Livvie could see it clearly.

"I thought she was the coolest thing on two legs and wanted to look just like her."

Livvie rolled her eyes. "Oh, please. Patty wasn't even a real person. She cut a picture out of Vogue magazine and handed it over to her plastic surgeon when she turned eighteen. You forget: Patty was a rich girl from the O.C. who came to Maine Law because the skiing was good."

Livvie was probably right, but I didn't care. I could still remember the way every head turned when Patty walked into the dance club wearing that miniskirt, and even today I could only imagine how amazing it would feel to cause that reaction.

I glanced down at my size twelve hips, well on their way to a fourteen after the amount of cake I'd eaten. Clearly the sight of me in a purple suede miniskirt would cause quite a reaction, and likely not the one I was looking for. As much as I hated to admit it, short of modifying my kitchen to zap me with an electric current every time I opened my refrigerator, hitting size six in twelve months was... well...*unlikely*.

And I hadn't even considered the challenge of finding a decent purple suede skirt.

I hopped down from my stool once more and crossed the kitchen to the refrigerator. Hidden amongst the wedding invitations, baby announcements and coupons for Lean Cuisine stuck to the door, I located the "skinny" picture of myself I kept taped there for inspiration.

"Look at this!" I thrust the photo at Livvie. "This is the thinnest I've ever been and it was still only a size ten! Sixteen years old at the Junior Prom with Mark Llewelyn. God, I'm depressed. I can't believe you showed me that letter."

"Get a grip, Sarah. I obviously didn't do it to depress you. I thought this would be fun!"

"Are you kidding? Take a look! All this does is show me how far away I am from where I thought I'd be. When I wrote this, I was practically living with Ryan, and was absolutely convinced he was

The One. I had it all planned out. We were going to graduate law school, get married, buy a house and be wildly successful attorneys who climbed mountains, went to concerts and travelled the world."

"And who apparently let each other sleep with celebrities."

"Shut up, Livvie."

I had a sudden desire to travel back in time and slap my optimistic, ignorant 25-year old self and report that "The One" was now commonly referred to as "That Rat Bastard". Worse even, in the four years since Ryan and I had broken up, finding a man with potential had been as rare as finding a Lifetime movie with a plot that didn't revolve around Tori Spelling in peril. Actually, my dating history resembled the synopsis of a bad sitcom or a Cathy cartoon.

"Oh, God." My head thunked on the counter as I realized that even Cathy the cartoon was married.

And cancelled.

Livvie dragged the edges of my hair away from the ice cream puddle where they had landed. "Stop thinking about Ryan."

"I'm not thinking about Ryan," I sighed. "I'm thinking about Irving." I lifted my head reluctantly from the table.

"Irving? Who's Irving?"

"Cathy's husb—never mind." I focused again on the list in front of me. "God, Livvie. Can you believe that four years ago I was close enough to a size six to even consider it a reasonable target? And look at this: a partner at a firm. Jesus, I was a dreamer."

"Before you sink too deep into the pit of despair, don't forget that you also thought you could sleep with George Clooney. Thus, it's possible that when you wrote this list, you were doing tequila shots like they were going out of style, my dear. Don't make more of this than it is."

"Well, we did see Springsteen last year," I mumbled, slightly mollified at the thought of being able to mark one of my goals as completed.

"True! And don't forget that when you, David, and Eddie took that trip to San Francisco last year you forced them to rent a car and drive you to Hollywood. You've got the stupid picture of you standing next to Jimmy Stewart's star sitting on your desk at work."

Good point, but one that made me feel even sadder for some reason. Being a freakish fan of movies, television, and all things celebrity, I had felt much like Scarlett O'Hara coming home to Tara when my friends and I took that side trip to Hollywood.

"Are you thinking about *Gone With the Wind*?"

"No."

"Right."

"Look at me, Livvie. I'm fat, single, and working at a one horse operation—"

Livvie rolled her eyes. "Stop. You love your job and you're not fat. I will admit that you're single, but correct me if I'm wrong, you were single yesterday and there was nothing wrong with it then."

"I was twenty-eight yesterday," I whined.

"And I'm thirty-seven! And divorced. It doesn't bother me."

"Of course it doesn't bother you. You're blonde, perky, and adorable. If you had a golden retriever, you'd be a walking LL Bean catalog cover." I touched the paper in my hands, contemplating the list again in the new light cast by desperation. "If I just tweak some of these items, I bet I can still make it."

"Make it? Make what?" I saw the moment realization dawned in Livvie's eyes. "God, Sarah, it's a silly joke. It's not actually a to-do list!"

"Why not? You've seen me accomplish some pretty impossible goals in the seven years we've known each other, and passing the bar exam doesn't even make the top ten. Have you forgotten the orange turtleneck sweater I knit in three days so I could go to a Halloween party dressed as Velma from Scooby-Doo? How about that dinner party I threw based entirely on Spam, eggs, and cheese fondue?"

"Sarah, sweetie, I love you, but that dinner was disgusting." She wagged her finger at me. "You may not want to count that among your great accomplishments."

Itchy to get started on my new plan, I grabbed the cake pan and proceeded to dump the remnants in the trash bin under the sink.

One small step for man, and all that.

Turning back to my friend, her mouth agape at my willful and unprecedented destruction of chocolate, I replied, "Piffle. Why can't I do this? You've always told me I can do anything I set my mind to!"

"I'm sorry, but did you just say piffle? How many drinks did you let Eddie pour you tonight, anyway?" Running her hands through her hair, Livvie tried to reason with me. "Look, there are certain things no one can accomplish, not even you."

I refused to respond or even make eye contact. Petulance was one of my favorite flavors.

"Come on, Sarah, just look at the list. The first item is, 'Be happily married'. Do you really believe even you can be happily married within a year?" Livvie's words lingered in the air even as she went to the living room to put in a new CD.

Happy that I didn't have to meet my friend's eyes, I chewed my lip in deep thought. I had to admit, as much as it pained me, that meeting a man, dating, getting him to propose and planning my dream wedding within a year might be a bit…let us say…*challenging*.

Still, though, there was something so heartbreaking about giving up on the goals I'd set for myself. Just four years earlier I'd believed that each and every item on this list was possible (so maybe the George Clooney item was a result of the tequila, but still…) I glanced at the hopeful handwriting of my younger self once more and seriously considered whether I had been an idiot, or just a better person than I was now.

And could I be that person – that hopeful person – again?

I straightened my posture. "Hey, Livvie?"

"Seriously, the apartment will smell like your brother's place if we don't clean tonight."

"Wait, Livvie," I touch her arm. She looked at me, her eyes already knowing my mind. "I think I can do this. I mean, I admit the list might need a few modifications—"

"Modifications?" Her eyes narrowed as she leaned toward me.

"God. Don't ever cross examine me, Ms. Assistant District Attorney. This isn't a plot. Just some simple modifications. For instance, I agree I'm probably not going to get married by next September. I could probably be in a happy relationship by then, though, couldn't I?"

I rushed over to the kitchen junk drawer, rummaged through the batteries and Chinese food menus until I triumphantly pulled out a pen. I scratched out the reference to marriage and replaced it with relationship.

"I mean that's possible, right? That I can be in a happy relationship by the time I'm thirty?"

God help me, it had to be possible.

"Yes," she agreed warily. "That's possible, I suppose."

Livvie leaned over my shoulder as we reviewed the list again. "What's with owning your own home? You have a great apartment. I didn't even know you wanted to buy a house."

"I'm going to be thirty next year. There's no reason I should still be sponging off my family in a cramped apartment."

Even as I spoke, I knew I was just being contrary faced with Livvie's resistance to my new (ahem, old) goals. In all honesty, my friend was right – I did have a great apartment, and I paid a fair rent to my Uncle who doubled as my landlord. However, the location was less than ideal as I occupied the second story of the building that housed the family diner where I still pulled as many shifts as possible with my busy schedule at the firm. While it was cozy being so close to the family I loved, the lack of privacy could also be stifling at times. I had squirreled away a small, but reasonable sum in my savings account, and there was no reason it couldn't be put to use as a down payment if I found the right property.

"Fine. I'll give you a happy relationship within a year and even a new house if you want one. But you aren't going to be able to manipulate the rest of the items quite so easily. Did you look at the one about being a partner in a Portland law firm? That's going to be mighty tough to accomplish since you're currently working for a sole practitioner who doesn't *want* any partners."

I pointed my pen at my friend. "Wrong! I work for a sole practitioner who doesn't *have* any partners. We don't know that he doesn't *want* any partners. I could still reach this goal in a year."

Livvie's left eyebrow rose in disbelief. "Do you really think Frank Murphy is going to make you partner? There is no way Frank would ever share top billing in his firm."

"You never know until you ask. Who knows – maybe Frank is ready to share the load. I mean, I've worked for him since I passed the bar. None of his other associates lasted more than six months. I must be doing something right."

"You're out of your mind, Sarah. If you start pushing Frank for partnership you might just find yourself out on the streets with no job at all. Besides," Livvie said, folding her arms across her chest and leaning her hip against the counter. "What with losing weight, getting a boyfriend, buying a house and screwing George Clooney this year, you'll probably be a little busy. Why not push off your professional accomplishments until next year?"

"I was planning to cross off the George Clooney item." I replied, starting to get annoyed at the levity with which my friend was treating my newly established life plan. "Now you're just mocking me."

"Of course I'm mocking you. You hate getting up from the chair to change the TV channel manually and this silly list has you climbing the tallest mountain in Maine."

"You've climbed Mt. Katahdin." I challenged. "Are you saying you can do it, but I can't?"

I could see in her eyes that Livvie knew she was treading into very dangerous territory.

"Sarah, I trained to climb that mountain. Started on some intermediate trails, smaller mountains. I went to the rock climbing wall when the weather was bad. Please, please don't take this the wrong way, but I work out on a regular basis." She pushed her hair back behind her ears, Livvie's only nervous tic, and one I'd seen her evoke only a dozen or so times during our friendship. "You...Well, you don't."

"It's okay, Livvie." I nodded, agreeing with my friend. "You're right. I don't work out. There is no way I could climb a mountain now. It doesn't make any sense."

"Well thank you." Livvie smiled, glad that I had finally seen things her way.

"But by next year I'll be in great shape. If I'm going to be a size six, I'll have to start hitting the gym more often. Maybe I'll even go to the rock wall with you. It'll be fine. Don't worry."

"Sarah!"

"What?"

"You're saying that over the next twelve months you want to change everything about yourself – your professional life, your body, your romantic life, your hobbies – everything! Why would you want to change everything about you?"

I took a moment, pretending for Livvie's benefit to give the matter a great deal of thought. It wasn't necessary, though, as I knew my reasoning before my friend had even posed the question.

"Because I'm not who I want to be. Isn't that reason enough?"

"You're gonna listen to a letter?"

"No." I tapped my finger on the signature line of the letter. "I'm gonna listen to myself."

Silent for a moment, Livvie held out her hand. "Alright then, let's take another look."

I handed over the slightly messy, marked-up list and ran around the counter to stand over my friend's shoulder to read:

I, Sarah Jackson Bennett, being of mildly inebriated (but sound) mind and body do hereby swear before God and these witnesses that by the time I reach thirty years of age, I will have accomplished the following:

1. Be ~~happily married~~ in an amazing relationship
2. Fit into a size six purple suede miniskirt
3. Be partner at a law firm
4. ~~See Bruce Springsteen in concert~~ (Done!)
5. ~~Sleep with George Clooney (preferably before #1, but if not, make it a condition of the pre-nup)~~
6. Own my own home
7. ~~Visit Jimmy Stewart's star on the Hollywood Walk of Fame~~ (Done!)
8. Climb Mt. Katahdin

Do-able, I thought, nodding my head. Very, very do-able.

And it would all start tomorrow.

October

"SEE YOU NEXT WEEK, STAN. Now button up your coat. It's getting cold out there."

I ushered Stan Walker – one of the regular patrons of my family's diner – to the front door as quickly as his bum hip would allow. With a quick glance at the Mickey Mouse clock on the wall to confirm what the empty diner already told me, I engaged the lock with a satisfying click and drew down the shade on the glass window. Sarge's Diner was officially closed for business and my Saturday shift was over.

Working weekends, holidays and early mornings at the family diner had played a huge role in supporting me through law school as I survived on leftover meatloaf and tips. Even now, at a time when I valued my free time even more than the diner's free coffee, I continued to work Saturdays whenever possible.

It was only right, after all, given that the diner was my father's idea in the first place. "Uncle" Jeremy Thornton and my father Edgar Bennett had been best friends and partners on the Portland police force for twenty years. Bored to tears after about two weeks of retirement, Dad convinced Jeremy to hock their gold watches and purchase a small diner located on the ground floor of the building where I now rented an apartment, and Sarge's Diner was born.

When Dad died two years ago, Jeremy made me a silent partner over my not-so-silent protests that the diner should instead belong fully to him and his two sons. After several negotiations where we each claimed to know what my father would have wanted, I finally agreed to share in the meager profits, but only if allowed to also share in the work.

It was an arrangement that worked well most of the time, the only exceptions being rare days like this one when I was left to close up alone. Before I could wallow too deeply in missing my makeshift family's cheerful chaos, though, I jumped at the piercing tone of the phone at my elbow. The ringer volume was set on high for the noisy diner crowd, but sounded like a scantily-clad coed auditioning for the next Friday the 13th movie when heard in an empty room.

"Sarge's Diner, may I help you?"

"Hi, Dad." I immediately recognized the sarcastic words of Jeremy's oldest son David. "Gosh, you don't sound quite like yourself today."

"Very funny, Thornton! What's up?"

"I wanted to talk to Dad. I can usually catch him when you guys are locking up. Is he there?"

I shook my head as if my friend could actually see the gesture. "Nope. Jeremy took the day off to take your brother to the airport. His flight back to Cozumel leaves Boston in about an hour."

"Poor Eddie." David chuckled, sympathizing with his brother's plight. The drive from Portland to Boston should normally take two hours, but with Uncle Jeremy at the wheel, the trip could easily take three or more. The man was still an old school police officer at heart, and one of his most endearing and infuriating traits was his failure to go even one mile per hour over the posted speed limit.

"You said things were going okay when we talked last week. How were they getting along when they left?"

"Do you mean, 'were they openly fighting?'" I scraped a fleck of dried pancake batter from the hem of my shirt. "Nah, no bloodshed yet. Although, when Eddie found out your father was driving him to the airport instead of me, I thought he was going to make a break for it. He had the same sad look on his face as Clyde when we took him to the vet."

"Why didn't you take him? Wasn't that the plan?"

"That was Eddie's plan. The minute Jeremy found out he had an opportunity of a captive audience for his thousandth recital of the 'Stop Wasting Your Life and Go to College' lecture, I was unceremoniously dumped as the family chauffeur and got solo diner duty instead."

While carrying on my conversation with David, I was simultaneously bustling around the diner in an effort to clean up as quickly as possible. My pace slowed automatically when it came time to retrieve the porcelain cream and sugar set laid out on the counter among the cheap silver napkin dispenser and plastic container of straws.

Jeremy hated the fact my father used my mother's wedding china alongside the rest of the diner's heavy-duty, chipless, crackless dinnerware and was sure they'd be knocked to the ground someday and shatter – my father's heart along with them. My dad just tut-tutted his friend and reminded him, "Anna used her best china every single day of our married life. She never understood people who kept their most beautiful things in a box on the shelf. If she were here, she'd insist we use her best dishes, and I never could say 'no' to that woman."

It turned out my father was right. As if recognizing it's value, burly truckers and shaky seniors alike all seemed to take reverent care when using the fragile cream and sugar set and Jeremy's worst fears were never realized. I was glad as I agreed with my father that fine things should be used, not hidden away. If not for its use in the diner, my mother's china would only have been enjoyed for a total of four years – two before my birth and two after.

The spring before I turned three, she and Jeremy's wife Connie had been hit broadside by a drunk driver as they returned home from a night out with the girls. Both women were killed instantly, leaving their grieving widowers – already best friends and partners on the police force – to raise their now-blended family of three children.

Eddie and I had been so young that we barely understood the change in family dynamics. All we'd ever known was a family of two fathers and siblings mingled together so that those of blood and those of choice were indistinguishable. David, though, had been old enough to register the seismic shift when his mother was taken away so suddenly. Whenever I took the time to reflect on the bond I shared with the eldest Bennett brother, I was humbled that he had embraced my father and me as true family rather than turn us away as fraudulent replacements. A perfectly understandable option for a motherless seven-year-old.

"I can't wait to get a text from Eddie to hear how the ride went this afternoon." David's tone turned to teasing as he continued, "So, is the diner still standing?"

I bristled in outrage.

"Hey, even the insurance guy said that wasn't my fault! I mean, even if I did use the wrong kind of soap... and I'm not saying I did," I quickly added, "you were here when he said dishwashers aren't supposed to just explode that way."

Tucking the receiver firmly between my ear and shoulder, I grabbed a rag to attack a particularly large, sticky pile of syrup.

"Did I say anything?" I'd heard the low tone of my friend's voice enough times since our childhood to know that he was barely able to contain his laughter.

"You didn't have to say it. You insinuated." I pouted. David may not have been my big brother by blood, but he certainly knew how to tease like he was. Having subdued the manmade lake of maple, I started stacking chairs on the now clean table.

"Fine, fine." David gave in to his body's need for release and barked out a laugh. "I'm sure the diner is in the best possible hands. What are you and Livvie up to tonight?"

"How do you know I'm going out with Livvie?" I was vaguely insulted by the insinuation that I was predictable and had nothing better to do on a Saturday night. "I might have a hot date with a gorgeous new man, you know."

"You might," David drawled out the last word. "But I'm thinking that if you had a date with a gorgeous new man, I would have seen the billboard."

My friend's comments would have been obnoxious but for the fact that he was right. In the two weeks since my birthday and new resolution to find a relationship, it was as if all the single men in Portland had crawled into a hole to hide. If and when I found someone to date, I might very well be excited enough to shout the news from the rooftop.

"Fine. You win." I admitted. "Livvie's coming over in a few minutes. We're going to take a walk around Baxter Boulevard then come back to my place for pizza and a Buffy marathon. I just picked up the season six DVD on sale at Best Buy."

As the words left my lips, even I heard how pathetic my Saturday evening sounded. Luckily, knowing that David's social life was not exactly written up in Page Six, I asked, "Before you even start in on me, what exciting plans do you have in the Big Apple tonight, Don Juan?"

"I'm staying in tonight. I've got an important presentation I've got to finish for Monday."

Precisely the response I'd expected.

"Be careful. All work and no play and you'll turn into Frank before you know it."

We both laughed, but mine was not an idle warning.

To my knowledge, my boss Frank Murphy had not had a social life since the day he graduated law school and opened his small civil litigation firm. He was at the office every morning when I arrived and stayed until well after seven every night. On the occasions I needed to work weekends, he always arrived first with the coffee and bagels. In fact, any random time of the day or night when my travels took me past our office on Wharf Street, I always saw the light burning in his office window. Livvie thought it was obsessive and creepy.

It just made me a little sad.

"Speaking of Frank," David pulled me from my musing. "Have you informed him yet that you're going to be his new partner by next year?"

"I'm not going to just spring that news on him, you know. I do have an actual plan." Having stacked the remainder of the diner chairs, I moved to the kitchen for a mop and bucket.

"You have a plan?" I heard David's chair squeak through the telephone line as he settled in and made himself more comfortable. "By all means, do tell."

"Fine. I'm going to spend the next few months working my ass off. Even more than usual. I'm going to make myself indispensable to Frank to the point that he'll do anything to keep me happy, including make me partner."

"And how is that working out for you so far?"

I hauled the janitor-issue bucket into the kitchen's large sink and said a small prayer that my chin muscles were strong enough to keep the receiver from plunking into the soapy water as I explained, "It's early yet, but I think it's going ok. Frank is stopping by the diner any minute with the paperwork I need to cover a hearing for him on Monday. I plan to be brilliant and thus further demonstrate how vital I am to the success of his law firm. As soon as I'm sure he knows he can't survive without me, I'm going to gently nudge him toward offering me a partnership."

"Well, it seems like a reasonable approach, but be careful, Sarah. You might have better luck gently nudging a beached whale back into the ocean. Just because it's a good idea, doesn't mean he's going to go for it."

"Yeah, yeah." Success in my professional life seemed far easier to execute than finding a relationship – heck, even a date. Work hard. Be rewarded for your hard work. How difficult could that be, anyway?

Knowing David's penchant for practicality – a quality I found terrifically overrated, I sighed, "I can't believe you forced me to tell you about my birthday list in the first place. It's enough that Livvie mocks me. I would think you could throw a little positive energy my way."

"First of all, I didn't force you to do anything. I received a post-birthday 2am call from you telling me your life was meaningless and wanting to know what time the animal shelter opened so you could start buying cats."

Oops. I'd kind of blocked that out.

After Livvie helped me clean up from the party, she'd gone home, leaving me alone with the list, an open bottle of Merlot and my thoughts. I read the list over and over, marveling at the spunk and optimism of the girl who had written down these goals, truly believing they were attainable. I couldn't get past the feeling she'd somehow slipped away when I wasn't looking.

Drunk dialing David had just been an unfortunate consequence of my despair.

"And secondly…"

Before my friend could finish his thought, I heard someone rapping softly on the diner door. "Hold on, Thornton."

Turning around, though, I was surprised that the silhouette shown behind the drawn shade was not of the tall, broad man I was expecting. Instead, it indicated a shorter, slighter figure. "Oh, shit."

"What's wrong?"

I sighed, walking toward the door to face my fate. "Nothing. I thought Frank was dropping off his own paperwork, but he sent his flying monkey instead."

"Play nice!" My friend ordered with a chuckle in his voice. David knew from the countless ranting phone calls he'd received from me in the last few months that the flying monkey at the door could only be Morgan Donovan, the second year law student who was interning at Frank's firm. "I know you don't like the guy, but Frank does. If you really want to make partner, don't piss off your boss by picking a fight with his Mini-me."

"The only reason Frank likes Morgan is because he's actually stuck around since June. That's a record for us when it comes to keeping interns."

"Sarah…"

"I know. I know. It doesn't matter why Frank likes him. He does and I just need to play nice." I agreed and grumbled my way through our goodbyes as I placed the handset back on the counter.

When I opened the diner door, I had every intention of playing nice. Really. Unfortunately, my brain was apparently not in league with my mouth.

"What are you doing here Morgan?"

The smile that had momentarily graced my co-worker's face disappeared. "Frank sent me. He said he'd be here in a few minutes."

I gestured for him to come in to the main room of the diner where we stood in uncomfortable silence waiting for our boss to arrive. As I tried to come up with something neutral to say, I did have to admit that if nothing else, at least my nemesis was fairly easy on the eyes. Morgan stood at about five foot ten with striking blue eyes and blonde hair that could only be described as "long-ish". Frank's receptionist Gloria and I agreed that Morgan looked just like the TV character Illya Kuryakin from the 1960s spy show *The Man from UNCLE*.

Unfortunately, good looks could only carry a person so far, and Morgan Donovan didn't have the allure of an international spy to fall back on.

Tired of staring at my shoes and having absolutely nothing to say to Frank's annoying lackey, I picked up my nearby dishtowel and concentrated on folding it into crisp, precise fourths. Just as I thought I could bear the silence no longer, Morgan must have felt the same way.

"Look, Sarah…" He began.

"Sarah." Frank's booming voice as he breezed into the diner, saving me from Morgan's awkward and ultimately insincere attempt at small talk.

"Hey, Frank. You're late." I vaulted toward the door to greet my boss. At fifty-one, Francis Murphy's tailor-made blue wool suit looked perfectly in place with Morgan and his button-down white oxford tucked neatly into his pressed Brooks Brothers slacks.

I looked down at my own denim shorts and faded green T-shirt, liberally freckled with grease stains. Hadn't these men gotten the memo that it was Saturday?

"How old is the coffee?" Frank asked, striding toward the coffee maker.

"Too old. I turned it off ten minutes ago, and I'm leaving as soon as Livvie gets here. I need to grab your paperwork and then you both have to go." My annoyance at Frank inviting Morgan to invade the sanctity of my diner burst forth despite my promise to David to reign in my temper.

Frank raised his eyebrows in surprise at my tone, but didn't say a word as he placed his briefcase on the counter, opened it and handed over the Astin divorce file. We were representing Monica Astin in a messy divorce from her husband, Portland's most successful orthodontist. I took a moment to familiarize myself with the document while Frank and Morgan chatted amiably in the background. Watching the two men bond, I remembered with a sickening feeling the list of my birthday resolutions. Instead of arguing with my boss, I was supposed to be buttering him up for a promotion.

"Sorry, Frank. I've been working the diner by myself all day and I'm a little short-tempered."

My boss snapped the buckles on his briefcase shut. "I hope you're not working for tips, Bennett. With that attitude, you'll starve."

A few years ago, when I knew Frank Murphy only by reputation, a rude comment delivered in his gruff tone might have actually frightened me. In fact, I had actually considered turning down the job interview due to Frank's terrifying reputation. Of course, I didn't know back then how carefully my boss cultivated that image and how sweet he could be if you really dug down deep.

Very deep.

Really fucking deep.

I had just graduated law school when Uncle Jeremy set up an interview for me with his friend, and I could recall vividly the first time I walked into the offices of Murphy Legal Services, LLC. I was a nervous wreck, but a glance toward the woman at the reception desk set me slightly more at ease. Gloria Daniels – according to the nameplate gleaming on her desk – looked up at me with a kind smile and twinkle in her pale blue eyes. I guessed she was in her mid-fifties, but dressed decades out of step with her cat's-eye black rimmed glasses and a pearl gray cardigan draped over her shoulders, held in place with a silver sweater chain. She had just opened her mouth to speak when a tornado masquerading as a large man in an expensive brown suit exploded into the room from behind a heavy mahogany door.

"Where is she? It's almost ten."

Without raising an eyebrow at the outburst, Gloria simply extended her right hand, heavy with expensive jewelry, in my direction.

"Oh." Frank looked me up and down and said, "Well, come on in, then."

I was ushered into a large office which appeared far smaller than it was due to the volume of files and papers littering every surface, including the chair I was presumably to sit in. I looked at the man expectantly, and after receiving a blank stare for longer than was entirely comfortable, I finally picked up the papers, placed them neatly on the floor and sat down. Again meeting a stare and silence, I finally started the conversation, nervously babbling about how I appreciated Frank taking the time to meet with me, understanding he was doing it as a favor to Uncle Jeremy.

At that point, and to my great distress, Frank leaned toward me and boomed, "I don't waste my time on people who kiss ass. If that's your style, we might as well end this interview now."

My head popped up at his words and I took my first close look at the man who according to reputation could cause the toughest, most time-hardened attorneys to cower in fear when they met on opposite sides of the courtroom.

Frank's size alone was certainly imposing. Easily six foot three and perhaps an inch more, he possessed the broad shoulders of a football player and the middle-age gut of a man who still ate – but no longer trained – as one.

His dull brown hair had receded from his head like Casco Bay at low tide, leaving the minute bumps and ruts in his sand-colored skull that resembled an eroded shoreline and completed the analogy. What little remained of his hair, though, was as neatly trimmed as were his nails and brows. Clearly a professionally manscaped job, but also a nod toward vanity to which Frank would never admit.

My gaze finally rested on the older man's eyes. A deep shade of brown, they were nearly hidden by the basset-hound heavy lids and bags of a man who obviously slept too little and probably drank too much.

As Frank Murphy leaned toward me, growling his request to end our interview, I realized much to my surprise that his attempts at intimidation had backfired. Raised by two gruff policemen into a family of men, soft and gentle words were often my undoing. Abrupt and grumpy, though, I was well-equipped to deal with.

"This interview is not over." I reached into my purse and handed over a sheaf of bound papers. "I was promised half an hour of your time, so would you like to look at my transcript or are you going to keep acting like a bully until our time is up?"

In the heavy silence that followed, I was terrified I had made a grave miscalculation and mentally composed the apologetic postcard I would send Uncle Jeremy from the leper colony where I planned to relocate.

Fortunately, after several painful seconds, a deep, hearty laugh erupted from the man sitting in front of me. "Well, now. Jeremy said you were a pistol. When do you want to start?"

I started working for Frank one week later, and my fear of him lessened as my respect grew in equal measure, but not all members of the legal community shared my opinion. Lawyers and judges around town fell into two distinct camps – those like me who admired Frank Murphy's brash style and those who thought he was an arrogant ass.

The bells over the diner door chimed, pulling me back to the present and heralding Livvie's arrival, an attorney who unfortunately fell firmly into the latter category.

"Murphy." She acknowledged my boss with a perfunctory nod of the head, and was met by one in kind.

"DiMarco."

I was momentarily thrown off my game when Livvie breezed right past Frank without pausing for even a snarky word or two until I realized she had immediately zeroed in on the young man standing to his right. While Livvie had heard all about the young intern I couldn't stand, she had yet to meet him in person.

Not waiting for an introduction, especially when an attractive man was on her radar, Livvie thrust out her hand. "Hi. Olivia DiMarco. I don't believe we've met."

"Morgan Donovan." The weasel replied, clearly intrigued – as were most people upon first meeting Livvie. What he didn't notice, however, was how the light left Livvie's eyes as she realized the identity of the man she was speaking with. Livvie's loyalty knew no bounds, and as cute as this boy may be, she knew I had pegged him as "the enemy".

I took the awkward silence that ensued as an opportunity to herd everyone toward the door. "Well, thanks, Frank. I think I have everything I need for Monday."

"I can take a hint." My boss placed his hand on Morgan's shoulder and I could hear the beginning of a lecture on the benefits of pre-nuptial agreements as I pulled the door firmly shut.

Turning to Livvie, I held my hands up, silently begging that she hold off on the inquisition at least until we started our walk.

Halfway to asking her first question, my friend rolled her eyes in acquiescence, grabbed two bottles of water from the cooler and said, "Well, come on then."

* * *

"So that's Morgan." Livvie didn't even wait until we reached the first ¼ mile marker. "I mean, after everything you've told me about him, I can't believe you let him in the diner."

"Not my fault. Frank sent him."

"Speaking of annoying men…"

"Don't start Livvie." I sped my pace in a passive aggressive nod to my friend's shorter legs. "He's my boss and I want him to make me partner in a year. I can't go around barring my door to his anointed heir apparent."

"Do you honestly believe 'Murphy Legal Services' is ever going to become a partnership, Sarah?"

Unable to deal with Livvie's question and my own underlying concerns, I chose instead to just remain silent and keep pounding the pavement.

Hop-skipping to catch up, Livvie sighed with the small amount of breath she was able to catch. "Alright then, slow down for God's sake and let's start with something easy. How's the rest of the progress on the brand new you?"

"I'm walking every day with you, aren't I? I've even priced a few stair machines to help when I start training to climb Mt. Katahdin. I haven't quite gotten on the diet bandwagon, but I'm doing pretty well with exercising."

"What do you mean you haven't 'quite gotten on the diet bandwagon'?"

"Well, I'm not really eating any less, but I've successfully completed my pre-diet purge."

No. Not that kind of purge.

The day after my birthday, when my to-do list was fresh in my mind and extra-strength Tylenol was keeping my headache at a dull roar, I went on a rampage and rid my refrigerator and cupboards of all dangerous snacks. Everyone thought those Keebler Elves were delightful little woodland creatures, but I knew they were secretly evil harbingers of diet doom.

Livvie laughed, "I've done the pre-diet purge before, too. Tell me, are you actually eating less or are you just making more trips to the grocery store?"

"Go to hell." I replied pleasantly, though not answering Livvie's astute question.

"Hi, Sarah. Hey, Livvie."

We both looked up, startled, as a young dark-haired man in his late twenties jogged past us at a good clip. Looking back over my shoulder, I yelled, "Hi, Scott!"

Livvie whistled softly, but appreciatively at the view as we both paused to watch him retreat. "I haven't seen Scott in years. What happened with you two, anyway?"

"I don't really remember." I shrugged. "He's engaged to Dianna Pownell over at the Legal Clinic. We all went out for a beer a few months ago."

Livvie stopped walking and shook her head in disbelief. "How do you do that?"

"Do what?"

"Collect men like they're Pound Puppies. Do you realize that you never really break up with anyone? They all just kind of drift away." She made a motion reminiscent of a hula girl statue on a Volkswagen dashboard.

"Of course I've broken up with people," I insisted.

"You have not. Name me one former boyfriend that isn't on your Christmas card list."

My answer would have been immediate had Livvie not delivered the pre-emptive, "And Ryan doesn't count."

"How can Ryan not count? The break-up to end all break-ups doesn't count?"

Livvie simply knelt down to re-tie her shiny white Nike cross-trainers and patiently waited for my response.

Fine. Trying to work within Livvie's rules, I tried to ignore her smirk as the silence stretched out. Finally, my memory cleared and I yelled triumphantly, "Jared! I have never sent a Christmas card to Jared."

Livvie shrugged, "One guy. Lame, Bennett." She began walking again before she suddenly stopped short and swatted me on the arm. "Hey! That's not fair! He's Jewish – of course you don't send Jared a Christmas card!"

"Hey, just because I don't have a big dramatic exit scene with every guy I date like some people I know…"

"Some relationships call for a big dramatic exit scene." She explained patiently. "Sometimes, you just don't have closure until the ugly words are thrown. And maybe a chair or two."

"And what, you don't think my words with Ryan were ugly enough?"

"It always comes back to the Great Ryan Debacle, doesn't it?" Livvie sighed.

She was right. It usually did come back to Ryan. "Why did I date that jerk for such a long time, anyway?"

"He was a hottie. A total ass, but a hottie." My friend answered, and then swiftly changed the subject before I got too morose. "Speaking of which, at least your new co-worker is easy on the eyes."

"I suppose." I agreed, reluctantly.

"You suppose my ass. Blonde hair, blue eyes. Great butt. If you wrote a book on the type of man you're attracted to, Morgan could pose for the illustrations."

I hated to admit she was right, but I remembered thinking the very same thing when Frank introduced the two of us on Morgan's first day at the office. In fact, we had gotten along great until he opened his mouth and started inserting his foot in it on a regular basis.

"I can't believe you looked at his butt."

"I can't believe you can't believe I'd look at his butt." Livvie laughed. "Speaking of your new co-worker, are you sure the guy is trying to sabotage you? From what you've told me, he might just be stupid. I mean, he's working for Frank, right? Present company excepted, that doesn't speak very well for him."

"Trust me, I would prefer stupid over conniving any day." I replied, no doubt in my mind that Morgan was anything but stupid. "The guy filches files from my desk so that I can't find them when I need them and keeps taking all the credit for the work we're forced to do together. Twice he even pointed out mistakes in my work directly to Frank without coming to me first."

"Well, did you make the mistakes?"

"Not the point!" I stopped in my tracks. "Okay, how about what happened last Thursday? He placed a call to the opposing counsel in one of my cases. That's way out of line in and of itself, but then he didn't document the file. I called the same guy later in the day and sounded like an idiot."

My friend nodded reluctantly. "I'll grant you that one. The guy is still in law school and shouldn't go around poaching your cases. Have you mentioned any of this to Frank?"

"Of course. It didn't help, though. Frank thinks Morgan is bright and resourceful."

"What do you think?

"I think those are the words Bette Davis used to describe Anne Baxter. Luckily you and David believe me. Thank God I've got a new unlimited minutes plan on my cell phone or my constant whining phone calls to New York would have seriously dipped into my new house fund."

"You know," Livvie said with the oddest look on her face, "I hate to change the subject from your psychotic paranoia. I mean, it's always so entertaining. But, the answer to your quest for an amazing relationship might be right under our noses."

"Oh no! There is no way I'm ever going to date Morgan Donovan!" I couldn't believe my friend would even consider such an idea.

"Actually, I was thinking about David."

I stopped dead in my tracks, stunned by my friend's suggestion. "Are you out of your mind? David? He's like my brother."

"*Like* your brother," Livvie repeated. "But he's not *actually* your brother."

"Ew." I resumed walking at a good clip, hoping somehow that distancing myself physically would shake off the unclean feeling I had at the mere mention of a romantic relationship with David Thornton.

Livvie, though, was not completely deterred. "Okay, if you insist that David is off the table, then why not Morgan? You mentioned him – not me."

"Were you not listening to me when I said the guy is trying to steal my job?"

"Oh please," Livvie dismissed my concerns with a flutter of her wrist. "If it ever came down to it, you could take Morgan. Besides, if you dismiss him as dating material just because he's opportunistic slime, you'd have to eliminate the entire Portland legal community from your list of potential suitors."

"Not making me feel better." I slowed down and gave my friend a chance to catch up. "I'll grant you the guy's cute, but even if he didn't make me insane, it wouldn't work."

"Why?"

"Because we work together. If Frank found out two of his employees were dating, he'd blow a gasket and fire us both. I'd be in a relationship alright, but have to sacrifice any hopes of a promotion – and my job itself."

Livvie pondered my logic for a moment. "Well, then, since we've struck out on the men you know, we need to get you out there and meet some new men. You've only got eleven months to go before you have to be in that amazing relationship, right?"

"Since when did you become so invested in my list?" I asked with distrust. "I thought you were just humoring me."

"I'm not against the concept of having goals. I just don't think you should meet every one of them within one year. But if you're determined..." She paused and gave me a once over. I felt like a dog at the pound, preening slightly in my hopes to meet with her approval.

"I'm determined." I rushed to assure her.

"If you're determined," she continued, annoyed at the interruption, "then you need to meet new men and that isn't as easy as it sounds. Look at our social circle. You hang out with me, a few other single girlfriends, Jeremy and his sons."

"Fine – we'll go to a bar or something tonight. You know, flirt a little." The very thought terrified me, but my friend was right. If I wanted a relationship, I first needed to meet some men.

Apparently that wasn't exactly what Livvie had in mind.

"Nope." She responded with a twinkle in her eye that caused my heart to drop to my stomach. "This calls for drastic measures. You need to make yourself available, and I know just the way to make that happen."

Drastic measures?

Make myself available?

The combination of my friend's words and the increased speed and lightness of her gait suddenly made me very nervous.

"Livvie?" I increased my own pace to a light jog. "Livvie, what exactly do you mean by drastic measures?"

November

"...SO THAT'S WHEN I TOLD HER to pack up her garden gnomes and get out. You can see my point, right? I mean, I'm right, right?" The man sitting across the table from me leaned in closer with each word, clearly expecting a response to his rants.

"Mmm hmmm." I nodded in agreement and reached for my rum and coke, taking a healthy swig and sending silent thanks to Captain Morgan for his help in surviving the evening.

I was in hell.

Actually, it just felt like hell. In reality, I was experiencing the 'desperate measures' Livvie had referred to in her attempts to assist me in finding a boyfriend.

My supposed best friend had sent me to one of the new "Drive-Thru Dating" services (patent pending, believe it or not) that had just come to town. For the bargain price of $50, I was spending the evening at a local bar with a group of other singles. Twelve women sat at small tables set up on the perimeter of a downtown club while every ten minutes a bell sounded and the single men at the event rose to rotate around them. It was a modern version of the complicated courtship dances found in a Jane Austen novel.

Unfortunately, instead of being wooed by the dashing Mr. Darcy or Mr. Knightley, I found myself staring vacantly at a greasy young man whose nametag read "Conrad", and counting the moments until he would go away and regale some other poor, unsuspecting woman with the tales of his ex-wife's garden gnomes.

"You don't own any garden gnomes, do you?"

"Who me? No. I don't even have a garden."

"Good, good. That's good." Conrad sighed his relief and I signaled the waiter for another drink.

The truly ironic thing about the entire evening was how difficult it had been to obtain a place at the table. It took nearly a month on the waiting list for a seat to open up for a single woman, but I understood they were still taking applications from single men at the door. It only went to prove what I had already suspected – there really were more single women than men in the Greater Portland area.

Of course, given the production it took to get me ready for the evening, it was probably a good thing that I had the extra time to prepare. As soon as I signed up for the event, Livvie had marched through my closet, an odd combination of General Patton and Joan Rivers. She barked orders while throwing accessories at me, then shook her head, pursed her lips and rejected each and every choice. In disgust at finally reaching the point where nothing remained on its original hanger aside from the bridesmaid dress I wore to my cousin Sidra's wedding, she forced me to go shopping.

At the conclusion of our death march through the mall, my credit card was at its limit but Livvie was finally satisfied with the slim black skirt and cashmere sweater I had purchased. I was a little uncomfortable about the skirt, thinking that it was too tight, but Livvie insisted that I always wore my clothes a size too big and she refused to let me buy another 'Maude-like caftan'. The v-neck sweater we picked caused no such arguments as I fell in love with it immediately. It was a pale shade of lilac, tapered just right to make my waist look smaller and my chest look bigger.

Very admirable traits in a sweater.

The night of the event, Livvie came over to help me do my hair and makeup. In her mind, leaving me alone in these endeavors would have been akin to Eisenhower hanging out at home and reading the paper to find out how the Normandy invasion had turned out. It took us forty-five minutes to attain the swept-back hair that was intended to look casual and effortless to the naked eye. Simple gold hoop earrings, sparkly eye shadow and a smear of pale pink lipstick finished off the ensemble.

Not wanting to admit all of that time and money had been wasted – since poor greasy Conrad was actually the cream of the crop – I rallied my efforts to try and make a connection. I felt I owed it to Livvie. And the sweater.

"So, Conrad...What do you do for a living?"

"I'm an actuary." Conrad wiped his cocktail napkin across his sweaty head. "It doesn't start out as an obsession, you know."

"Being an actuary?"

"What? No. The gnomes. It doesn't start out as an obsession. She only had one at first. Cute little guy. He had green suspenders and a red hat. We named him George."

"Yes, well, speaking of George, I hear Clooney has a great new movie out." I silently congratulated myself for the inspired, if a bit clunky, transition. "What genre of movies do you like, Conrad?"

"I think the obsession started when she thought George might be lonely, so we brought home Leo. His hat was blue. We'd been married about a year then and things just got out of hand from that point on. Every time I came home there was a new gnome on the lawn. After a while, the neighbors started to complain." Conrad's eyes began to well with tears. "At the end it got so I couldn't even maneuver the mower between the... the..."

"The gnomes?" I supplied helpfully.

"The gnomes." Conrad whispered, head dropped low between his shoulders.

Ring

At the sound of the bell, my gnome hater rose from the table. "It was great meeting you, Sarah. I feel like I can really talk to you."

I smiled vacantly, imagining my future as Mrs. Conrad and waited a respectable three seconds before scratching "No" as indelibly as possible on my handy "Drive-thru Dating" scorecard. Rummaging through my purse in search of a thick black Sharpie to ensure my lack of interest in Conrad was fully understood, I didn't notice as my final match of the night arrived and settled down across from me.

"Well, well, well. What do we have here?"

Oh God.

I recognized the voice of my new dating partner immediately and wondered what I possibly had done to so offend the God of Happy Relationships.

"Aren't you going to say hello?" My companion asked, the smirk on his face obvious from his tone alone.

Unable to avoid eye contact any longer, I looked up and confirmed my worst fears. "Hi, Donnie."

Donnie DiMarco. Livvie's ex-husband and an insufferable bag of wind in his own right was my last scheduled date of the evening. Even Jane Austen working in tandem with O. Henry couldn't have imagined this twist.

I looked at Donnie with a critical eye and supposed I could understand why Livvie had once fallen for him. Dark hair liberally sprinkled with gray, he had an old movie star quality that seeped through his wide smile and hearty laugh. He was also a partner at the largest law firm in Portland, earning a salary to support his upper class lifestyle of boating in the summer, skiing in the winter and island vacations scattered in between.

As shallow as it seemed, that was not an unattractive trait.

Luckily, I was well-versed in Donnie lore by the time I'd first met him. Livvie and Donnie were already divorced when she and I started law school, but Portland's law community was surprisingly small and the two DiMarcos often ran into each other at bar-sponsored events. Since I was usually my friend's escort of choice, it was only a matter of time before I became acquainted with her ex-husband. While every divorce is unpleasant, theirs more closely resembled Demi and Bruce than Demi and Ashton, leaving the ex-couple free to maintain a cordial public façade so as not to tarnish their professional reputations.

As was the best friend's prerogative, however, I reserved the right to hate my best friend's ex on principle alone.

"So how have you been, Sarah?" Donnie didn't even try to disguise his leer as he followed up with, "You're looking good."

"Thanks," I stabbed my cocktail straw into my glass, trying desperately to find one remaining drop of rum. "But don't waste your energy."

"Just calling it as I see it, Sarah. No need to get testy." He looked around the room. "Where is my lovely ex-wife, anyway? I assume you came together?"

Giving my first sincere smile of the entire evening, I explained, "Livvie isn't here. She's seeing someone right now. A parole officer named Ben. Great guy. They met when..."

"A parole officer you say? What do they pull in? Forty K? Maybe forty-five?"

"Money is not important to Livvie."

"Clearly."

I wished for a moment that Conrad had left behind a garden gnome that I could lob at my new companion's head. Unfortunately, I had no weapons at hand and knew I would have to simply suffer through the remaining few moments.

"So, how are things over at Harris and O'Toole? I read that you're representing the new wind farms off the coast. That has to be pretty interesting."

"I'm involved in it." The older man preened. "Of course, I've got a heavy workload myself, so I'm mentoring Ryan. He's really the guy in charge of the account."

"Ryan?" I registered the fact that a sudden lack of any moisture in one's mouth apparently left one with the inability to swallow. "Ryan who?"

"Ryan Corruchi."

I'd been referring to my ex-boyfriend as "Rat Bastard Ryan" for so long, that I'd almost forgotten the power his full name had over me. Like Superman confronted by a rock of kryptonite, I felt myself wilt back into my chair.

"Oh, didn't you know Ryan works at my firm now? Has for almost a year. I was assigned as his mentor and we hit it off right from the start. Good guy, that Ryan."

If only I'd known the horrific turn this evening was going to take, I would have bolted from the bar after my date with Conrad and called the event a rousing success.

"He talks about you, you know." Donnie smiled as he leaned impossibly closer. "You really should call him."

Ring

With a parting wink, Donnie DiMarco rose and scouted the room briefly before leaving me sitting alone at my table to make a beeline toward a well-endowed blonde hovering near the bar.

Donnie and Ryan work together?

Ryan talks about me?

I should call him?

Did Donnie mean that *Ryan* wanted me to call him or that *Donnie* wanted me to call Ryan? And if *Donnie* wanted me to call Ryan was it because he thought *Ryan* wanted me to call him?

Head swimming and failing in my attempts to catch the waiter's eye to bring me a much needed drink, I slumped back into my chair and checked my watch, waiting for Livvie's arrival. She may have sent me into battle alone, but my best friend promised to drop by for a drink after the event for an immediate debrief. True to her word, at exactly quarter past the hour Livvie entered the bar, looking the very image of "sporty casual".

She was apparently so focused on finding me, though, that she didn't notice the couple canoodling near the door. I watched with a mix of amusement and horror as Livvie crashed directly into her ex-husband.

Actually, she walked into the stacked blonde that Donnie was trying to usher out of the bar to admire his house on the bluff, or boat in the bay, or whatever random material possession had been used to lure Blondie back to the lair.

The perfunctory kiss to the cheek Livvie gave and received from her former spouse would have looked the very picture of civility to anyone who didn't know her. Of course, since I knew her as well as anyone, I picked out the set of her eyes and the firmness around her mouth. I believed these were the same characteristics noted in wild panthers just before they took down their prey.

The threesome appeared to be making polite small talk and I was too far away to hear the conversation. I turned my head for just a moment, trying and failing to attract the waiter who briefly buzzed by, and when my attention returned to the group by the door I saw the blonde look at Donnie with disgust and stomp into the night, alone.

Well, now, that was interesting.

Donnie and Livvie continued talking for another moment before they finally parted, she toward my table and he presumably trying to chase after his date.

"What was that all about?"

"What do you mean?" Livvie smiled as the waiter appeared at her elbow before she had even removed her coat. "A house merlot for me, and another rum and coke for my friend."

"That girl ran out of here like she was on fire. I'm thinking you may have had something to do with that."

Livvie twisted her finger through a lock of her hair, looking ever the innocent waif we both knew she was not. "I simply thanked Donnie for referring me to his doctor and mentioned that the round of antibiotics I'd been given had worked wonders."

"You, my friend, are evil." I raised my empty glass in salute. "He didn't even look that mad."

"Nah. I bested him at his own game. Donnie actually admires a worthy adversary." Taking a sip from the wine that had magically arrived the moment she sat down, Livvie abruptly changed the subject. "So, how did it go?"

"Well, let's start with the show stopping news of the evening. Did you know that Ryan and Donnie worked together?"

Livvie sighed and muttered something under her breath that sounded suspiciously like, "Shithead."

"So you knew?"

"I knew. I just didn't see any reason why I should tell you. Donnie's firm focuses on corporate work. Intellectual property and whatnot. I figured you and Ryan would never come into contact. Sorry."

I waved off the apology as a minor breach in the girl code. "Don't worry. The only interesting thing about those two working together is that Donnie told me I should call Ryan."

This time when my friend said, "Shithead," it was clearly audible.

To most of the room, actually.

"Look, Sarah, Donnie says a lot of things. For starters, he told me he'd love and honor me till death do us part. Clearly that didn't happen. The man is a liar and an idiot, and if you take his advice, it will make you an idiot, too. Take it from one who knows."

"You're right, you're right. I know you're right."

"Well, then, stop channeling Carrie Fisher and tell me how it went with the men you're actively trying to date and not the one you need to forget about. Any prospects?"

"Settle in and get comfortable." I warned as I began to describe the complete disaster my evening had been.

Even as I started telling Livvie about my first "date" with Carl (the bisexual, unemployed dog groomer) another part of my brain started to hum.

I was seriously thinking about calling Ryan, even knowing down to my toenails it would be a mistake of epic proportions. Maybe I was so caught up in my list of goals to accomplish before I hit thirty, and the need to be in a relationship that I was beginning to lose perspective.

"I think I need to reorganize," I blurted, apropos of absolutely nothing.

"You know I've asked you to put on your signal when you're going to take a conversational left turn." Livvie crossed her legs and leaned back in her chair. "So, reorganize. Your purse? Your closet? What exactly is the scope we're looking at here?"

"My life. I'm going to reorganize my list of life goals." Anticipating Livvie's groan, I rushed ahead. "Look, creating a happy relationship and professional success are fairly tall orders for me to tackle first. After all, reaching those goals is dependent on external factors and other people. The other items, though – losing weight and buying a house – those are totally within my control. All I need is will power and a good credit rating."

"So you're saying…"

"I'm saying that I'm going to momentarily put thoughts of single men, Ryan and gnomes named George out of my mind for a little while."

"Gnomes named George?" Livvie reached over and pulled my cocktail out of my reach.

"Forget about George. Listen to me. I'm just going to take a little break from my more difficult goals on my list before I do something really stupid. Instead, I'm going to focus on getting one or two easy successes under my belt."

"Easy successes. Like losing two dress sizes or buying a house?"

"Exactly!" I was so glad to see my friend finally begin to understand. "Really, what could be easier than losing a little weight or signing a purchase and sale agreement?"

"What, indeed." Livvie took a long sip from her wineglass and gifted me with a look I couldn't quite place. I chose to believe it was an outward expression of her admiration for the reasonable alterations I'd made to my life plan.

Unfortunately, even three fairly strong drinks didn't allow me to buy my own explanation. Livvie clearly thought I was insane.

And I would just have to prove her wrong.

December

BANG. BANG. BANG.

Ugh. I burrowed my face deeper into the couch pillow, wanting to ignore the sounds coming from the diner below me. It was almost eight pm and I had spent the last hour trying to marshal the energy necessary to brush my teeth and go to bed. Now faced with an unidentified racket winding its way upstairs, I flexed my left leg in another attempt to push off from the couch.

Ow! My calf cramped and I collapsed back in a whimpering heap.

I wasn't sure if my pain and malaise was caused by the spinning class yesterday, the belly dancing lessons Livvie and I had taken over the weekend or both activities combined with too few calories ingested over the past several days.

Closing my eyes to realize that even my eyelids hurt, I decided the most likely culprit was the lunchtime cardio yoga session at the gym that included a self-realization power stretch.

Cardio yoga. A room full of seemingly intelligent men and women jumping and stretching their bodies into unnatural positions – many of which were probably illegal in some states – all to the musical accompaniment of Kelly Clarkson. Yup. My attempt at losing weight and getting healthy instead had me draping myself like a chalk outline across the couch.

Of course, the rest of my lingering ugly mood couldn't be attributed to my exercise regime so much as the lousy day I'd had at the office. Putting out fires, dealing with unreasonable clients and topping off the day was the vicious argument I'd had with Morgan.

"What the hell is this?" I'd barged into the office law library that doubled as our intern's headquarters.

"What?" Morgan had jumped at the sound of my voice when I first entered, and then blinked owlishly as I first waved the sheaf of papers in front of his face then thrust them down on the desk in front of him. After taking a moment to read the typed pages, he answered, "Um…I think that's the Garfinkel Motion for Summary Judgment, right?"

"Wrong! I finished the Garfinkel Motion last night, signed it and put it in Gloria's inbox for her to copy and file with the court this morning. This is not the Garfinkel Motion."

Morgan opened his mouth to speak but I didn't give him the chance. "I'll grant you, it looks like the Garfinkel Motion. It's even labeled, 'Garfinkel Motion for Summary Judgment', but since my motion is finished and signed and this motion is unsigned and quotes a new case I've never even heard of, this cannot be the Garfinkel Motion. Try again, Morgan. What the hell is this?"

Morgan glanced up at me briefly before turning his attention to the papers on his desk which he then took great exaggerated pains to straighten into a neat pile. Wheeling his chair back, he stood and handed me the stack once again. "What this is, Sarah, is the new and improved Garfinkel Motion. I saw your motion in Gloria's inbox and noticed you didn't include the Bryers case that was decided by the Third Circuit last week. I added the citation, printed off a new copy and put it in your inbox to sign."

"You…you did what?" I was barely able to sputter out.

"A simple thank you will suffice."

"Thank you?" My head threatened to explode at the thought of thanking this man for his attempt at undercutting my work.

"You're welcome." Morgan deliberately misunderstood my tone and walked around me to step out of the room.

It was a smart move since as soon as my shock-induced paralysis lifted I was planning to chuck a stapler at his head.

From halfway down the hall I heard him yell, "Read the case, Sarah."

In the sanctity of my apartment at the end of the day, I groaned in pain at the memory because I had read the Bryers case as Morgan had suggested.

It was on point, favorable to my client and hugely supported my argument.

Well, shit.

Maybe I could work out my resulting frustration at the kickboxing class I'd signed up for the next day. If I ever got off the couch.

My stomach gurgled loudly, voting that I get off the couch and make supper, but it was unaware that the only food items remaining in the safety zone of my house were fat free cheese and low carb bread. Since both had the consistency of wet cardboard and were therefore not exactly the siren call of a cheeseburger and fries, I suspected the lure of the couch was going to win this round.

Bang! Bang! Bang!

Oh, right. The unidentified noise from the diner – which was closed and should have been empty for several hours – infiltrated my dreams of greasy beef and fried potatoes. In my heart I knew burglars would likely attempt to be quieter, but I couldn't shake the mild concern that I might be ignoring the warning sounds of someone trying to break in. With one final grunt, I finally rolled my body into a sitting position.

Grabbing my tennis racket from the hall closet, I crept down the stairs of my apartment that led directly into the diner's pantry. I stopped short on the third step from the bottom when I noticed that between the banging sounds I could distinctly hear the strains of Barry Manilow's Christmas album.

Burglars rarely came with a soundtrack.

But Eddie Thornton did.

"Eddie!" I ran down the rest of the stairs – muscle weakness forgotten – and threw myself into the arms of Jeremy's youngest son, home for the holidays three weeks earlier than expected. Hammer in hand, he was decorating the diner with holly, garlands and twinkling lights.

"Hey, Bennett! I was wondering how much noise I would have to make before you got your ass down here."

I gave one final bone-crushing hug before de-tangling myself long enough to take a good look at the handsome man before me. Tall and lean like his brother, Eddie's hair was light where David's was dark, and streaked lighter still by the warm sun of Aruba, his most recent destination.

The Caribbean sun must also have been responsible for the deep tan accentuated by Eddie's faded blue T-shirt and ripped jeans. Teva sandals – in December because my friend had no sense of weather or season – finished off the picture that was my youngest unofficial brother.

"Look how long it is." I remarked pulling on a strand of hair.

"That's what she said."

Rewarding his crude remark with a smack to the back of the head, I reached for one of the diner's carafes and filled it with water from the tap behind the counter. "Regular or decaf?"

"Is that really a question? High octane, please."

"Put down your hammer and get over here," I ordered. "We can catch up while it's brewing. Why are you in Maine so early?"

"I got a great deal on an airline ticket flying right into Portland. I don't have another assignment until the middle of January. Figured I deserved a nice long break."

Eddie – my father's namesake – was born just a few months before me, but we were different as night and day. While I was content to live in Maine forever with the occasional plane ride to a different location just to make life interesting, Eddie couldn't wait to leave Portland and see the world. He got his high school diploma and set sail, camera in hand and was now a sought-after travel photographer. While he returned to his hometown often, each visit was usually very brief and generally unannounced.

Showing up weeks earlier than expected was not at all unusual for Eddie, but his explanation sounded a bit flimsy. I'd seen him change his plans in a moment for an interesting assignment, family emergency or attractive fellow traveler that he wanted to accompany back to the States. But a deal on Expedia? That wasn't exactly Eddie's style.

"Stop thinking so hard, Sarah," Eddie observed with a mixture of affectionate amusement and resignation. "What do you want to know?"

Putting aside my questions about why he was in Portland – knowing Eddie and that they would therefore be deflected – I asked, "Have you seen your dad yet?"

"Nope. I called the house when my plane landed but he didn't answer. It took me about two hours to get my bags, make it through customs and rent a car, but when I got home he still wasn't there."

"Weird," I commented, looking at the time. "He didn't mention any plans to me."

Eddie shrugged, and then waved his hammer around with a flourish. "I got bored waiting and figured I might as well come by and start decorating."

I poured a cup of coffee for each of us, his black and mine lightened with fat free cream. Of course, I might as well have added Elmer's glue for all the flavor it provided.

"Well, I'm thrilled to see you. You should have called me and I would have picked you up."

"I figured you'd be busy. Writing the great American novel. Brokering world peace. Curing cancer – you know, the usual gig for a twenty-nine year old."

I took a sip of coffee – tasteless caffeine was better than no caffeine at all – and rolled my eyes. "I take it you've been talking to Livvie?"

"She may have sent me an e-mail or two about your plans to be perfect by the time you're thirty. I heard all about that horror show where she somehow set you up with her ex-husband. Classy. So, any new prospects since then?"

"None at all. The downturn in my love life has replaced the Dow Jones watch on the local news. Besides, if you are getting your intel from Livvie, she should have told you I decided to put the boyfriend hunt on the back burner for a while. At least until the holidays are over."

Eddie stood and stretched, placing his cup on the drain board. "Speaking of holidays, move your lazy ass and help me finish hanging the garland by the door."

It was good to have my friend home.

Working as we talked, Eddie and I soon had the diner almost fully bedecked in all its Christmas glory. One final touch that remained was placing my mother's crèche in its home of honor in the front window. A hand-me-down from her grandmother, it saddened me to think how many more years I had enjoyed the beautifully carved figures than had the intended recipient.

Unwrapping St. Joseph, a donkey and the other manger residents from their newspaper cocoons, I grasped for a topic that would lead me away from the melancholy I felt as thoughts of my family's losses assaulted me.

"Hey, Eddie." I caught my friend's attention, deciding to get a man's opinion on a subject I'd been stewing over for a month. "When you talked to Livvie, did she happen to mention that Donnie said I should call Ry…"

"Jesus Christ, Bennett! No!"

Baby Jesus flew out of my hands and into the air. Catching him just before he smashed into the ground, I took a breath to collect myself. "God, Eddie! Give me a heart attack why don't you? 'No' what?"

Eddie descended the ladder he had used to hang more lights, reached into my storage box and started shredding a paper bundle that emerged after a moment as a wise man. "No. We are not going down that road again."

I didn't insult him by asking which road – we were obviously talking about Rue de Ryan. "Why not?"

"Why not?" Eddie shook his head and for a moment I thought he wasn't going to answer. Then finally he said, "Well, let's start with the fact that the first time you had a fight, he got drunk and screwed his tarty ex-girlfriend."

Wow.

It was amazing how brutal the truth sounded coming out of someone else's mouth. The details were correct, I supposed, but in my head I had made the event so much more complicated and gray. Not sure quite how to respond, I instead pulled at a tangled heap of garland from a nearby box and busied myself trying to find the end.

"I swear to god, if you say that you two were 'on a break' I will go upstairs and smash every Friends DVD you own."

Against my will, I felt a smile tug at my lips at Eddie's attempt to lighten the mood. "Hey – you can hate Ryan if you must, but that's no reason to take it out on Ross and Rachel."

"I'm sorry. I'm not exactly known for my bedside manner. It's just that I know you loved him, but Ryan was a dick."

"Yeah. I know." Finally finding the garland's end, I concentrated on winding it around the stairwell banister, strategically putting my back to my friend as I confessed, "I just get lonely and forget sometimes."

The silence stretched uncomfortably as my pseudo-brother worked out an appropriate reply. Poor Eddie. The man would run into a burning building for me, but couldn't give emotional support if it were wrapped in a box with a bow.

Deciding to give the guy a break before he hurt himself by thinking too hard or resorted to the ever-popular and corny squeeze of my shoulder in a show of nonverbal, manly understanding, I moved away from the heavy topics of death, love and betrayal. "So, was that Barry Manilow I heard on the stereo when I came downstairs?"

"Yup. You have a problem with that?" Relieved to be let off the hook, I heard the Clint Eastwood toned challenge. When I turned to face him, I was pleased to see Eddie's playful glint was back.

"I wouldn't have a problem if it was still 1978, but it's not. Bell-bottoms and the Bee Gees had the good grace to fade away, so why is Barry still around?" Tying off the garland, I rummaged through the remaining decorations, trying to find the silver bells Jack liked to hang from the front door.

"Hey. Just because you have issues, it's no reason to take it out on Barry."

"He's a plastic, Muzak freak."

"He's an icon."

"He's a lounge singer who would be singing at the Exit 8 Howard Johnson's if he hadn't met up with Bette Midler," I argued, emptying the big guns.

Eddie straightened his posture to his full height, towering over me by more than a foot. Glaring down, he emphasized each word as he said, "Barry Manilow is a misunderstood genius."

I couldn't hold back my smile at our fake fight any longer. Chuckling, I shook my head and said, "My god, you are so gay."

"True," Eddie admitted. "But, lots of straight people like Barry, too. Or so I hear, anyway."

"No straight people I know." I remarked, pressing a box of ornaments to his abdomen and pointing to the small tree in the corner while I confiscated the ladder to hang a sprig of mistletoe over the door. "So, what does Shaun think of the amazing Mr. Manilow?"

Eddie shrugged. "I don't know. Probably not much considering he was more of a Metallica fan."

"Was?" I asked, picking up on the past tense.

Eddie crossed the room and began placing the silver and red ornament on the tree. Shrugging in an effort to appear nonchalant, he said, "I suppose he still is. I don't know."

Oh. The unexpected trip home to Portland suddenly started to make a little more sense.

"I take it that Shaun didn't come back to Portland with you?"

"Nope. We broke up." Eddie turned to the coffee pot, emptied the remaining liquid into the sink and began scrubbing with a bit more vigor than was truly called for.

"Do you want to talk about it?" I asked, folding up the ladder and placing it carefully against the wall.

"Nope."

Gay or straight, why was talking to a man about feelings and relationships – actually, talking about anything other than pop music – such a chore? "Let me rephrase. Do you think you *should* talk about it?"

Eddie sighed, put down the coffee pot and turned to make eye contact. "There's really nothing to discuss. We broke up. Mutually. Two people decided that they didn't have enough in common to make it work. No drama. No third parties involved. Just us deciding that we shouldn't be together."

I searched my friend's eyes and found only the truth. I found something else, though – something that perhaps Eddie hadn't intended to share. Whether or not they had anything in common, Eddie still loved Shaun. Not knowing what to say, I decided on the only thing I could.

"I'm sorry."

"Yeah, me too." Smiling again, he continued, "At least I don't have to figure out how to explain Shaun to Dad at Christmas. He was getting a little suspicious about the 'work colleague' routine I kept pulling."

"You need to tell him." I advised, going down a well-worn road. Eddie's father was the only person in the continental U.S., most of

South America and many small villages in Europe who didn't know the truth about his son's sexual orientation. Unfortunately, another truth was the fact we were fairly sure Jeremy – conservative, former military, former cop, devout Catholic – would likely prefer not to know.

"Let's save that subject for another day, okay?" Eddie looked up, hopeful that enough angst had been sorted through.

"Fine, Scarlett. Tomorrow is another day," I agreed, letting him off the hook. "What do you want to talk about?"

"How about Christmas? Have you set the menu?"

I groaned and threw myself into one of the diner chairs. "I've been trying to avoid thinking about holiday food. Rum cake. Turkey with all of the trimmings. Aunt Marion's ginger cookies."

I began to drool just thinking of all the tasty treats that Christmas would bring. None of which were on my "Thin by Thirty" diet plan.

Eddie, who had been around for both the enthusiastic beginning and slow fade-out of numerous diets over the years just rolled his eyes. "It's Christmas, can't you make an exception?"

"Sure," I responded. "Just like I made an exception for leftover Halloween candy. And the pumpkin pie at Thanksgiving and those little fried dumplings at Judge Garand's retirement party last week. Nope. I'm on the wagon with a vengeance."

"Sarah, I know you want to lose weight, but I think you look terrific just the way you are."

A perfunctory compliment, but I lapped it up nevertheless.

"Thank you, but again let me remind you that you are speaking as a gay man. Your people like women who have a few extra pounds, but straight men, not so much."

Eddie sighed deeply and rubbed his hand across his eyes. I couldn't tell if the gesture was jet-lag related or a result of his amused frustration at our conversation. "I have people? I'm sorry, but when did I get people?"

"Your people." I explained, waving my hand at the imaginary throng surrounding him. "Men who love Liza and Liz and Bette in her chubby, pre-blonde days. I love your people, and they love me, but they aren't going to keep me warm at night."

My friend stared at me for a moment before shaking his head briskly, apparently trying to clear my words from his head in much the same manner as one would clear an Etch-a-Sketch screen. "I'm going to ignore that semi-homophobic stereotype for a moment. Mostly because it's true. I will remind you, though, that I am not the only Thornton man who thinks you look terrific. And the last I checked, my brother David was not one of 'my people'."

Not that old argument!

"I am putting a stop to your e-mails with Livvie. That's the same thing she's been saying to me for weeks, but you're both reading David completely wrong. Sure he loves me, but he doesn't *love* me."

"Care to explain the distinction?"

"I can't believe I have to, but fine. You remember when Jeremy and I went to New York this summer? We saw a few plays with your brother and went out to a fabulous dinner. Everything was perfect, but there were absolutely no romantic undertones between your brother and me. David and I love each other, but in the platonic, 'Donny and Marie' kind of way."

"Okay, first of all, you were there with my dad. Of course the weekend didn't feel romantic. That really would be creepy. And as for Donny and Marie, they're related." Eddie paused a moment. "And they're Mormons."

"What difference does that make?"

"I'm not sure, but I think it does. No, you and David can't be compared to Donny and Marie. You're much more like Greg and Marcia Brady. Not related by blood, but you know there was some action happening in that attic bedroom when the rest of the family was out practicing for the potato sack race."

As amusing as the comparison was, I was surprised to find that Eddie wasn't smiling. Actually, he looked quite serious.

"Eddie…" I began, but my words were cut off as Eddie held up his hand to stop me.

"I'm not going to get into this tonight, Sarah. I'm just saying that if you really want a relationship, you can have one any time."

I shook my head and decided to take the conversation in a different direction. Taking my coffee with me, I plopped into one of the counter swivel chairs.

"Hey, Eddie. You like to hike, right?"

"Yes..." His eyes telegraphed a deep sense of distrust at my question. "Why do you ask?"

I grabbed a straw from the canister on the counter, ripped it open and concentrated on a careful accordion fold of the wrapper. "Well, part of my to-do list includes climbing Mt. Katahdin. I thought you could give me a few tips, maybe go with me to L.L. Bean to pick up some boots and gear."

"Climbing Mt. Katahdin?" Eddie put his mug down heavily, eyes open wider than I'd seen them in some time.

"Yes."

"You want to climb Mt. Katahdin?" His loud, guffawing laughter filled the small diner.

I hopped out of my chair and kneeled on the floor, gathering newspapers and shoving them in the box that had once contained my manger scene. "Your disbelief is less than flattering, Thornton. I can climb Mt. Katahdin if I want to, you know."

"Sorry, Sarah." Perhaps sensing from my lack of reply that his lukewarm apology wasn't making any headway, my friend carried my coffee from the counter, placing it on the table nearest me. "Hey, I'm sorry, really. It's just...It's just that you're not really the mountain-climbing type. You hate nature unless it comes packaged as a white sandy beach with a cabana. I'm not saying you can't climb Mt. Katahdin if you want to. I just can't understand why you want to."

I had to admit that Eddie wasn't wrong.

"Because it's there?"

"Lame answer, Sarah. Why do you want to climb Mt. Katahdin, really?"

Deflating, I went from kneeling to sitting like a cross-legged toddler. Closing the box and moving it to the side of the room, Eddie took its place on the floor beside me as I confessed, "Because she wanted to."

"She, who?"

"She, me. She, 25-year old Sarah. She wanted to climb Mt. Katahdin and be married, and successful at her job and own her own house. She had all these dreams that are so far away from my reality that I don't even remember having them. I want to remember what it's like to be her again."

I dipped my head, hiding my face behind my fringe of bangs and the mug of coffee, drinking deeply.

Yuck.

The only thing worse than coffee with fake cream and sugar was cold coffee with fake cream and sugar.

"Climbing Mt. Katahdin, huh?"

I nodded, too drained from my admission to speak further. Emotional conversations clearly required an energy level I couldn't sustain on my current low-calorie regime.

"Well, luckily I haven't had time to get your Christmas present yet. Let's head up to Freeport tomorrow and get you some sturdy hiking boots."

"Really?"

"Really."

I rose from the chair and gifted Eddie with a hug that made my sore shoulders wince.

"Oh, Christ, Bennett. Get off me. It's just a pair of boots."

It was more than the boots, and he knew it. Willing to end his embarrassment, however, I ended the hug with a smack to the back of Eddie's head. "Shut up and come upstairs. I'll make you a twelve calorie sandwich."

"Mmmm. Sounds yummy," Eddie replied. "I traveled thousands of miles and that's all you can offer me?"

"That's all I have. Just try it." I knew his sense of adventure and morbid curiosity at what I would serve him would win out over his revulsion at the dish. Grabbing his hand and pulling him up from his seated position and toward the stairs, I belatedly realized that Eddie had about forty pounds on me. My strained muscles that had lain dormant during most of our conversation made themselves known once again with a vengeance and collapsed. Unfortunately, the combination of our forward momentum, the fact Eddie hadn't yet gotten his feet beneath him from his crouch and our aggregate weight tipped us both headfirst toward the pantry stairs where we landed in a tangle of limbs.

"Bennett!" Eddie's muffled disgust was heard from somewhere under my left armpit.

"Have I mentioned how nice it is to have you home, Thornton?" I laughed, then yelped at the sharp pain it caused in my ribs.

Perhaps kickboxing class should wait just one more day.

*   *   *

A few days after nearly breaking the younger Thornton brother's collarbone by merely trying to stand erect, I found myself in a heated debate with the elder brother on my way home from work.

"You need to talk to your father." I insisted, clutching my cell phone to my ear as I walked the half mile home from the office, my puffs of breath visible in the frigid December air.

"No."

"What do you mean no?"

"I mean no, Sarah." David repeated, sounding just as frustrated with me as I knew I felt with him. "I agree with Dad. If you want to buy a house of your own, that means moving out of your apartment. If you do that, Dad should buy you out of your share of the building. Your dad and mine bought that building together. Uncle Ed left his share to you. If you move out, you should be compensated accordingly."

"Compensated accordingly?" I mocked. "Seriously, David, you sound like a tightass corporate borg. Oh, wait, that's right. You *are* a tight…"

"Hey, before you finish that sentence you might want to remember that you're the one who called me asking for a favor."

Crap.

I really needed to stop annoying the people I wanted help from.

"I'm sorry." I tried to sound as contrite as possible, even if I didn't feel it. "I just don't understand what the big deal is. Sure, if I buy a house I'll move out of my apartment. I figured I'd just rent it to someone else and the rent would pay my part of the mortgage on the diner building. I mean, that's all my rent covers now, anyway."

"Sarah, it's not going to be that easy." The rush of air from David's sigh could have powered a small wind farm. "First of all, you can't rent that apartment to just anyone. It opens up into the diner, so we need to make sure we rent to someone we can trust. Besides, do you really want to be an absentee landlord? Dealing with complaints about water pressure and days when the snowplow blocks you in and all of the little things that you deal with as a homeowner but tenants wouldn't be so tolerant of?"

My friend did have a point. I loved the charm and character of the old Victorian near the waterfront, but someone paying rent might not want to put up with the closet doors that didn't shut tight, the toilet with the very sensitive handle or the north wind that came down from the attic nine months out of the year.

I bit my chapped lip, trying to control the tears of frustration that threatened to fall. This was supposed to be one of the easiest tasks on my list. I was sick of stumbling blocks and just wanted to see one task through to completion. "God, David, I just want to buy a house. That's all. I've got some money saved up. I figured I'd call a realtor, sign some papers and rent a moving van. No biggie. Now your dad is hiring an appraiser and talking about refinancing his place to buy me out. That's not what I wanted at all. This is all getting way too complicated."

"I swear, Sarah. If you thought buying a house was 'no biggie', I'd like to see what you consider an actual big deal."

My tears dried immediately at David's condescending tone. Just because I'd called him for advice on how to manage his father and expected my friend to make my problems evaporate with a sweep of his hand didn't mean he had any right to act like he was in charge of me.

At least in my head that was true.

"Look, my decision to move doesn't have to impact Jeremy. We'll block off the pantry entrance to the apartment and I'll find a trustworthy tenant before I leave."

"Great. Block off the pantry and you leave only one method of exit to the apartment which you know is illegal. Besides, you've known my father your entire life. In that time, what has led you to believe that any major decision you make doesn't impact him?"

"I'm hanging up now, David."

"Sarah, don't be like that."

"I'm not being like anything." I lied. "I'm home and its cold and I can't unlock the door and hold the phone at the same time. I'll call you later."

"Fine."

"Fine." I snapped the phone shut and jammed my key in the door. Once inside I slammed it shut behind me and stomped up the stairs to my apartment. Ready to stab another door open with my key, I was only mildly surprised to find it already ajar.

Of course. Martha Stewart and Bob Villa must have beat me home.

I walked over to the counter and placed my purse beside the day's mail that was sitting in a neat pile. Scanning the rest of the apartment I saw my morning coffee mug washed and sitting upside down in the dish drain and a neatly folded drop cloth and ladder in the corner of the room.

That explained the smell of fresh paint.

"Uncle Jeremy? Eddie?" I yelled out as I wandered through the living room, pausing to turn on the computer that sat on the desk near the side window. When I walked into my bedroom, I found the closet door off its hinges and lying sideways across my bed. At its foot stood Eddie who was running a plane across what I assumed was the bottom edge of the closet door. Wrinkled curls of pine wafted down and surrounded him in an odd looking nest. Jeremy leaned on my closet threshold, a beer in one hand, issuing instructions to his son.

"Hi, kiddo." Jeremy stood to his full height which was just a hair shorter than Eddie and crossed the room to give me a warm hug. "Are you home already? I didn't realize it was so late."

"It's after seven. I would have been home sooner, but Frank was at a hearing in Augusta and I spent most of the day keeping Morgan from committing malpractice before he actually gets licensed."

"Hey, pest." Eddie raised his plane in salute. "Morgan? Is that the intern you've been complaining about?"

"Yup." I rolled my eyes. "Spare me from talking about him tonight, please."

Eddie shrugged, returning to the task at hand while I took another look at my doorless closet and the fresh carpet of shaved wood. "Um, what are you guys doing?"

"You said the closet doors were sticking, so I thought Eddie and I could take care of them."

"And the ladder in the kitchen?"

"The paint on the kitchen ceiling was looking a little dull. I'll get to the living room tomorrow or the next day."

"Uncle Jeremy..." I would have dropped to my bed with exhaustion at having this conversation yet again, but there was a six foot closet door reclining on it at the moment.

The mere fact of which actually made me even more fatigued and in need of lying down.

"This is crazy. Just because you've decided to get the building appraised doesn't mean you have to fix every little thing that's wrong with the place in one week."

"Now, now. Don't spoil my fun. One of the few things Eddie and I have in common is our love of Home Depot. You wouldn't want to deprive me of bonding time with my son, would you?" I looked to the aforementioned son for confirmation and had to admit he seemed fairly content.

"You know me, Sarah," Eddie gave me a lascivious wink. "Nothing I love more than HGTV and a chance to use my drill."

No way was I going up against all three Thornton men.

"Well, then, thanks for the door. And the paint. I guess." I grabbed some casual clothes that had been balled up on the closet floor and slipped into the bathroom to change.

Listening to Jeremy express satisfaction at Eddie's work, the next sounds I heard were the two men reassembling my closet.

"So, Sarah, have you spoken with my other son lately?" Jeremy initiated a new conversation through the closed bathroom door.

"Um, yes. I talked to him earlier." I emerged from the bathroom and tossed my work clothes in the hamper across the room, abruptly changing the subject. "Two points. So, are you staying for dinner?"

"If you have enough." Jeremy said needlessly, knowing I always made enough for company when Eddie was in town, expecting that he and his father would arrive for most meals.

"I think tonight is that big charity event David's attending at the Metropolitan Opera House," Eddie piped in, already moving toward the kitchen.

I nodded, remembering David mentioning his plans before I'd launched into the conversation about the building appraisal. "I think you're right. Do you know who he's bringing? Barbie or Midge?"

Eddie burst out laughing at my comment, drawing his father's narrow gaze and low growl. I was lucky to sidestep any admonishment as I went to heat up our supper in the kitchen. I might have felt bad if my characterization of David's girlfriends was in any way wrong.

A very intelligent and sensitive man in most areas of his life, David Thornton's criteria for choosing women hadn't changed much from the time he was thirteen years old. Namely, the flashier, blonder and better endowed a woman was, the more David was attracted. I was never quite sure where he found these women, but after one or two dates he always ended up sorely disappointed and highly surprised that dinner conversation was limited to stories covered in US Weekly. In fact, knowing David's type of woman was one of the main arguments I used against Livvie's theory that my friend was attracted to me.

I hated to label him as shallow, because David always ended his relationship with the bimbette of the week when he discovered they couldn't make a deep connection. The tragedy was that he never quite figured out that a woman with a lifelong dream of being shaved by Howard Stern might not be able to hold up her end of a conversation about the Dow Jones Industrial Average.

"Get out." I grabbed Eddie's arm from where he was already pawing through my refrigerator in search of something edible and coming up short. Luckily, I had recently prepared a vat of homemade spaghetti sauce – a low fat dish that even my traditional meat and potato uncle would enjoy. A quick zap in the microwave and we could eat.

"What do you boys have planned for the week?" I asked, rummaging through my silverware drawer while my guests took turns washing the sawdust off their hands at my sink.

Eddie answered first. "I need to run up the coast for a few shots of snow-covered lobster boats. I was commissioned to do the pictures for a piece that's going to run in Yankee magazine in March."

"If you go on Wednesday I can leave Sammy in charge of the diner and go with you." Jeremy called from over his shoulder, looking through my cupboards for bread – which he was not going to find. "We can stop for lunch in Augusta and visit my friend Earl."

Eddie caught my eye briefly, before responding, "Earl, the dean of students at U Maine Augusta? That Earl?"

"Well, yes, that happens to be Earl's job."

Uh, oh.

I popped open the microwave and gave the sauce a stir, trying to make myself one with my appliances, thereby somehow avoiding the imminent fireworks.

"Dad! We are not having this conversation again. I decided ten years ago that college isn't for me. I haven't changed my mind. Why do you keep pushing?"

My uncle put the plates on the table with a little more force than was necessary. "I'm not pushing. I just don't think you've thought through your decision. When I was a boy, I would have given my eye teeth to go to college, but there just wasn't the money. I've offered to pay your way time and again..."

"And it's not that I don't appreciate it," Eddie interrupted. "But I don't need to go to college. I have a career and I'm very happy."

Jeremy turned to me, trying to gain support. "Would you listen to my son? Have you ever heard anyone so bullheaded and stubborn?"

"Yes. You and David every time you open your mouths." That earned a ghost of a smile from each of the Thorntons.

Jeremy shrugged, hating to lose the point, but lapping up the comparison of his sons to himself. At heart, my uncle was nothing if not the proud father. "Of course I'm glad my boys have forged their own way in the world, and I know it's a cliché, but sometimes father really does know best. Call me old fashioned, but I liked it when they used to mind me."

"Don't worry, Dad. We still mind you. Well, *most* of the time." Eddie winked, playfully mussing his father's hair and earning himself a well-placed punch to the bicep. The two men shadow-boxed around the kitchen while I put the pasta on to boil, an amazing show of choreographed chaos that would have made Jerome Robbins proud.

Finally the microwave bell alerted us that dinner was ready. I tossed the sauce through the pasta and both men piled their plates high. I took a small, reasonable portion and aside from my feelings of jealousy and bitter deprivation at the differences in our caloric intake, we ate in comfortable silence until the food disappeared. Following a long sigh of content, Jeremy peered at me over the top of his glasses. "You know, what I said about my boys goes for you too."

"What's that?"

"I mean that part of me wishes you'd stayed a little girl so that you would mind me, too. I know you want to buy a home and I think that's a wonderful thing. Everyone should aspire to be a homeowner, but Eddie told me it really has something to do with some harebrained scheme you have to make your life perfect by your next birthday."

I kicked my friend under the table. Eddie always had been the rat in the family.

"I don't know what Eddie told you, but it is not a harebrained scheme. You said yourself that aspiring to be a homeowner is a good thing. There's nothing wrong with trying to improve myself, is there?"

Jeremy furrowed his brow in thought. "No. No. I think improving oneself is a noble goal. I'm just concerned about some of the other things I've noticed recently with the strange exercise classes you've been attending and I heard Gloria is setting you up on a date with her nephew next week."

Jeremy finished his milk in one long gulp. "I just don't want you to turn out like that Mary-Kate girl that wasted away to nothing, or those boy-crazy girls that party all night and don't wear any underwear."

Knowing that my uncle's concern was sincere, I bit the inside of my lip and avoided eye contact with Eddie. When I was in enough pain to ensure I could keep a straight face, I solemnly swore that I would be reasonable in my weight-loss efforts.

And always wear panties.

"I'm just doing a few things to get healthy and meet new people. I mean, don't you ever get lonely sometimes, Jeremy?"

An unexpected smile crept across my uncle's face. "Well, no. Not so much as of late, that is."

"What do you mean?" I couldn't believe what I was hearing. From the shocked look on Eddie's face, I could tell this was news for him, too.

"Are you seeing someone, dad?"

"I don't know. Is 'seeing someone' the word you kids would use for keeping company with a lady friend? I think I would consider it 'courting' if I had to give a name to it."

"Who exactly are you 'courting'?" I pressed, dying for details.

"Oh, now, a gentleman doesn't provide details. It's not polite." Jeremy rose from the table and kissed me on the forehead. "Speaking of which, I have to take off. I'm afraid I have plans later. Will you drop Eddie off at home after he helps you with the dishes?"

"Sure."

With a pointed look at his son, indicating that he *would* be helping me with the dishes, Jeremy left, leaving two gaping mouths in this wake.

* * *

Exactly one week after my uncle dropped his conversational bomb at my dinner table, the two of us stood in the middle of the diner placing the last strands of tinsel on the now overly-decorated tree in the middle of the room. As far as I was aware, we were the only family left on the planet that still strung the fake silver threads from their tree. Mrs. Borbozzi from the dollar store told me she ordered a few boxes special for us every year.

"You really don't have to do this, Jeremy," I reminded him for the hundredth time. "It's only a few days before Christmas. David will be here on Saturday, or we could put it off until after the holidays altogether."

"Sarah Bennett. I swear to all that is holy, if you don't stop telling me what I do and do not have to do, I will sell this building outright and donate the profit to the Portland Home for Wayward Cats."

I moved my fingers to my lips, zipping them tight, a timely gesture as the bell over the diner rang at the same instant, heralding the arrival of the real estate appraiser David had scheduled us to meet with.

Even if I could have talked, I wouldn't have had the words. The woman who entered the diner was a tiara and flaming baton short of a beauty pageant escapee.

Caryn Carmichael was roughly my height – five foot four or five – but with the added height of her stilettos and beehive-styled hair, she barely made it past the top threshold of the door. I couldn't help myself from wondering exactly how much of the destruction of our ozone layer could be directly related to keeping that bouffant aloft.

I didn't realize I'd been openly staring at the woman until I heard Jeremy clear his throat beside me, a warning signal from my childhood that really meant, "If you kids don't behave, I will start knocking heads together. Don't tempt me."

Duly chastened, I swallowed the giggles that crept up my throat and tried to avoid eye contact in order to keep them at bay.

"Mr. Thornton?" Caryn's high squeaky voice didn't disappoint and completed the picture.

"Please call me Jeremy." My uncle's impeccable manners kicked in over his shock as he grasped one well-manicured hand. "This is my business partner, Sarah Bennett."

Business partner. Wow. That sounded so grown-up and official. Knowing that the title actually belonged to my father, it also sounded very, very wrong. Fortunately, I was prevented from walking down that maudlin road, since just as Jeremy mentioned my name, Caryn gasped and both hands covered her mouth.

She was either channeling Fay Wray or had just swallowed a fly.

"You're Sarah Bennett?"

"Um, yeah."

"*The* Sarah Bennett?"

"I suppose..."

Caryn grabbed my right hand between both of hers and began pumping like she was Annie Sullivan and I'd just discovered the word for water. "David has told me so much about you. I am just so pleased to meet you!"

"Well, thanks. It's nice to meet you, too." An awkward moment passed as Caryn stared at me, Jeremy stared at her, and I wondered exactly what reputation 'the Sarah Bennett' would have to live up to. "So, should...um...should we get started?"

"Of course. Of course." Walking toward the kitchen, Caryn said, "So, Davey tells me you two are planning to sell this place."

I wasn't sure whether I was more disturbed by her affectionate nickname for my friend or his apparent characterization of our meeting today. "No. No. We're not selling the building. We just need to know its value so we can think through some refinancing options, right Jeremy?"

An inexplicable look passed over my uncle's face as he turned toward the petite woman. "Well actually, Caryn, we're probably just looking at the value of the building, but we do want to keep our options open."

"We do?"

Squaring his shoulders, Jeremy turned back toward me. "Well, yes. I mean, I'm not going to want to run the diner forever, Sarah, and I know you and my boys have other plans for your lives. If I'm going to buy your share of the building anyway, it might just be a good time for me to think about selling the whole kit and caboodle outright."

I suddenly felt the guilt of the world settle firmly around my shoulders. "Jeremy! I told you that you don't have to..."

"Just hush, Sarah. We're not making any decisions today. We're just going to listen to what Caryn here has to say."

I glared at my uncle, feeling somehow shanghaied by this entire experience. "We're just listening," I agreed warily. "But we *will* be talking about this later."

Caryn gave me a brilliant smile, probably meant to sooth my obvious nerves. Instead it only made me wonder how many thousands of dollars she'd invested in dental work. If the number was as high as I expected, it was possible that her teeth may have cost more than her breasts.

And those puppies were clearly worth a bundle.

"We're just here to talk, honey." Caryn put her arm around me and gave my waist a little squeeze. "Don't you worry now. We won't make any tough decisions today."

The annoyance I felt when men patronized me by reaching for the keys to my car, silently asserting that because they had a penis they should never deign to sit in the passenger seat didn't even come close to the rage I felt when women pretended we all belonged to one big sorority, linked by our double X chromosomes.

Sensing that if he didn't get Caryn away from me he might have to sweep up bleached blond chunks of hair from his floor before the morning shift, Jeremy jumped between us. "Should we start in the diner?"

"That sounds like a lovely place to start, sugar. Let me grab my clipboard and we'll get you both the information you're looking for."

Watching Caryn work I hated to admit that she was surprisingly competent. She crawled through the basement, walked the property line and even commented on the walk-in freezer Jeremy and I had invested last year's tax return check in. She was familiar with the model and said it would add a great deal of value to the price of the property. I should have known David wouldn't have hooked us up with someone who wasn't good at her job, despite appearances to the contrary.

"Well, let's have a look upstairs now, shall we?" The overly perky agent asked, finally arriving at the only part of the appraisal I was actually prepared for. I led the way up the stairs and found myself opening closet doors, demonstrating the pressure in the shower and explaining away the water stain above the couch. I felt Jeremy twitch beside me, clearly annoyed he'd missed a spot on his own gigantic to-do list.

Two hours after the visit began, Caryn was standing at my kitchen counter going through her notes, her faux-Chanel suit still crisply pressed while my cotton t-shirt felt like it had wilted and crumpled under the strain of the day.

"Well, I think you've answered all of my questions." Caryn snapped her briefcase shut. "I'll need to go down to City Hall later this week for some more information and then you should expect to receive a report in a week to ten days."

I handed the woman one of my business cards. "That sounds great. Thank you. You can mail it to my office."

"You work for Frank Murphy?" She squealed.

"Um. Yes..."

"You don't happen to know Morgan Donovan, do you?"

Just when I thought this experience couldn't get any worse...

I considered jumping in with a sarcastic reply. After all, I worked in a law office with four employees and while I may not be happy about it, chances were good I knew Morgan Donovan. However, not wanting to risk another chastising throat clearing from Jeremy, I answered the question straight. "Yes. Morgan and I work together. Do you know him?"

"Only a little bit. That boy is just a gem, isn't he? Just a gem."

"Yup. He's a gem alright."

"I mean, the Church Street Womens Shelter would never have made their goal without his donation. It put them over the top." Caryn held her hand to one ample breast. "And don't even get me started about the Elder Agency picnic. He and the foster grandfather he was paired with could not have been cuter at the horseshoe pit. It just about brought a tear to my eye."

Jeremy piped in as he walked Caryn to the door. "Is that the same Morgan I've heard you speak of, Sarah?"

Translation: Why have you been slandering this poor boy?

"I guess it's the same person, but I can't say I've ever seen a charitable side to him." I turned back to the diminutive bearer of this odd news. "Are you sure the Morgan Donovan you're talking about is the one who interns for Frank Murphy? It isn't a common name, but it isn't that unusual either."

"Oh, I'm sure. Morgan Donovan, formerly of the Donovan Trust. When he gave up his position a few years ago and went to law school it was in all the business sections of all the papers."

"Wait a minute. 'The Donovan Trust', as in the charitable division of Donovan Industries?" My brain was having difficulty processing at an appropriate rate of speed. "Donovan Industries employs half the mid-coast region."

"Didn't Frank ever mention Morgan's previous line of work, kiddo?"

I shook my head at my uncle. "You know Frank. He walked Morgan in on his first day, said, 'Here's the new intern', and told me to teach him how to make coffee and unjam the copier."

"And Morgan has never mentioned…"

I had the good grace to be a bit embarrassed. "Let's just say that our relationship hasn't exactly fostered a lot of productive conversation."

Caryn watched the back and forth between me and my uncle with much interest. "Well, it doesn't surprise me at all that Morgan didn't talk about his family business or all the amazing work he does for charity. That boy is just something else."

"He's something alright," I agreed, ushering the woman to the door. "So, you said we'll be getting your report in a week or so?"

"Ten days at the most!" Caryn smiled brightly as I closed the door not completely in her face.

Flopping on the couch next to my uncle who had collapsed himself a moment before, I asked, "If we call Eddie do you think he'll bring over Chinese take-out?"

"Probably."

We both stared at the phone sitting mere feet away, but still well out of arms reach.

"So, what did you make of that business with your co-worker?"

I shrugged. "I'm still not convinced it's the same Morgan Donovan. Even if it is, it doesn't surprise me in the least to find out he's a spoiled trust fund baby. The charity work is probably all just a write off."

"You are not a very trusting soul, Sarah. How did that happen?"

"Well," I explained while wriggling my body to lay flat as possible so as to snag the leg of the end table on which the telephone rested with my ankle, dragging it forward. "I was raised by two men who carried guns and gave me a can of pepper spray the first time they let me go to a co-ed roller skating party when I was thirteen."

"I suppose that could have had something to do with it," Jeremy nodded wisely in agreement. "Don't forget the extra garlic soy sauce on my dumplings."

"Wouldn't dream of it." I dialed Eddie's cell phone, my eye catching on the "Bachelor Lobstermen of Maine" calendar on my kitchen wall.

December 19th.

Soon I would be a third of the way through my 29th year and I hadn't checked off any of the items on my to-do list. Still, I rationalized that I'd just met with a real estate appraiser who was going to put me on the road to get the financing in line to buy a house. That was progress!

I'd also lost six pounds. Of course, if I was honest with myself, I'd realize I wasn't actually that much closer to my dreams of wearing a size eight. If anything, it just made my size twelve jeans fit a little bit better.

Listening half-heartedly to Eddie repeat back our take-out order, I thought about the ill-fated trip we'd taken a few days ago to buy hiking boots. He labeled all of my choices as impractical and I'd nixed his as ugly and heavy. It was going to be tough to climb a mountain without boots.

And then there were the men in Portland who were still mostly undatable and the fact it seemed I would have to outshine Albert Schweitzer to be noticed by my employer...

"Sarah!"

"Huh?" I heard my name being yelled both from the receiver in my hand and from the man sitting beside me on the couch. "Oh, sorry. Just got distracted there for a minute."

I directed Eddie to meet us in my kitchen with food half an hour later before turning to my Uncle who was looking at me with a mixture of bemused fondness and alarm.

It was a look I was used to receiving from each of the Thornton men.

"Sorry about that. I just caught a glance of the calendar and freaked out about everything I have to get done."

"Don't apologize, kiddo. The holidays are a very busy time." Jeremy said, misunderstanding the scope of my anxiety. "As much as I love the season, I also look forward to January. There's something about hanging a new calendar for a brand new year. Full of promise and a fresh, clean slate."

I brightened at my Uncle's words. He was absolutely right! Between the holidays, David's impending homecoming and the Lyman trial due to begin on Tuesday I couldn't possibly expect to make any progress on my to-do list in the next week or so. January, though, would be an entirely different story. The New Year holiday was all about fresh beginnings and resolutions.

A new year would make all the difference!

January

IT WAS THE FIRST MONDAY of the New Year and it turned out Uncle Jeremy had been right. The fresh turn of the calendar filled me with new energy and inspiration. A few days earlier I'd printed my "Before 30" list on lavender scrapbooking stationery and armed with renewed motivation and a 50% off coupon, I'd gone to Kinko's to have it laminated. It now held a place of honor on my refrigerator door, stuck there with my favorite magnets – one a photo frame of Livvie and me in our law school caps and gowns, sticking our tongues out at the camera and the other my name emblazoned on a plastic Hollywood star. Free from its original cross-outs and rewrites, the list now read:

By the time I reach thirty years of age, I will:

1. Be in an amazing relationship
2. Fit into a size eight purple suede miniskirt
3. Be partner at a law firm
4. Own my own home
5. Climb Mt. Katahdin

There. Five items printed in black and white (well, black and lavender anyway) didn't look that scary. Despite some early and fairly spectacular setbacks, the clean slate of a new year had convinced me I could meet every goal I had set for myself. After all, my birthday was nearly nine months away.

If I could only ditch my residual New Year's Eve hangover and actually get out of bed, I would be unstoppable.

I finally tore myself from my cozy bed with a groan and made the mental note to never let Eddie play party bartender again. Thanks to his amazing punch which should probably be administered by prescription only, I had only vague memories of the holiday two days ago. I remembered that the food was delicious and think we watched the ball drop in Times Square on TV. That was about it. The fuzziness started setting in just about when Livvie and I jumped up on the bar for our rendition of "I've Got You Babe". Thank god I had the foresight to confiscate the camera phones at the door.

One scalding hot shower and extra primping time later and I was a new woman. Looking at my reflection in the mirror, even I had to admit I looked pretty snazzy in my best go-to-court suit. I certainly looked appropriate for tackling the item on my to-do list I had been the most successful at avoiding head-on.

I wanted to become a full partner in Frank Murphy's law firm.

I knew, despite my renewed vigor in changing my life that this would be no easy task. Frank was very proud of the fact that he ran a successful solo firm and was beholden to no one. The Law Office of Francis G. Murphy was a surprisingly successful firm given its small size and accepted most civil cases with the only Frank-imposed rule being a refusal to take on any criminal defense work. As a former police officer himself, Frank refused to argue a case whose outcome hinged on the cross-examination of a cop.

In fact, Jeremy's friendship with Frank – which had led to my interview with the man in the first place – began in the late seventies when my boss was a fresh-faced rookie. During his initiation period, Officer Murphy was briefly paired with seasoned Detective Jeremy Thornton and the two hit it off immediately. When Frank decided to change jobs and left the force to enter law school, he kept in touch with my uncle sporadically through Christmas cards and the occasional phone call. In between, Jeremy tracked Frank's progress through newspaper articles cataloging the younger man's skyrocketing legal career.

If Frank was going to accept me as a partner and share a name on his letterhead, I had to prove my worth to him and demonstrate that the firm simply couldn't function without me around. For that to happen I needed to morph into the perfect employee, and beyond producing flawless work I needed to actively take time to point out my accomplishments to my boss.

That was the easy part.

As much as I had to admit it, being the perfect employee also meant getting along with Frank's protégé. I had to accept the fact that Flying Monkey Morgan was here to stay. He was going to graduate from law school in the spring and if he passed the bar, all signs pointed to Morgan joining as a full time associate. If that was what Frank wanted, then by god I was going to be supportive, even if it killed me. If my boss wanted to hire a Geico caveman to argue motions in District Court, then I would offer to sign the timesheets myself.

In short, my grand plan was that if I conducted myself as Frank's partner, making it official would seem like a natural progression when I pitched the idea.

Walking toward the courthouse – my first stop of the day – I considered whether this particular goal needed more specific planning, and composed a mental sublist:

To be Frank's partner I must:

1.   Point out to Frank how hard I work for him
2.   Work even harder
3.   Submit only flawless work product
4.   Be nice to the Flying Monkey

Oops. I meant "Be Nice to Morgan".

Ignoring the last item for the moment and focusing on the first, I increased my pace. While I logically knew my boss was aware I worked hard, I never thought it was particularly important to keep him apprised of the numerous things I took care of around the office to make his life easier.

That was about to change.

I slipped quietly into the back of Courtroom B where Frank was just finishing up his trial and took a seat on one of the uncomfortable oak benches reserved for observers. Court was still in session and Frank paced back and forth in front of the jury members who were clearly captivated by his storytelling. When not confronted by "Trial Frank" on a daily basis, I forgot his ability to make and hold eye contact with each individual juror, magically drawing them into his version of the events that had unfolded throughout the trial.

With a moving plea for a finding in his client's favor, Frank completed his closing argument and the presiding judge dismissed the jury, leaving them to their deliberations. I had never argued before Judge Kristoff before – she was fairly new – but I had served her scrambled eggs and toast once or twice at the diner on a busy Saturday.

A lousy tipper.

I sat back down after the jury shuffled out of the courtroom while Frank took the break as an opportunity to speak to his opposing counsel. Mike Newell was in his early 60s and owned many versions of the same expensive looking suit, each in a more unflattering color than the last. Today he wore the suit I privately referred to as "Mud Season Brown". I couldn't hear the conversation, but from body language I could tell Mike did not appear to be enjoying Frank's comments. After a moment, he turned his back to attend to some papers while my boss was still talking to him.

While I'd never taken a class in interpreting body language, even I knew that couldn't be good.

Grinning when Mike finally grabbed his papers and stormed out of the courtroom, no longer able to ignore him, Frank caught my eye and nodded. I smiled back in return and walked through the small swinging door and down the aisle until I stood alongside him at the plaintiff's table.

"What are you doing here?" He asked in the clipped tone reserved for trial. Luckily, I was long since immune. Frank's gruff manner was nothing to be afraid of, but when he grew overly polite and smiled his large, toothy smile it was time to run for the hills.

"I came to see the master at work, of course."

Narrowing his eyes, suspicious of the unsolicited flattery, Frank simply ignored it and looked at his watch. "Never mind. Tell me what you want on the way back to the office. I have to get back and return some messages."

Frank purposely chose the overpriced rent of an office next door to the courthouse for the convenience of running back and forth several times a day. Snatching his briefcase from the table and walking at his normal fast pace, Frank assumed I would keep up. Not an easy task considering Frank was nine inches taller than me and not currently wearing the new three inch Jimmy Choo pump.

Trotting beside my boss, I tried very hard not to pant.

Finally arriving at the office building, Frank held the door open for me as I tried to wipe the sweat from my forehead, covertly masking it as a half-wave to Gloria sitting on her usual perch at the reception desk.

"How was the trial?" She asked, handing Frank his stack of pink out-of-office slips.

As Frank was engrossed in reading his messages, I jumped in with a response hoping my attempt at seamlessly meeting my boss' needs would be noticed. "Frank was awesome. He had Mike Newell running scared."

"I can speak for myself, Bennett," Frank growled.

That was not exactly the notice I had been hoping for.

Experienced in the art of redirecting bad behavior, Gloria deftly asked, "Why were you at the courthouse this morning, Sarah?"

"I wanted to file the Hendricks deed before noon. Since Frank was finishing up his trial, I thought I'd stop by and meet him. I'm going back later this afternoon to file the Abrams motion if you need me to pick up any forms."

Frank's head popped up from his messages at the mention of the Abrams case. I was working on a particularly difficult property division case that could lead to a precedence being set in state court, so he was very interested in its progress.

"Did you make the changes we talked about? Introduce the handwritten amendment and cite the Jansen case?"

I rolled my eyes. "Yes, Frank. I did everything you asked, and it's in your in-box for a final once over. When you tell me it's perfect

– which it is – I'll sign the motion and have Gloria prepare a filing package. I'm going to hand deliver it to the clerk myself."

Frank grunted, mollified for the moment, and returned to his pile of messages.

"Just one more thing," I said as casually as possible. "I thought I'd ask Morgan to join me today. You know, give him a little tour of the courthouse and show him how things are done."

Frank just stared at me, mouth agape. Gloria, usually unflappable, sputtered a bit and repeated, "Morgan?"

"Yes." I decided to try for wide-eyed innocence. "Is that a problem? I thought he was working a full day since the spring semester doesn't start until next week, but did you have other plans for him today?"

Frank exchanged a glance with Gloria, then seemingly having regained his composure, perched on the edge of her desk, long legs stretched out in front of him, crossed at the ankles. Leaning heavily on his arms, he asked, "Are you planning to do him in by any chance? If so, I think the courthouse is a poor choice. Lots of witnesses and several of them are in uniforms and carry weapons."

Gloria frowned in disapproval at Frank's words, without seeming altogether unconvinced he was wrong. "Sarah, Morgan is a fine man. I don't know what you're planning for him this afternoon, but I just don't see why you two can't get along. "

Hearing a chuckle beside me, I looked up and into Frank's smirking face. "Gloria thinks he's a fine man. What more of a ringing endorsement do you want?"

"I don't want a ringing endorsement and I'm not going to have him killed, for crying out loud. You keep telling me to be nicer to Morgan. That's all I'm trying to do, so stop looking a gift horse in the mouth."

Frank shook his head, clearly disbelieving my good acts came without an accompanying trick up my sleeve. "I didn't get to be where I am by trusting things at face value, Bennett. I know you're up to something. I just don't know what."

It was difficult to be too offended in the face of my boss' mistrust given that I actually did have an ulterior motive.

I just didn't have to admit it.

Luckily, before the bell rang to mark the beginning of round two, Gloria stepped in to my corner. Turning her back to me, she faced my boss. "Well, Francis, since we have no tangible reason why we shouldn't, I think we really must trust Sarah and believe her offer is based on a sincere desire to do as you've asked."

"Thank you, Gloria," I replied, trying and failing in my effort to keep the smug look off my face.

"Oh, don't misunderstand me, dear." Gloria whipped around, now directing her words to me. "I think Frank's right. You're up to something. I just believe a person is innocent until proven guilty and I hope my faith in you will be well founded."

Well, crap. One smug look effectively erased. Gloria had an incredible skill at letting someone know that she was on to them, without ever making it look like they'd actually been admonished.

If I wasn't sure before, I knew at that moment why I'd left this as the last self-improvement item I would tackle. I loved Frank and Gloria – admired them and respected them, too. But they didn't let me get away with anything. Diets and relationships were kid stuff compared to dealing with these two.

"Look guys, I'm just trying to be a team player here." I again tried to remind them that regardless of my motives I really was offering to do something nice. My comment, though, was met with two disbelieving stares.

Did I mention already that these two were a tough crowd?

"Okay." I held up my hands in supplication. "I will admit that this attitude may be coming out of left field, but can't you just chalk it up to a new leaf for the New Year or something?"

Before I was able to get an answer, the object of our discussion walked through the door.

"Hello, Morgan," Gloria chirped.

"Morgan." Frank nodded in acknowledgement.

"Hi, Morgan," I said, smiling brightly.

In retrospect, I don't think the shock of my greeting was the *only* reason Morgan stopped dead, his continued forward momentum causing him to catch his foot on the entry hall rug.

And I certainly shouldn't be blamed for him windmilling his arms in an effort to recapture his balance, thus flinging his full cup of coffee across the room, catching Frank squarely in his broad chest.

"Jesus Christ!" My boss bellowed.

"I am so sorry, Frank!" Morgan grabbed at the Kleenex box from Gloria's desk and moved toward our boss, as if to wipe him off. However, an invisible force field consisting of straight-man testosterone and fortified by Frank's glare kept him from actually following through with the deed.

"Never mind," Frank said, rubbing his hands vigorously across his nearly hairless scalp, a rare show of frustration. "Never mind. I have some spare clothes in the office. It wasn't your fault. Not your fault at all, Morgan."

Even if Frank hadn't been staring at me when he said that last bit, it would have been hard to miss the subtle inference there.

Gloria, Morgan and I flinched as one as the door to Frank's inner office slammed with a final fury. The moment the reverberations stopped, I was met with two very pointed glares.

"What?" I asked, daring them to place the blame on me.

Gloria merely sighed and gestured toward me as she turned to Morgan. "Sarah is going to the courthouse this afternoon to file a motion. She thought you might like to join her so she can show you around a bit."

"Why?" Morgan's openly puzzled look was my final undoing.

"Oh for God's sake!" I exploded, giving voice to the persecution of my good deed which I'd felt since the moment the unending discussion had begun. "I am trying to be nice! I am a very nice person! What the hell is wrong with you people?"

Instead of inciting anger with my words, I was surprised to see Morgan break out in a grin. A mighty handsome looking grin, actually. "I'd love to go to the court with you this afternoon, Sarah."

"Fine. Come get me at one o'clock." I shook my head and walked toward my office, completely befuddled by the morning's events. Following Frank's lead, I slammed my door behind me.

Being nice was not supposed to be this hard.

* * *

When I entered the safe cocoon of my office, the amount of work piled on my desk provided me with the happy distraction I needed. As the next several hours ticked by, my blood pressure slowly retreated to a life-sustaining number, and I barely registered the soft tap on my door.

I glanced at the clock on my wall. One o'clock on the dot.

"Come on in," I yelled. Somewhere over the course of the busy morning, Frank had approved and signed the motion that I needed to run over to the court and I was as ready for this outing as I would ever be.

I opened the door to face my nemesis, annoyed anew at the bright smile and nice packaging that greeted me. You would think the spawn of Satan would at least have the decency to look the part. "Ready, Sarah?"

"Sure."

Morgan helped me on with my coat – two points for being a gentleman – and Gloria and Frank were nowhere to be found when we escaped through the front door. I had no doubt that Gloria purposely distracted my boss to ensure we did not have a repeat of this morning's performance.

The walk toward the courthouse was fairly uneventful. We spent a few minutes discussing the weather as we walked through the brisk, cool wind, but really, how much time could that kill? "Cold, huh?"

"Yeah, cold." It was January in Portland, Maine. Once you acknowledged the cold, conversations about the weather grew pretty dull.

I took a sidelong look at Morgan and caught his eyes flitting suddenly away, caught in his own furtive glance. Squaring my shoulders, I acknowledged that the entire outing was going to be a disaster if I didn't at least try to be a little friendlier.

"So, has Frank ever taken you to court and showed you around?" I tested the waters.

What appeared to be a grateful smile ghosted across Morgan's lips. "No. Not yet. I had to come with my civil procedure class last semester, though."

"Is Professor Daniels still teaching that course?" I asked, relaxing as we found a safe topic. I was an alumni of the same school he attended. Certainly we could find some common ground at good old Maine Law.

"Yeah. He took a sabbatical last year, but he's back now."

"Is he still as scary? I shook in my boots through most of his classes." I remembered back to my first year when there was a rumor going around that Professor Daniels' annual bonus was based on the number of students who dropped out after tuition was deemed nonrefundable, solely due to fear of his class. Livvie often remarked that he made John Houseman look like Santa Claus.

"You think John is scary?" Morgan asked with a note of surprise.

John? I had never really known the man's first name, but supposed that could be it. Of course, I would have found it just as likely that his first name was Lucifer, Damian or "Rabid-Old-Man" which is how he was most commonly referred during the years I'd been at school.

"I guess I never really thought of him as scary," Morgan continued. "Intense, maybe, but I really liked that about him. I spent a lot of my time first year hanging out in his office, just shooting the breeze. He's a good guy."

Son of a bitch.

Although I didn't give voice to my thought, it must have telegraphed loud and clear through the look on my face, because suddenly Morgan's eyes grew much too large for his face and he began backpedaling.

"I can see where he could come across as pretty scary, though. I mean, he knows so much. I can understand why some people would be intimidated by him."

Some people who were inferior to the great Morgan Donovan, perhaps? Frank's suspicion that I was luring Morgan to the courthouse to meet his violent end suddenly seemed even more inviting than the idea of my making partner.

Partner. That's right, I reminded myself, blowing my bangs away from my face. My laminated lavender refrigerator list shimmered like an oasis on the horizon. This outing was aimed at helping me make partner at Frank's firm and if I contemplated pushing Morgan into a snowdrift every time he said something infuriating, it was going to be a very long afternoon. I turned my head side to side until my neck cracked with relief and plastered on a fake smile, leading Morgan through the metal detectors as we arrived at court.

Luckily, the first person we ran into was a truly friendly face – Trenton, my favorite bailiff. I introduced him to Morgan and explained with a wink that Trenton knew all the secrets of the courthouse – who was having affairs, which attorneys secretly took a nip of something stronger than coffee between cases and which judges relied on their law clerks to do all of their work. Trenton was a man you wanted on your side.

"So, what do we owe the pleasure of today's visit?" Trenton asked, crossing his long arms across his chest, giving the slightest bit of bulk to an otherwise lean and lanky frame. "I don't remember seeing your name on the docket sheets this morning."

"Nothing scheduled today. I just came to drop off a filing," I explained, holding up my manila folder.

"You do know that you can file those electronically, don't you?" Trenton said, a twinkle in his eyes anticipating my answer.

"As if Frank would trust his practice to technology," I laughed. "Speaking of which, have you checked out the new website? I still need to play around with some of the links, but it's looking pretty good."

"Wait a minute. You set up Frank's website?"

I tried very hard to curb my annoyance at the disbelief dripping from Morgan's tone and explained, "It's not that big a deal. I took a weekend course at the community college a few years ago to set up a site for the diner to grab some of the tourist traffic."

"I haven't been online much lately except to see pictures of the grandkids on Facebook," Trenton replied to my original question, returning my focus to the older man. "I'll be sure to check it out."

"Great. Hope the rest of the day goes well." I turned to leave, but found my progress halted by my friend's arm on my sleeve.

"One second, Sarah. I saw the Freeman case settled. That looked like it was going to be a doozy of a case. What happened?"

"It went right to the last minute," I answered, wishing desperately that attorney client privilege didn't apply so I could regale Trenton with the tale of two business partners dissolving their firm based on their affair with the same woman. In the end, it was our client's willingness to expose the tax returns to the public record and the other side's unwillingness – based on a separate but even messier divorce case caused by the same affair. "Let's just say Mr. Freeman walked away pretty happy."

"I'm sure he was." Trenton turned to Morgan. "You could learn a thing or two from this woman. She tries to settle her cases, but at the end of the day she'll take her case to trial. That's the mark of a good lawyer. You need to be unafraid of the courtroom."

Morgan glanced at me quickly, eyes alight with a spark I couldn't name and hadn't seen before. My opportunity to identify it passed quickly, as he returned his attention to the bailiff. "I've seen too many men and women walk these halls who secretly hate going to court. They want to make deals from their office and practice law over the phone. This girl – and Frank's another one – they are here to practice law."

Embarrassed, but pleased by the praise, I said a hasty goodbye and dragged Morgan to the clerk's office where we took our place at the back of a long line.

While I leaned back to study a particularly interesting water stain on the ceiling, Morgan decided to break the tedium in a different way. "So, Sarah, is this part of a New Year's resolution or something?"

"What?" I snapped my head down, completely thrown by the question.

"Come on, Sarah, why are you trying to be nice to me?" He gave me a hint of a smile. "It clearly isn't easy for you."

For crying out loud. Were we really going to go through this again?

"Believe it or not, I am a very nice person." I bit out and shoved an errant strand of hair behind my ear, wondering why everyone was acting like it was so out of character for me to behave in a civil manner. "If you remember, Mr. Donovan, when you first started at Frank's office, I was very nice to you. Super, sticky, sugary sweet nice."

Morgan's hint of a smile was gone in an instant, replaced by a look that I could only call bewildered. "And, she's gone again. You are the most maddening woman. Five minutes ago we were having a nice conversation with your friend Trenton and now you're made of ice again."

I glanced quickly to my left and right, ensuring that Morgan's words weren't overheard. Partner or pauper, I had worked hard to build my professional reputation and wouldn't stand to be part of the courtroom gossip mill. "Keep your voice down. I don't know what you're talking about."

He shook his head from side to side, this time his ghost of a smile could no longer be mistaken for mirth and the flash of his blue eyes were no longer surprised.

The man before me was angry.

And damn if it didn't make him look a little bit hot.

"No." Morgan held up his hands. "Just no. I am not letting this go again."

Knowing that I had mere moments before we really were the talk of the town, I grabbed my co-worker by his wool overcoat, trying not to be distracted by the firm bicep that filled out the sleeve and yanked him out of the clerk's line and behind a stairway leading to the balcony seating above. It was too much to hope that we hadn't been noticed, but at least I had hopefully minimized the damage.

"We are not doing this here!" I insisted.

"Oh, we're doing it! We're doing it here or we're doing it in the middle of the lobby. You decide." Morgan yelled, and then took a step back as he heard his own words and how they might be interpreted.

"Fine." I chose to ignore the double entendre. I was tired of Morgan trying to play the innocent victim when I knew the truth. "Every time I turned around, from that very first week you started working at the firm, you threw me under the bus at every opportunity. What did you expect? That I'd just sit there and take it?"

The lines in his forehead deepened into something that was less anger and more confusion, but still a strong mix of both. "I threw you under the bus? What are you talking about? What does that even mean?"

"You know. Throwing someone under the bus." From Morgan's continued confusion, I could tell that repeating the phrase was not helpful. "You tried to sabotage me in front of Frank whenever you could so that you'd look good and I'd look incompetent."

"You thought I was trying to sabotage you?"

"Of course you were!" I shook my fists in frustration.

"How was I sabotaging you?"

Was he completely daft? "You kept pointing out my mistakes to Frank, instead of me. You took work off my desk so that I couldn't find it when I needed it. You returned phone calls that came to me so I didn't know what was happening with my own cases. You made me look stupid in front of other attorneys."

"But, there were mistakes in your work. And Frank or Gloria asked me to take some of those assignments from you."

"And you couldn't leave a note? I didn't care that you did the work and might have even appreciated it if you'd told me about it, but you should have sent me an e-mail to tell me what you were working on or that you had returned a message so that I didn't have to." Seeing a glimmer of understanding in Morgan's expression, I continued, "You could have pointed out my mistakes directly to me and given me the opportunity to fix them instead of bringing them to Frank's attention."

"You thought I was purposely sabotaging you?" I was still scrutinizing the way Morgan cocked his head to the side as if seeing me for the first time when he turned sharply away and walked dazedly toward the small bench across the lobby, outside the main courtroom.

Feeling the tectonic plates of my life shift beneath me at what I was rapidly beginning to believe may have been a misunderstanding of epic proportions, I gave us both a moment to gather ourselves before following Morgan to the bench where I hovered over him.

"She thought I was purposely sabotaging her work." Morgan muttered, head down, apparently talking to the voices in his head. After a moment, he raised his wide, apparently guileless eyes to me and remarked, "Well, I guess that does explain some things."

"So you weren't doing those things on purpose to make me look bad?" I held my breath, awaiting the answer, but knowing this performance could not have been faked.

"No." He denied vehemently, before breaking into a sheepish grin. "Well, I mean, of course I was trying to make myself look good in front of Frank. But I swear I wasn't trying to do it at your expense."

"If that's true, why didn't you come to me when you found a mistake in my work?"

Morgan shrugged. "In the beginning it just made sense that if the work was on Frank's desk, it would be easier for him to fix it and I wouldn't have to bother you. Later on, though…"

"Later on?" I prompted.

Morgan glanced at me from under his fringe of blonde. "Well, later on you kind of made it clear that you hated me. I tried not to talk to you at all if I could avoid it."

Fair enough.

"Move over." I lightly pushed Morgan's leg which was unfortunately every bit as firm and distracting as his arm, and sat on the bench next to him when he made room. He opened his mouth to say something, but I put up my hand to stop him. "Wait. I'm still processing."

I ran my hands through my hair, mentally evaluating every exchange I'd had with Morgan and running it through the new filter of information I'd received.

Another few moments of quiet passed before I turned to him and asked, "Have you always acted this way around co-workers? Hasn't anyone else complained about your work style?"

Morgan mumbled something under his breath, but I couldn't hear him. When I asked him to repeat his words, he said, "I've never had co-workers before. This is my first job."

"How old are you?"

"Twenty-eight."

"Twenty-eight? It isn't possible that you're 28 years old and you've never had co-workers before." I dismissed. "I don't mean in an office. I'm talking about any co-workers."

"I've never had co-workers." Morgan shrugged, feigning nonchalance, but the way his eyes darted toward and away from mine belied an unexpected vulnerability.

"So you're telling me you've never had a job before this one? Waited tables? Worked retail?" Each question was met with a negative shake of the head. "You've never folded t-shirts at The Gap?"

"Nope," Morgan replied.

I suddenly remembered Caryn's words from a few weeks before and snapped my fingers together. "The Donovan Trust. Donovan Industries. That was you, wasn't it? You worked for your family. Well, that's a job. Giving away thousands of corporate dollars to charity certainly counts as a job."

My companion shrugged. "Yeah. I guess, but not really. My job consisted of going on the internet and Googling charities. When I found one I liked, I'd spend a few weeks volunteering to make sure it was legit. If I liked what I saw, I'd talk to my dad and show up with a check."

"Huh. So you weren't trying to be a creep. You just didn't know any better."

"Hey..."

"Shut up Morgan." I said, my smile removing any heat from the statement. I rose from the bench and put out my hand. "Let's start over. Hi, I'm Sarah Bennett."

Morgan smiled as he stood. A true, dimple-inducing smile. "Morgan Donovan." He grasped my hand firmly. "Nice to meet you. I understand we'll be working together."

I didn't know if it was the warmth of his hand or feeling the cloud of anger I'd always felt in Morgan's presence lifting, but in that moment, my breath came a little easier and I didn't have to reach very far to find a smile that answered the one I received.

"Great. Before we start, let me tell you a few things about working with other people. Lesson one, when you want to make changes to someone else's project..."

Unfortunately, my words were abruptly cut off by a loud shriek to our left.

"Ohmigod! Sarah!" The grating, fingernails-on-a-chalkboard voice was unmistakable, but I hoped against hope that I was wrong.

Turning to my left, I acknowledged the woman behind the voice with as much enthusiasm as I could muster.

Which wasn't very much at all.

"Hi, Cory." God really does like to play mean, horrible jokes on me.

With long copper curls and a smile that could make the Osmonds jealous, five foot ten Cory Latham slithered between Morgan and me. He wore a startled, wary expression and I wasn't sure whether it was in reaction to Cory's eardrum-rupturing hello or my less-than-friendly greeting.

My marked displeasure at seeing Cory must have looked even more unusual to an outside observer given her apparent *thrill* at running in to me.

Of course, Cory and I both knew it was all an act.

"I, like, never see you here anymore!" She cooed, and then moved her attention to Morgan.

Which, of course, was the only reason she had accosted me at all.

"And just who do we have here?" She asked, pointing a perfectly manicured nail at Morgan.

I supposed I was expected to make introductions at her prompt, but where Cory Latham was concerned, social graces were just not something I cared about. I'd already been a player in her games and lost.

After waiting a moment for me to say something – anything – Morgan finally stuck out his hand in reply and introduced himself. I pretended to ignore the confused look he gave me.

"Oh, you're the fresh meat that Frank Murphy hired, huh?"

I did bite my lip to hold in the chuckle at that choice of terminology and the glare that ghosted across Morgan's face, transmitting his distinct displeasure. "Frank hired me, yes. I don't know quite what you mean by 'fresh meat'."

"Oh, you know." The young woman responded, clueless to her new acquaintance's change in mood. "Frank has a reputation for hiring inexperienced law students and working them to death. Right, Sarah? You should know."

I wanted nothing more than to be able to jump to Frank's defense, but unfortunately Cory's characterization wasn't entirely untrue. Frank did like to hire interns right out of law school. He worked them hard, and therefore most did not stay with him for long, but he also gave them amazing opportunities that they would never have in a larger firm. Not wanting to engage Cory in any way, I just shrugged and became incredibly interested in gnawing at the cuticle on my right thumbnail.

Morgan gave me a pointed glance, again waiting for me to properly introduce the annoying redhead.

Wasn't going to happen.

"I don't believe I know your name." He was finally forced to say.

"Oh, sorry. I'm Cory Latham, a secretary in the District Attorney's office. I work with Livvie DiMarco, and I've heard all about you." The last sentence was said with what could only be called a come-hither glance.

I took a look around the clerk's office, calculating the number of bailiffs and deputies in view and decided Frank was right. A murder – this time I was contemplating Cory's untimely demise – should wait until I was in a room with a slightly less visible show of law enforcement.

"Oh, I remember Livvie. I met her at your diner a few months ago, right?" Morgan turned, desperately trying to engage me in the conversation. He looked a bit like cornered prey, and he wasn't far off the mark.

By the time Cory commented, "Oh, I haven't been to the diner in ages!" I decided it was time to come to Morgan's aid.

"If I remember correctly, Uncle Jeremy told you that you weren't welcome at the diner, which would be why you haven't been there in ages. Well, we really must be going." I pulled at the arm of Morgan's coat and yanked him out of the danger zone. "Bye, Cory."

Cory glared at me for ratting out her forced expulsion from the diner but flashed all of her pearly whites as she said goodbye to my companion. "It was awfully nice meeting you, Morgan. Any time you want a tour of the DA's office, you just give me a call!"

We bolted for the clerk's office, and it wasn't until we were safely behind closed doors that Morgan turned and asked, "What in the world was that?"

"That was Cory Latham," I replied. "She works for Livvie in the DA's office and is just the laziest, most inappropriate, mildly crazy, indiscrete, gossipy wench that you will ever meet."

Morgan nodded, apparently agreeing with my characterization despite only a brief encounter. "Why doesn't Livvie fire her?"

"She can't. The state office of Human Resources hired Cory, and unless she does something outrageous, it's impossible to get rid of her."

If only Morgan knew how hard Livvie had tried.

"You seem to get along well." He smiled at his own joke.

"We share a bit of history," I admitted. I wasn't sure how much of my history with Cory I was willing to share with Morgan. He and I had definitely made some progress, but I didn't know if I fully trusted him yet, and some things should stay buried.

"That was pretty obvious." His lips quirked in a smile. "I was a little jealous for a moment there. I mean, I thought you reserved that kind of intense nastiness just for me."

I stopped short and turned to face him, glaring. "Morgan Donovan. Did you just make a joke at my expense?"

He looked a bit nervous, but nodded his head. "Yeah. I guess I did."

"Well good for you." I smiled and continued toward the clerk's office to again stand in line. "I probably deserved that."

Morgan grinned, pleased at my reaction. "So, are you going to tell me about your history with Cory? Or why your uncle banned her from his diner?"

"Not today." I worried my lip between my teeth for a moment. "Probably not never, but not today. Okay?"

Morgan gave me a reassuring smile. "Sure. I was just looking for some tangible reason to dislike her."

"Listen, not for anything, but you might want to watch out for Cory."

"Don't worry," he assured me. "She's not my type. She's a little too predatory for my taste. Besides, I like my women a little smarter, with a little bit of an edge. You know, women like you."

Women like me?

Women *like* me or women like *me*?

My face flushed a bit as I tried to decipher the inflection in Morgan's tone while he cleared his throat and looked away quickly, apparently as surprised at his words as I was.

"Hey," he said at a volume probably louder than intended, an obvious attempt to quickly change the subject. "Weren't you about to start my lessons for being a good co-worker before we were so rudely interrupted?"

Thankful and more than willing to go along with the the abrupt change in direction, I smiled and responded, "Yes, I was. Lesson one.

If you find an error in my work or think I should make a change, bring it to my attention first."

"Done. Next?"

This might actually be kind of fun. We shuffled closer to the clerk's desk. "Lesson two. Hard as it is to believe, I really am a decent person. If you ever end up working at a bigger firm, make sure you document any instructions you get from your boss or co-workers. Never underestimate the importance of CYA."

"CYA?" Morgan tilted his head to the side. "What's that?"

"You've never heard of covering your ass?" I linked my arm through his and led him up to the clerk's desk, unable to hide my amusement. "Morgan, I think this may be the beginning of a beautiful friendship."

February

"NOT THOSE." I INSTRUCTED DAVID as he pulled the most expensive lasagna noodles off the grocery store shelf and put them into our cart. "Get the store brand."

My friend rolled his eyes and instead continued to walk down the aisle plucking various canned ingredients from the shelves, expecting I would just follow behind.

Which I did.

"I'm not getting the store brand, Bennett." He called back over his shoulder. "They taste like cardboard. If money's the issue, I'll pay the difference."

From my vantage point, I couldn't see David's cocky grin, but knew all the same it was there. All David had to do to win an argument was take a shot at my pride. "You're not paying the difference, Thornton. If you're going to be a baby about it, I'll make your father's birthday lasagna with the noodles you like."

"...but the store brand would have been perfectly fine." I muttered under my breath as David's attention turned to Livvie, who had rounded the corner with a loaf of bread in each hand.

"French or Italian?"

"French." "Italian." David and I spoke together in one breath. Livvie stood by silently waiting for a final ruling while David and I conducted an unspoken conversation. Sighing, I nodded, again acquiescing to my friend's wishes.

"French!" He joyfully reported to Livvie.

"French bread with lasagna?" I whined, punching David lightly on the arm. "You've got no couth, Thornton."

Ignoring the children's antics, Livvie peered into the cart at the ingredients we had gathered while she was in search of bread. "Man, Sarah, this is going to be one fantastic dinner. I'm glad you're not on a diet anymore."

"I haven't given up on my diet." I was taken aback by my friend's assumption. "This is just a special occasion because all three of my favorite men are home at the same time for Jeremy's birthday."

Feeling insulted and needing to defend myself, I proudly reported that I had even lost seven pounds during the month of January. Amid the sincere congratulations of my friends, I somehow failed to mention that I'd actually gained six pounds between Christmas and New Year, so really I had only netted a loss of one pound.

Hey, seven pounds was seven pounds, right?

"So who is coming to the big birthday shindig?" Livvie asked as we continued through the store. "I ask, because I haven't been officially invited yet. I'm only assuming I'm on the list because it would be pretty crappy of you to have me help shop for dinner I'm not allowed to eat."

I laughed at Livvie's backward request for an official invitation. I forgot sometimes that for all her bravado, Livvie wasn't at all the rabid pit bull she projected.

Also realizing Livvie's presence had been only assumed and not actually requested, David bent on one knee in front of the fresh kale. "Ms. DiMarco, would you please accompany me to my father's birthday dinner tomorrow night?"

Livvie put out her hand and adopted the accent and coquettish manner of a southern belle as she answered, "Why Mr. Thornton. This is just so sudden. I simply don't know what to say."

"Eddie is making cheesecake."

In an instant, Scarlett O'Hara left the building. "Oh yeah. I am totally there!"

"Who else is coming?" David turned, knowing that I would be on top of most of the details.

"Jeremy invited about a dozen of his cronies from the force and a few of the diner regulars. I thought I'd invite Frank, too."

I avoided Livvie's loud huff at the mention of my boss.

"Have you invited Gloria?" David asked.

"I wasn't planning on it. Do you think I should?"

His lips quirked in a knowing smile. "I have a feeling Dad already has. Since they're dating each other and all..."

"No way!" Livvie and I pounced for details. "He hinted a few months ago that he was seeing someone. Are you sure it's Gloria?"

"Yup."

"How do you know?"

David straightened his shoulders and buffed his fingers against the collar of his jacket. "Because I am clever, cunning and have keen deductive skills."

We waited a beat for the punch line.

"Yeah, okay." David slouched into a more natural, relaxed pose. "I caught an earlier flight home yesterday than Dad expected and walked in on them having dinner."

"Good for them," Livvie replied.

We strolled through the frozen foods for a moment, each lost in our own thoughts of considering this seemingly unlikely match when Livvie asked, "Since it looks like the rest of your office is coming, should you invite Morgan? Now that you're getting along it would be too bad to piss him off."

David jumped in before I could answer. "No. This guy has never met my father. We're not going to just invite him to a family party."

While surprised by David's vehement response, I agreed. "No. I don't think it would be appropriate."

Livvie just clicked her tongue at the both of us and kept walking.

"Since you mentioned Morgan, did I tell you that he and I ran into Cory at the courthouse a few weeks ago?" I asked, pushing the cart lightly into the back of David's thighs to stop his dawdling and prod him down the aisle.

David winced at the name. "I take it you behaved yourself? My father didn't call and ask me to wire bail money, so I assume you did."

"I was the picture of charm and grace," I replied, ignoring the chuckles of my friends. "Okay, let's just say I didn't kill her."

David turned to Livvie. "Tell me something. With all of that hot

Italian blood of yours, how do you work with her day in and day out knowing what she did to Sarah?"

"It isn't easy." We turned into the wine aisle where Livvie immediately zeroed in on her favorite brand of Chianti. She selected two oversize bottles from the shelf, then thinking better of it, went back for a third. "Most of the time I try to ignore her. When I can't do that, I make a game out of insulting her in ways that go over her dumb, pretty little head."

"That can't be hard," I commented.

"Nope. Not hard at all." Livvie gave her most wicked grin and I was reminded anew that people who counted Olivia DiMarco as a friend were very lucky.

Those who counted her as an enemy were pretty much screwed.

Without a list and with barely a word exchanged, we continued to walk through the store silently, a well-oiled, three-armed machine. Aside from David's continued and snobbish insistence on the most costly ingredients, there was barely a misstep between us as we landed at the checkout line.

For some reason I could not explain, my mind kept returning to Cory and our most recent exchange at the courthouse. "Do you know what I really don't understand about Cory?" David and Livvie, both standing slightly in front of me in line shook their heads in the negative. "I think sometimes she honestly wants to be my friend and can't figure out why I won't play nice."

"Wanting to be your friend is a lovely idea in theory, but the last time I checked the friendship manual, there was a rule against sleeping with your friend's boyfriend." Livvie announced, loudly enough that the cashier paused mid-scan and glared at me, probably assuming I was the offender and not the onerous Cory.

"Well, we did say Cory was dumb," I said, digging through my purse for my wallet. "I actually feel sorry for the men of Portland."

"Speaking of, how are things on the manhunt front?" David asked, casually slipping his debit card to the cashier before I had a chance.

"Not so great. The drive-thru dating was horrible. I took a brief hiatus, but now I'm back in the saddle and hoping to meet someone at the singles party next Friday night."

"Oh yeah. Tell me about that," David commanded. "How on earth did you talk my father into turning his diner into a whorehouse for the evening?"

Not even bothering to address the 'whorehouse' insult, I replied, "If you remember, Mr. Thornton, the diner is also half mine. At least for the moment. I have every right to use it as I see fit."

David pinned me with a knowing look that said there was no way I would do anything at the diner without Jeremy's approval and he was well aware of that fact. Having another person know your every thought could be a bit disconcerting at times. Oddly comforting, but disconcerting.

"Okay, fine," I explained as we walked out of the store and began loading the groceries into the back of the Jeep David rented for the trip from the airport. "I talked Uncle Jeremy into letting us throw a singles party at the diner the Saturday after Valentine's Day. It was Livvie's idea."

"Nice. Pin it on me, why don't you?" Livvie complained with no heat. Turning to David, she explained, "I did talk Sarah into it and I think it's a great idea. We put up posters all over town. A few trays of munchies, soda, coffee. No overhead and no cover charge. The only rule is that each woman who attends must bring at least one single man.

"Who are you bringing, Livvie?"

My friend had the good grace to look embarrassed. "Donnie."

David stopped loading and just stared. "You're bringing your ex-husband to a singles party? You two really do have a very odd relationship."

Livvie shrugged. "I needed a single guy. What do you want?"

David turned my way, "How about you, Bennett? Who is your single male ticket to this party?"

"Morgan saw me hanging up posters and volunteered to be my single man. Of course, that was before I knew you'd be in town for your dad's birthday." I smiled suggestively and let the unasked question hang in the air.

"No." David slammed the trunk shut. "No way."

"Why not?" I whined

Ignoring my lament, he deflected attention. "How about my brother? He's in town, too. Why didn't you ask him instead?"

"No thanks," I shook my head. "He already has enough single, attractive men on his team. The last thing I need is for Eddie to infiltrate our ranks and actively try and recruit new members."

David laughed – one of his rare, deep laughs. "I'm sure he'd be flattered by the faith you have in his powers of persuasion."

We hopped in the car and rode in amicable silence for a few blocks until David mused, "You know, a room full of single girls might be interesting."

"Those single girls live in Portland, Thornton. Have you forgotten that you live in New York? What would be the point of meeting someone here?"

David grinned, "I know you find this hard to believe, DiMarco, but there are jobs available in New York. Perhaps with my dazzling smile and charming personality I could convince someone to relocate for me."

I considered this possibility and poked my friend in the shoulder. "A peek at your fat bank book probably wouldn't hurt."

"Thanks, Sarah. That's very flattering." My friend took a left at the light and continued on toward the diner. "Or…I suppose I would consider moving back to Portland if I met the right girl."

I was shocked. David never mentioned such a possibility. "You would? I thought you loved New York."

"I do. I just like to keep my options open."

I knew David sensed my shock when he grabbed my hand as it lay loosely in my lap. "Don't look so freaked, Sarah. I'm just kidding. Don't worry. I won't crash your little party."

I smiled and squeezed his hand back, but couldn't respond, knowing my friend and I were not on the same page. It wasn't the idea of David crashing a singles mixer that bothered me, but instead his casual suggestion that he would consider moving back to the Portland on account of a woman.

That bothered me a great deal.

* * *

On the night of the singles mixer, as I stood to the right side of the diner counter, two thoughts warred each other for attention in my head. The first was, "Why did I think this party would be a good idea?"

The event reminded me of every junior high dance I had ever attended. Most of the boys stood in one corner of the room talking about the latest video game technology while the women stood together on the other side, pretending to chat with one another, but instead actually checking out the gaggle of men across the room.

The second thought that beat a consistent tempo through my skull was the insecure thought that all of the other women were prettier than me. Thinner. Cuter. Younger. It didn't help that the only mixed-gender interaction taking place occurred in the middle of the room between the twenty men who had peeled themselves from the pack and the two or three skankiest women in attendance.

The true insult came in the fact that I had even "skanked-up" for the occasion. Knowing we would be competing for attention against women who were likely five years or more our junior, Livvie had convinced me to join her in both raising our hems and lowering our necklines. Extra makeup had been applied, and I even dragged out my curling iron from its home in the back of the linen closet for the occasion.

While I basked in my own personal insecurities, I could at least hold onto one pleasant fact. Livvie had "arranged" for Cory to go to a conference out of town, so I didn't have to worry about her showing up at the diner. I should have felt guilty at the thought of the State budget footing the bill to increase my chances at a date, but I didn't have the heart to care.

It took a while, but an hour or so into the party it looked like the men and women were starting to mingle a bit more. I noticed Livvie talking to a nice-looking man with a blue button-down oxford and I gave her "the look" to silently ask if she needed a rescue. I was happy to receive a very subtle headshake in return – she was having a good time.

Livvie had made me promise that we would work the room separately. We normally stuck together, which might make us too intimidating for some men to tackle. Seeing Livvie having fun gave me the courage to square my shoulders and leap into the fray. The first eye I caught, though, was actually another female friend of mine – Claire – who looked every bit as uncomfortable as I felt. She tapped the shoulder of the man standing next to her and they both walked my way.

"Hi Sarah. This is my brother, Keith."

"Hi Claire. Hi Keith." I took her brother's hand with a smile, but was disheartened to find that he didn't even pretend to make eye contact. Something behind my left shoulder had caught his attention and wouldn't let go. Claire and I made small talk for a few minutes, but every time I glanced back at Keith or tried to draw him into the conversation, it was obvious that his interest was elsewhere.

Getting annoyed, I finally looked over my shoulder where I was less than surprised to find a perky brunette standing behind me making googly-eyes at the smitten Keith. She nibbled on her swizzle stick in a manner that would have been considered public obscenity in at least twelve states.

I turned back to Keith and waved dismissively toward the girl behind me. "Oh, just go already."

"Thanks!" I finally got one sincere smile out of Keith before he bolted.

Claire at least had the good grace to look annoyed by her brother's antics. "Sorry about that."

I shrugged. "No worries."

I understood brothers. While David would never have shown such bad manners, Eddie had stood me up numerous times over the course of our lives for a better offer.

She smiled and pointed to my right, in the direction of the diner door. "Don't look now, but someone's giving you the eye."

I looked up, slightly nervous at what I might find, but was pleasantly surprised to see Morgan smile and nod in my direction. When he hadn't shown up when he said he would, I figured he just chickened out. Smiling, I excused myself from Claire and we walked toward each other, meeting in the middle of the floor. "Hey, you showed up!"

"Sorry I'm late."

"I'm just glad you showed. Livvie almost didn't let me attend my own party without a single man." I took a good long look at

Morgan as he explained the automotive catastrophe that had led to his tardiness. As my knowledge of cars was limited to adding gas, oil and windshield wiper fluid, I found my mind – and eyes – wandering.

The boy cleaned up good.

Actually, it was more accurate to say that he cleaned down good. I was used to seeing Morgan in khakis and tucked-in, button-down oxford shirts. Once in a while he even mixed it up with a jacket and tie. He always looked very nice at the office, but clearly this was a man that was much more at home in a pair of jeans and a grey thermal Henley. He even sported a gorgeous turquoise stone tied around his neck with what looked like a bohemian looking length of braided hemp. He looked good, but more than that, he looked comfortable.

"So," he asked, "how did you talk Livvie into letting you in without a single man on your arm?"

"Lucky for me, her single man is late, too. Oh, there he is now." I spotted Donnie letting himself into the diner, and slipping comfortably through the diner door next to him – as he had done hundreds of times before – was my ex-boyfriend, Ryan.

Crapcrapcrapcrapcrapcrapcrap.

"Sarah, are you alright? Your face just turned really pale."

"Um, yeah. I'm fine." I knew that Morgan was less than convinced by my answer, but I was too busy trying to remember if locking your knees prevented or caused someone to pass out.

I thought things couldn't get worse, until Ryan's eyes caught mine and the moment nosedived from horrible to devastating. Devastating, because after two years, a destructive breakup and painful recovery period, my stupid heart still leapt a beat when Ryan Corruchi zeroed in on me with that smile.

That stupid, charming, gorgeous, cock-sure, room-illuminating, heartbreaking smile.

Oh, man, I was going down fast.

Luckily, I remembered a life preserver was standing immediately to my left. "Put your arm around me!" I hissed.

"What? Why?" Morgan's confusion at my behavior turned to concern. "Are you going to pass out? Should you sit down?"

I watched Ryan part through the throng of people, intent on approaching me. Luckily, I still had time to implement my hastily thrown-together plan as he was stalled by the sea of women who – like me – were not immune to his charms.

"The guy with the black coat coming our way. He's my boyfriend. Ex-boyfriend." I inhaled sharply, wishing I had a brown paper bag to breathe into, my words tumbling out faster than I could stop them. "Do you remember Cory from the courthouse? He cheated on me. With her. Donnie's the other guy. He's Livvie's ex-husband. I don't know why he's here, but I'm afraid that he wants me back."

"Donnie?" Morgan asked.

"No, Ryan! Keep up!" I hissed. "I think Ryan wants me back. Donnie kind of hinted he did, anyway. I don't want him back, but he's not going to believe me unless I'm with someone else. Why should he? I'm not even sure I believe me. Maybe I do want him back. But I shouldn't. Anyway, I need you to put your arm around me and pretend you're interested. If you do that, I swear you can make fun of me, undermine my career, do anything you want. I don't care."

"Sarah, take a breath." I complied while Morgan continued, "I think I actually caught enough of that to figure out what's going on. Okay – I'll play along, but you owe me."

I took another breath as the weight of Morgan's arm settled on my shoulders. "Anything."

My companion smiled – perhaps the correct term was smirked. "Great. You owe me. If you really agree that I can collect anything as payment we'll put on a show that will send this guy packing. Otherwise, I walk."

"Are you kidding? You're blackmailing me? No way." I turned away from Morgan and his appealing shoulder. "I'm not going to agree to something unless I know the terms."

Morgan shrugged. "Okay then. Have fun talking with your ex."

Oh god. I had one instant to make a choice between two inevitably bad decisions. On my right was Ryan, approximately three steps from reaching me for what purpose I didn't know. Actually, that was a lie. I knew what Ryan wanted. Sure he was a cheat, but he wouldn't have come to the diner just to rub my nose in my single status and he wouldn't try to pick up other girls on my turf.

He wanted me back.

While I didn't want Ryan *back*, I was honest enough to admit that I did *want* him – at least on some levels – and I didn't know if I was strong enough to turn him away without help.

On my left, we had Morgan. Sure we were getting along pretty well lately, but he was insane if he thought I would just agree to owe him a favor without knowing what I was signing up for. Had he never seen a mafia movie? These things never ended well.

My brain clicked into gear as I suddenly realized I couldn't think of anything that I wouldn't agree to do.

Free diner food for life? Done.

Take the bar exam for him? No problem.

Re-enact his favorite scene from Showgirls? Let me just grab my pasties and I'm good.

No, I needed to promote the charade that I didn't need Ryan sniffing around. Realizing I really didn't have an option, I jumped in with both feet.

"Sure, Morgan." I faked a coquettish giggle, both volume and pitch several notches higher than usual as I clamped Morgan's arm back down over my shoulder. "Anything you say."

"Hi, Sarah."

I turned to the men who greeted me. "Hi Donnie. Ryan."

"Hi, Sarah. You look good."

"Thanks. You too." And damn if I didn't mean it.

As if sensing my resolve about to crumble, I felt the squeeze – a bit harder than entirely necessary – of Morgan's hand on my arm. "Sarah, honey, aren't you going to introduce me to your friends?"

"Sure. Morgan, this is Livvie's ex-husband Donnie and his friend Ryan."

Ryan's blue eyes caught mine as he said, "There was a time I was your friend, too, Sarah."

At the soft cadence of his words, I began to second-guess myself. There really was a time when Ryan was my friend. There was a time I thought we were going to spend our lives together. I started to remember the good times before that one foolish moment with that one foolish girl when it was all gone.

I was about to shrug Morgan's arm off my shoulder and ask Ryan to join me in a corner of the diner to talk about another chance. My shoulder muscles twitched in anticipation, but just before I took action, I noticed Ryan's eyes wander from mine to the swizzle-stick twirling blonde who was now standing just to my left. His eyes were back on me in a moment.

An instant, really. But in that instant my resolve returned.

Maybe Ryan was sorry. Maybe he did miss me. And maybe I missed him, too. But there was no maybe about the fact that I just didn't trust him.

"There was a time you were my friend, Ryan, but that was a long time ago."

The four of us stood, not knowing quite how to pull the conversation back from its serious tenor when the hostess in me bubbled up. "Does anyone want a drink? I can show you where they are."

Too many years of serving coffee in a diner led to the odd defense mechanism that left all of my companions looking at me in disbelief.

"Um. No. Thanks anyway." Ryan looked around the diner, taking in the few changes Uncle Jeremy had made over the last two years. Nothing drastic – a fresh coat of paint, a few more pictures on the wall. "The place looks good. I've missed it."

I assumed that was my cue to invite him back to the diner during regular hours and end his exile, but that was Jeremy's decision to make.

Before I could think up a safe, inane conversation starter, Ryan again turned serious. "Are you happy, Sarah?"

Morgan took on his role with gusto, giving me a protective squeeze as he pointedly answered for me, "We're very happy. Thanks for asking."

Ryan turned to Morgan, the soft emotions he reserved for me erased from his face until only an arrogant shell remained. "Yeah. You're both so very happy that Sarah planned a singles party to meet men. Give it a rest, fella."

Oops. I had forgotten that crucial little detail. Looking at Morgan's face and the way the two men were squaring off, I decided to end the charade.

"Now isn't a good time Ryan."

My ex turned his attention back to me. "I'm not staying. I just wanted to say hello and ask if I could come by sometime. You know, get a cup of coffee at the old place."

"No, Ryan. That's not a good idea."

"Well, if you change your mind."

"I won't."

Ryan sized me up and nodded. "You know how to get in touch with me."

Breathe. Breathe. Breathe. Breathe. Don't respond. Don't respond.

He waited a moment, than Ryan turned and left the diner without another word.

An awkward silence reigned as Donnie remained behind. Never awkward for long, though, Donnie looked around the room and rubbed his cupped hands together. "Well, since I'm here in a room full of single girls, I think I'll have a drink."

I pointed him in the general direction of the refreshments, pulling away from Morgan, and took a moment to collect my thoughts. My first thought, strangely enough, was not about Ryan. It was that Morgan's arm remained around me after Ryan left and I had been the one to pull away.

"Thanks, Morgan. I know that was really awkward for you, but you helped me out of a bind."

He shrugged. "I think it was a lot more awkward for you. Listen, I think I'm going to take off now, so I'll see you at work on Monday."

I was confused. He had arrived just moments before the Ryan fiasco and now he was leaving? He hadn't even had a drink or scoped out the local color. "You're leaving?"

"Yup. I got what I came for."

Nervous by the grin that came over Morgan's face, I questioned, "What does that mean?"

"What does any man want when he comes to a singles party? A date with the prettiest girl in the room." The grin widened and my nerves ratcheted up a notch.

I saw Morgan when he came through the door, and to my knowledge I was the only one he had spoken to. Who...?

Oh.

OH!

"So, does next Saturday work for you? Do you have anywhere special you'd like to go or do you want me to choose?"

"Morgan, I never agreed to go out with you," I stammered, completely at a loss.

"Yes you did." Morgan smiled indulgently as if anticipating my response. "I asked you to agree to a favor, no questions asked. This is the favor. You agreed, so we're going out on a date."

"But we can't."

"Why not?"

It seemed like a very simple question, but really the reasons were multiple and incredibly complicated. I decided to start with the easiest roadblock first. "Morgan, we work together."

"So? I work for Frank, not you. What's the problem?"

"Frank would have a cow. He would go bat-shit crazy if we started dating."

"I'm not afraid of Frank Murphy."

I was stunned into silence. Everyone was afraid of Frank. As much as I denied it, even I was a bit afraid of Frank at times. I tried another track. "Until a few weeks ago we barely spoke to each other. This is not a good idea."

"We're getting along fine now, right?" Morgan waited for me to disagree, but I couldn't and unfortunately, my silence was apparently taken as consent.

"Great! Next Saturday night I'll pick you up at seven."

Morgan paused, one hand on the door handle, and turned back with a deep smile. "Oh, and by the way, this singles mixer was a great idea. Tell Livvie I said thanks."

* * *

Considering that we'd only served appetizers and non-alcoholic beverages, I was amazed at the number of dishes a group of fifty odd singles could create. For an hour after the party ended, Livvie and I efficiently cleaned the diner. We were the only two remaining in the large room, having flicked the lights at midnight, announcing to the crowd in accordance with the song, "You don't have to go home, but you can't stay here."

Finally, I reached into the sink of soapy water and released the plug and we launched into our standard post-show wrap-up with full attention and gusto.

"Did you see the tramp Donnie went home with? I mean, seriously. Can you see him bringing her home to meet Nana DiMarco?" Livvie pouted. "Cataracts be damned, when that old woman sees all that bleached hair and press-on nails, she'll keel over from a stroke."

"I don't think Donnie's plans with that girl included his granny's place for tea," I gently broke to my friend. "Why do you care, anyway? I saw you being chatted up by at least three guys. Any prospects?"

Livvie perked up considerably at the mention of her good fortune. "Well, there was this one guy – Thomas. Mildly interesting and pretty cute."

At that moment we both heard the distinctive 'snick' of a key turning in the lock of the diner. As it was closing in on two in the morning, we might have been alarmed – if we hadn't already been expecting a visitor.

"Of course, none of the men here tonight were nearly as cute as that David Thornton guy. He's just dreamy…"my friend remarked in an exceptionally loud voice which was meant to be overheard.

"I'm dreamy, huh?" The object of her comments walked over to our table, swung a chair around backward, and straddled it. I handed over my coffee cup and watched him take a sip before continuing, "I couldn't sleep and figured you two would still be up gossiping."

I shook my head. "Sorry, buddy. You missed the dishes, so you miss the gossip."

"That's okay. I know how to make you talk." David smiled, stealing another sip from my mug, then rose and went behind the counter to get a beverage decidedly more adult than the coffee that had grown cold.

In a fluid motion borne from ritual, David reached for the tequila while Livvie got up to grab the shot glasses, and I headed into the kitchen for the limes and salt. We converged back at the small round table and began lining up the drinks.

Apparently convinced I was going to chop off a finger, David sighed and took the knife, cutting board and lime from my grasp. Without looking up from his task, he asked, "So Bennett, how did it go? Did you meet Prince Charming?"

"Nope. But I did meet his brothers the Duke of Halitosis and the Lord of Bad Hair Plugs."

"Don't let her kid you, Thornton," Livvie interjected. "Sarah here got herself a date with a promising young attorney-to-be."

David didn't comment, and instead handed me a lime to go with my shot glass. The three of us clicked our glasses together and performed the age-old rhythm of lick, salt, lick, shot, lime.

Ew. Our faces grimaced and contorted as one.

"So, that Morgan guy finally asked you out?"

David's assumption shocked me and it must have shown by the look on my face.

"Yeah, I figured." David poured another finger of tequila and downed it without the benefit of a tangy lime distraction.

"How did you know?"

"I'm a guy. Guys know guys, and I know Morgan." David replied as he rose and turned his chair over, placing it upside down on the table's surface.

Preparing the floor for a good sweep and mop, I followed my friend's lead as I questioned his odd statement. "You haven't even met Morgan."

David paused in his actions, pinning me with his gaze. "Doesn't matter. I know him."

Turning to Livvie he asked, "So, changing the subject, how was the rest of the evening?"

"The highlight was the special guest appearance by Ryan Corruchi."

Even David was surprised by that piece of news. "Ryan showed up? My, my Sarah, you just had all the boys clamoring over you tonight, didn't you?"

My cheeks burned with a touch of shame that I didn't quite understand and after a few minutes more of idle chatter, excused myself to go upstairs to bed, leaving Livvie and David to clean up. The goal of the evening had been to meet men, and yet my success somehow sounded like an insult when coming from David's mouth.

* * *

The Saturday after the party at the diner arrived despite my every effort to mentally stop time.

In defeat, I'd spent the entire week blocking out everything and everyone outside the looming date circled on my calendar. My uncle called numerous times to discuss the appraisal Caryn had prepared – a very lucrative number – and talk about possible financial arrangements. A realtor colleague of Caryn's had also called to set up dates to go shopping for houses. Livvie kept calling me to ask when I was going to meet her at the gym. David and Eddie had flown back to their respective lives, but even their e-mails to check in went ignored.

The only person I couldn't ignore – as the evil fates would have it – was Morgan. Since making a good impression on my boss included actually showing up for work, Morgan and I spent every moment following the singles party dancing awkwardly around each other. We were professional enough that Frank never picked up on our odd behavior, although in my opinion, anything short of our prior active hostility wouldn't hit his radar. I was suspicious, though, that Gloria might have picked up on the shared hesitant smiles as we watched each other out of the corner of our eyes. If she thought something was going on, though, my friend kept it to herself. Perhaps she had adopted a "don't ask, don't tell" motto as the result of her own budding romance with Jeremy.

Finally, though, the night of the Big Date arrived. Applying a final coat of lipstick in the bathroom, all I hoped was that it would be more successful than my first post-Ryan date two years earlier.

I cringed at the memory that time hadn't begun to dull.

Some people need to contend only with sweaty palms, but that wasn't enough for me. I was forced to wear a turtleneck sweater on the date because I had broken out in full-body hives. Unattractive, rash-like blotches that appeared as a side effect to my nerves. The more blotches appeared, the more anxious I got which caused yet more blotches until I was practically a walking circus freak.

That evening, after the date was finally over and Greg walked me to the door and planted the perfunctory good night kiss, my only two thoughts were "Whew, I survived that hurdle," and, "Where is the calamine lotion?"

Needless to say, with passionate feelings like that, Greg and I didn't have a second date.

Since that night, as Livvie often pointed out, my dating life had been fairly bleak. On the rare occasion I did meet someone and was asked out, I generally approached the event with mild regret that I would miss a Friends rerun on Channel 12.

Tonight, though...

I had to admit that my feelings about dating Morgan were slightly different. If I had to put a name to the emotion I was feeling, it might be nervous anticipation. The butterflies in my stomach were definitely not the same ones I felt before arguing a motion I knew I'd probably lose, or those I felt sitting in the dentist office when I knew a lecture on gingivitis was imminent.

Waiting for Morgan, I felt exactly the same as I did on vacation at Disney, sitting on the Tower of Terror just before it plummeted toward the ground. I was unquestionably terrified, but knew in the back of my mind that as scary as the ride might be, it also just might be a hell of a good time.

I checked the clock again. Quarter till six.

"Well," I said to my reflection, taking a final look in my bathroom mirror. "You don't look horrible." I was wearing a cute, flippy print skirt and white boat-neck top. The results of my "diet" were still non-existent, but according to the latest issue of Vogue, my choice of a dark skirt and light top should make me look "Ten Pounds Lighter in Ten Minutes!"

I was a little concerned about my hair which might have been a tad too coiffed. Somewhere deep in the heart of this Maine native lived a Jersey girl when it came to big hair and makeup. I fought these instincts on a daily basis, and as a result, my hair contained just enough hairspray so that the look would stay in place, but no so much that I would need medical intervention to remove my fingers from my hair if I touched it at some point during the night.

My cellphone chirped, startling me from my narcissistic view of my reflection. Even more surprising was the name printed on the screen.

"What's wrong?"

"Geez, nothing's wrong, Sarah. I just called to wish you luck tonight."

David taking time away from his Saturday night to call me before a date was unprecedented. Calling to wish me "good luck" was just downright weird.

"What do you mean, 'good luck'?"

"Just that. Good luck," he said, adding absolutely no clarity. "So tell me, do you need any help figuring out your strategy or are you all set?"

"Strategy?" I was now officially confused. I thought for certain I had mentioned my date to David, but he clearly had my plans confused. Maybe he thought I was going to trivia night at one of the local bars?

"Yes, Sarah, I want to know your strategy." He sighed, slowing down his speech as if I were a small child or particularly simple adult. "I mean, Morgan is your goal, right?"

"My goal?" I moved to the couch and plopped down. The mental stamina it was taking to decipher this conversation had suddenly sapped all of my strength.

"Sure. You want to be in a relationship by your thirtieth birthday. It's been months now, and Morgan has been your only hot prospect. You need to move in for the kill."

Perhaps David was in the midst of having a medical crisis.

"Move in for the kill?" I asked, my mind wandering to the segment on the Today Show I'd watched that morning about the early warning signs of a stroke. "You don't smell burnt toast by any chance, do you David?"

"Stop repeating after me Sarah. And, no. I'm not having a stroke. I watch the Today show, too, you know." The sharpness of his tone made me wonder absently if perhaps I was the one experiencing cognitive deficits.

"Well, what am I supposed to think? You're saying ludicrous things, David."

"What am I saying that you consider ludicrous? You set a goal for yourself and Morgan is a tool you can use to meet that goal."

Wow. While I supposed David's statement was technically accurate, the way he'd phrased it sounded so cold and tactical.

My silence must have clued my friend into the fact that he'd really hit a nerve as he started down a different road, "Look, Sarah, there's nothing wrong with putting a plan into effect to meet a goal, right?"

"Yeah..." I hesitated, as any good attorney would, sniffing at the bait of a trap about to be sprung. "I suppose that's true."

"Okay, then. You have a goal. You have a tool at the ready to help you meet your goal. That brings me back to my original question. What is your strategy in utilizing this tool?"

I brought my hand to my temple, rubbing the headache that was beginning to form. "Look, if I continue with this discussion, will you at least stop referring to Morgan as a tool?"

"Only if you insist."

"I insist." I then collapsed bonelessly against the back of the couch, deciding to humor my friend. "Let's just pretend for a minute that I should have a strategy. To meet my goal. What do you think it should be?"

"Well," I heard the creaking of David's expensive leather armchair through the phone line, signaling his shift of position as he considered my question. "Here's the thing, Sarah. You're a pretty straightforward girl. I think you should be honest with Morgan."

I hadn't realized I'd been dishonest with Morgan up to this point. "What exactly am I supposed to be honest about?"

"I think you should tell Morgan about your goal to have a boyfriend by the fall, and that you'd like it to be him."

"Jesus, David! You can't be serious." My friend had clearly lost his flipping mind.

"I'm very serious. Why shouldn't you tell Morgan what your intentions are?"

"Tonight is our first date." I responded, shocked that I actually had to spell it out. "First dates are for getting to know someone. Finding out if you have anything in common. Seeing if you're compatible. Getting serious about future plans on the first date goes against every rule of dating I've ever heard."

"And these dating rules have served you well up to now?"

Ouch. That kind of hurt.

Of course, it was also kind of true.

"Sarah, you already know Morgan. You know you have things in common and are compatible." David paused, giving my brain a moment to catch up with his logic. Forging ahead. "He asked you out, right? You didn't pursue him or even show any interest the night of the singles party. It's not like he doesn't *want* you to take an interest in him.

"Maybe so, but there's a big difference between being interested in someone and asking that person to be your boyfriend," I countered.

"I know I'd be thrilled to find out a girl I liked wanted to be my girlfriend," David said, perhaps a bit wistfully.

"Really? Even on the first date?" I tapped my finger on the edge of the arm rest, considering.

David's confident tone left little room for doubt. "Absolutely. The sooner the better."

"I just don't know…"

"Think about it, Sarah. I'm a guy and therefore can speak to you as a member of your target audience. Besides," he lowered his voice and went for the jugular, "have I ever steered you wrong?"

"No," I admitted. David's advice was the gold standard.

"Then go for it. Be aggressive. Tell Morgan what you want."

"Okay." While still unsure, I had to admit to David's point that following my old dating rules hadn't worked out so well in the past. What was the saying about insanity? Doing the same thing and expecting a different result was insane? Maybe David was right and I should change my tactics to tell Morgan what I really wanted.

Happy to have gotten his way, David abruptly changed the subject. "So, is Livvie there to supervise the wardrobe?"

"Nope. She's been banished to her own home tonight. She's devastated that I wouldn't agree to let her come over here and tart me up properly."

"Why did you banish her?"

"It was just a little creepy. Morgan's picking me up here and if Livvie was here, it would have felt too much like Ma Ingalls sending Laura and Almonzo off to their first barn dance."

The silence spanning the phone line reminded me that most straight men didn't understand my frequent Little House on the Prairie references. I noted to keep Laura back in the big woods for the rest of the evening and translated. "I thought it would be awkward to have Livvie here acting like my chaperone when Morgan arrived."

"Gotcha." I barely heard the word over the sound of the doorbell, marking Morgan's arrival.

I leapt up and brushed the wrinkles from my skirt. "Gotta go. He's here. I'll talk to you soon."

"Let me know how it goes."

"I'll give you all the details." I assured my friend.

"Um…" David hesitated. "Maybe not all the details."

I laughed, realizing there were some things that even honorary big brothers probably didn't want to know. I said one final goodbye, returned the phone handset to its cradle and passed the mirror for one final inspection.

As ready as I would ever be, I crossed the room and pressed the button that would allow access to the downstairs entrance. "Come on up!" I yelled, having told Morgan – as I told all of my guests – to come by way of the building's side door which had a buzzer access. As the only other entrance to my apartment was through the diner and up the pantry stairs, when on a date I tried to avoid traipsing guests through the grease pits of the diner.

"Hi. Come on in." I opened the door to the apartment and ushered him across the threshold. Morgan was wearing his generic office attire – khaki pants and a button down oxford. While he looked very nice, I somehow found myself disappointed that he hadn't chosen a more casual outfit – like the one I'd seen him in at the singles party. Ever since that night, I had been having very inappropriate thoughts about every man I passed that just happened to be wearing a grey Henley.

It was most disconcerting, and beginning to be quite awkward.

"That's the first buzzer I've seen in Portland," he commented. "I felt like I was on an episode of Seinfeld for a minute."

"There aren't that many large apartment buildings in Portland, so there's not much of a need for them. This building has one for deliveries to the diner." I explained, and then we both fell silent and simply smiled at each other.

God, the first few moments of a first date were always so awkward. It didn't help that I had David's advice swirling in my head, making me wonder when I should put my 'strategy' into action.

"You have a nice place here." Morgan's voice rescued me from my musings only to find that once again in time of stress my manners had failed me. I should have offered to show him around.

"Would you like to take the ten cent tour?" I offered belatedly, desperately trying to remember whether I'd put my wet towels in the hamper, rather than hanging them on a convenient doorknob as was my usual habit.

"Sure. I'd love to see the place."

"Well, it shouldn't take long. This is the living room and kitchen." I gestured to the small counter jutting out from the wall, separating my couch from the small nook that held my refrigerator, sink, and two-burner stove. Two barstools were tucked underneath the counter which doubled as my kitchen table. If I planned to entertain more than a few guests at a time, a need for elbow room meant asking Jeremy permission to use the diner downstairs.

And then I saw it.

Lighting up the room like a lavender beacon.

I wouldn't have to tell Morgan about the list of things I wanted to do before I hit thirty. The list, which I'd forgotten to remove from its pretty perch on the refrigerator would be able to tell him, itself.

Leaping across the room, I grabbed the offensive item, flinging refrigerator magnets in every direction, and shoved it in the freezer. Draping my body against the door, I asked casually, "Would you like something to drink?"

"Um, no. Problem?"

"What? That? Oh, no, no. That was nothing."

"Ooookay." Morgan dragged the word out, making the point that he hadn't been fooled, but was willing to let it go.

For now.

As he walked around the couch, taking time to peruse my book, DVD and music library, I was hit by another wave of insecurity. My music wasn't edgy enough. My books too bourgeoisie. And I knew, as the tour led to my bedroom, that he secretly judged me for my "Buffy the Vampire Slayer" box sets.

"This is nice." He commented, walking into the room and peering through the doorway and into the bathroom beyond. I followed him, relaxing slightly as I noted the fresh towels hanging neatly next to the sink.

Morgan crossed to my dresser and looked at the three framed photographs I kept there. "I love looking at pictures." He sheepishly admitted, picking up the largest of the frames.

"Those are my folks." I explained, although the resemblances probably made it unnecessary. Mom was the picture of elegance on her wedding day in a white halter top gown, and small puff of tulle atop of her Jackie O-inspired bouffant. I was sure that my father had never looked more handsome than he did that day standing in his blue wool police uniform, beaming with pride at his young bride.

"They made a very attractive couple," Morgan said, reverently putting the frame back in its place. "And they have a very attractive daughter."

Oh my. I prayed that my nervous blotching problem had resolved itself in the last few years.

"That's a picture of Jeremy and my father at their retirement party." I blurted, rushing past the compliment and pointing to the second, 5x7 photograph. "And there's David, Eddie, Livvie and me at my law school graduation." Morgan picked up the third picture frame and studied it carefully.

"You mention David quite a bit, but I haven't heard much about Eddie. What is he like?"

I took a moment, considering a way to describe the Thornton brothers. "Let's just say that when I wanted a fake ID in college, Eddie's the person I called and he came through. When I got caught with it, I called David."

Morgan laughed and replaced the photo on the dresser. "Well I don't know about you, but I'm starving. Are you ready to go?"

"Yes." I locked the apartment door, set the alarm and followed Morgan down the narrow stairs and out into the unseasonably mild evening.

He led me to an expensive hybrid car – the current model year – and opened the passenger door before making his way to the driver's side. I would have liked to pretend it was Morgan's environmental responsibility that impressed me, but that wasn't the truth.

In truth, I was a closet car whore.

That's right. As much as I liked to believe I wasn't taken in by material possessions, I was incredibly shallow and easily distracted by pretty, shiny things on four wheels.

There was no specific method to my madness – my love of cars and wine were much the same. I didn't know anything about grape crops or wineries; engines or transmissions. I just knew what I liked, and just as a good bottle of wine could save an otherwise dull meal, the appearance of a gleaming car – whether vintage, muscle or brand new off the showroom floor – made the owner infinitely more interesting in my eyes.

"So, where are we going?" I asked as we turned on the highway toward the ocean.

"Company Road," he replied, naming the city's best seafood restaurant. Again, I was impressed. Even with reservations, getting into that restaurant on a Saturday night was no easy feat. Morgan was not kidding about his status as a trust fund baby – he apparently had friends in all the right places.

Destination decided, we settled back into the silence, broken only by a Springsteen CD playing softly on the car stereo. While not uncomfortable, I was happy when our chatter picked up as we arrived downtown with matters to discuss such as a search for parking on the crowded Portland streets. Our small talk continued comfortably as we entered the restaurant and shuffled around getting settled at a table with menus and a nice bottle of Pinot.

I heard Livvie's voice in the back of my head as I perused the menu for my dinner choice. I knew to stay away from dishes with thin sauces – they had a tendency to splatter. Not the most attractive look to project on a date. No food with too much garlic or onions, either…for obvious reasons.

I spared a glance to Morgan who was making appreciative noises at several of the dishes listed and wondered if men ever went through the same torture when trying to make a good first impression. I doubted it, but according to David, I knew very little about men and what they were thinking or expecting from women.

Suddenly, the romantic table for two became very crowded between Morgan, me, Livvie's voice in my head telling me what to order, and memories of David instructing me what to say and how to act.

"What are you going to order?" Morgan interrupted my thoughts.

"I'm not sure. Everything looks good."

"I was thinking of ordering the salmon special."

I considered the description our waitress had provided – a lightly grilled fish with no onions, no garlic and no sauce. We had a winner. "That sounds good. Let's make it two."

Meal ordered, I had a momentary attack of anxiety. Everything up to this moment had been just an overture. The opening act. Like Natalie Wood dropping her scarf at a drag race, by ordering dinner and ridding ourselves of our menus, the date had officially started.

"Stop it."

"What?" I brought my startled eyes to meet my date's.

"Whatever you're doing, you need to stop. I lost you somewhere when the waitress walked away. I don't know what you're thinking, but come out of your head and talk to me."

I studied the smart, handsome man sitting opposite me. He had already seen me at my worst and was miraculously interested in coming back for more. I took a deep breath and leaned back in my chair as I realized I was making things much harder than they needed to be. I mentally pushed Livvie, David and even my own insecurities away from the table for the moment and smiled in acknowledgment of his words. Picking up my glass of wine, I asked, "So, you like Springsteen? Have you ever seen him in concert?"

It was amazing, the wave of serenity that swept over Morgan's features as discussion turned to the relative safety of music. God love Bruce Springsteen. His name unlocked the invisible barrier between us and soon the conversation, like the wine, began to flow. "Yeah, I've seen Bruce a couple of times. The best show was…"

I really liked this guy.

Our discussion ebbed and flowed over the evening as we touched on politics, movies and books, finding ourselves both to be fans of an obscure science fiction writer.

"You can't read the third series until you've read the first two," he argued.

"You're wrong." I leaned over the table. "All of the series stand alone just fine and none of the characters overlap."

I waited for Morgan's counter-argument about the author progressively building upon a theme, but it didn't come. Instead, I found my date staring down at my hand which I'd casually draped over his arm when making my point.

"Oh, I'm sorry." I pulled back immediately, only to find my hand captured and returned to its place on Morgan's arm.

"It's okay." He smiled, placing his hand on top of my own.

"Oh. Okay, then."

By the time coffee and dessert were delivered – cheesecake for him, gelato for me – we had broached more personal topics.

"So, my older brother Will is helping my dad run the business. They were disappointed when I quit and went to law school, but they've pretty much adjusted."

"You weren't interested in moving from the charitable end into the business itself?" I asked, still a little sketchy on the details of Donovan Industries. I knew from the news that it employed tons of people, manufactured some kind of computer parts, was well-respected and made scads of money.

"Nah." Morgan brought his napkin to his lips and then dropped it on the table "I've just never been interested in spending two million dollars researching ways to save eight cents per widget. I know that sounds cold, but I'm just not made out for corporate America."

"What are you made out for?"

Morgan looked almost wistful as he answered, "Honestly? I want to be a lawyer that protects the integrity of the legal system by taking the cases no one else does. I really want to be a public defender."

"If that's the case, why are you working in Frank's office? You know he refuses to take on criminal defense cases."

"I know. The truth is, my father would have a cow if I worked where I wanted. He thinks being a public defender is beneath me. Dad knows Frank and his reputation and is proud to tell his friends where I work. I don't want to mess with that."

Not wanting to walk into a touchy family issue on the first date, I attempted to deftly change the subject. "I know how dads can be. As proud as my dad was of my law degree, I think he was a little sad that I wasn't interested in taking over the diner. He loved that place."

The waitress arrived with the check which Morgan exchanged for his credit card before turning my way. "Not interested in taking it over some day?"

"No." I took a final sip of coffee. "I mean, I love the place and can't imagine a day when Uncle Jeremy is actually ready to retire, but I definitely found the right profession for me."

We continued our conversation about the diner while Morgan signed the bill and during the walk to the car. Part of me was engaged in the discussion while another part tried to dissect the feeling I was experiencing as the night wound towards its conclusion. There was a definite level of comfort and ease I felt being around Morgan, but underlying it all was a small thrum of energy dancing around the edges of the evening.

The drive back to my house was not the silent trip to the restaurant we'd experienced a few hours earlier with each of us sitting rigidly in our own space. During the return trip, we wrestled with the demands placed on adult children in the modern family structure, all the while my hand was held gently in Morgan's, rested on the side of the passenger seat.

Even I had to admit that this date was kicking ass.

My euphoria lasted approximately another twelve seconds before we were parked in front of the diner and I was back in panic mode. It had been a very long time since I'd been on a first date with a man – and much longer still with a man I really liked. I was no longer clear about the direction the rest of the evening should take.

Namely, should I invite Morgan up to my apartment? What would that mean? What would he think it meant? I considered every exponential possibility of asking the man beside me upstairs, and as I did so, I also watched the hopeful light in Morgan's eyes dim.

Had I missed my window of opportunity?

Did Morgan assume I didn't want to continue our date in a more intimate setting, while the truth was that it was exactly what I wanted? I dithered around in my head trying to figure out what Morgan would read into such an invitation and whether it was too early to go there.

Screw it.

I was twenty-nine years old and no blushing virgin. Remembering David's words from earlier in the evening, I decided to be the strong, independent, decisive woman Morgan had originally pursued.

"So, Morgan," I leaned in and asked. "Are you interested in a relationship?"

He leaned back, startled and made a gurgling sound in his throat that could have been interpreted as, "Huh?

"Are you interested in a relationship?" I repeated. "With me. Do you want me to be your girlfriend?"

I saw and felt Morgan go from mildly disappointed at not receiving an invitation upstairs, to a man in the throes of blind panic. I put my hand lightly on his shoulder and his entire body went rigid at my touch.

And not in the good way.

David's advice was abruptly pushed out of my head and instead I heard Livvie's voice screaming, "Abort! Abort! Abort!"

"Oh my god, you should have seen your face!" I joked with a high pitched, keening laugh that in no way resembled my own. "I'm kidding of course. Just kidding. Well, anyway, thanks so much for a lovely evening. It was fun. Let's do it again. Again. Yes, let's. Okay, then, I'll see you at the office on Monday."

I leapt from the car and ran to my building, jammed my key into the door and raced upstairs. There was one final task I needed to complete before I let myself over-analyze my insane behavior. Stalking to my laptop, still running and open to the internet from when I checked my e-mail that afternoon, I quickly opened a new message screen, typed in David's address and a very succinct message.

"You ruined my life."

* * *

Bzzzzzzzzz.

I raised my head from the edge of my desk where it had collapsed in a pathetic heap several minutes earlier, and glared at the office intercom.

"What is it Gloria?" I picked up the phone, failing to hide my irritation.

"Two things." She replied in her crisp, efficient manner. "First, you have a delivery at the front desk that you need to pick up. Second, you will not take that snippy tone with me in the future."

"Sorry." I said, meaning it. It wasn't fair to take out my bad mood on anyone but the person responsible for it.

That would be me.

My next words were in a much friendlier tone. "Can you bring my delivery down to my office?"

"So you can continue to hide in there like you have all day? No, dear, I cannot."

I took great offense to Gloria's classification of my behavior. I wasn't hiding. Just because it was the Monday following my date with Morgan and I had gotten in early, shut my office door and not emerged for a coffee or bathroom break in nearly five hours? I wasn't hiding.

I was focused. Very, very focused.

"Morgan just left for lunch." Gloria informed me, once again astounding me with her amazing deductive skills.

Realizing I really could use a fresh cup of coffee...and really needed to pee..., I turned off the intercom and walked down to the reception area where I was surprised to find a beautiful arrangement of yellow tulips, a small card with my name on it tucked neatly in the center.

Perhaps I was overreacting, I thought with a smile as I reached for the card. Sure the last five minutes of our date had been horrible, but maybe Morgan was willing to grade the entire evening on a bell curve, ignoring the fact I had flunked the final exam.

"They're lovely, aren't they?" Gloria remarked. "Who are they from?"

I opened the card and found a neatly typed message.

Don't be mad.

Love, David

"They're from David." I reported, disappointed, but at the same time not altogether surprised.

"Your uncle's son, David?" I leapt a foot in the air, not expecting to hear Morgan's voice a few inches from my ear as he leaned over my shoulder to read the card.

"Sorry. Didn't mean to startle you."

"No problem," I assured him, my next words directed to Gloria. "For some reason, I thought you'd gone out to lunch."

My death glare elicited merely a noncommittal shrug from Gloria before she turned back to her computer screen, shutting herself off from the conversation.

"So, David is sending you flowers. I thought you guys…I mean, I didn't think…" Morgan cleared his throat and squared his shoulders just as I caught on to what he was trying to say. "So, when we went out on Saturday, that wasn't really…"

"No!" I jumped in, anxious to nip his incorrect conclusion in the bud. "I mean yes. I mean, Saturday night *was* really…I mean, David is just a friend."

Was it relief I read on Morgan's face at my clarification? Or, more likely, was it relief I saw because that was so desperately what I wanted to see?

"David, he, um…" I wondered precisely how to put words to what I wanted to say. "He tried to help me with something and it got hopelessly screwed up. These are apology flowers. That's it."

"Oh, okay." Morgan picked up his work from the printer and turned down the hall back to his office.

"Wait!" I yelled, causing him to stop and turn but not take any steps back toward me.

Great. Now that I had his attention, what was I supposed to say?

"I had fun on Saturday."

Morgan's lips moved in an upward motion, but I would have been hard pressed to call his expression a smile. "Yeah, me too. See ya."

The man then turned and scuttled away down the hall like I was on fire.

If I'd had any doubts regarding whether I'd irrevocably screwed things up with Morgan, they had just been answered. I turned toward Gloria and just held my hand up to stop the flow of questions I knew were coming my way.

"Don't. Please." My tone must have been just pathetic enough, because while an inquisitive eyebrow was raised, no questions were asked.

Just as I began slinking back to my own office, the main door slammed open and Frank burst through with a booming, "Good afternoon, people!"

I once again jumped at the unexpected greeting and remained startled by Frank's over-the-top good humor. There was an actual, sincere smile on his face as he clapped me on the shoulder – nearly knocking me over with the unknown strength of his exuberance – and continued on down the hall yelling for Morgan to show his face.

"Mandatory meeting in the conference room now." He turned to Gloria. "Switch the phones over to the answering service."

I took a seat as far from Morgan as possible without raising Frank's suspicions, but had the feeling that my boss was too wrapped up in his own thoughts to notice my behavior at all.

"I have excellent news that I want to share." Frank smiled his toothy, predatory smile. "We have an important new client."

That was unexpected. Usually Frank carted me to the required contact-building lunches where my social skills prevailed and he could happily scowl from the corner. Gloria's face registered surprise as well, which was even more astounding. If it was unusual for me to be out of the loop, it was downright shocking that Gloria was also in the dark.

"Who's the client and what's the case?" I asked.

"I went to college with Mark Ekbert." My boss stretched back in his chair, getting comfortable as he began to tell his story. "Mark lives out on Lightship Island in Casco Bay. The island is currently considered a part of Bayside City, but its citizens have signed a referendum outlining their plans to research seceding from Bayside and creating a new town of their own."

Lightship Island was a forty minute boat ride from Bayside, a city just up the coast from Portland. If I remembered correctly, it had a year round population of a hundred people which swelled by ten times during the summer months when rich families from Massachusetts and New York returned to claim their summer homes.

"Secede? I thought people stopped doing that after Fort Sumter," Morgan remarked.

"Actually, secession is quite popular in Maine," Gloria interjected. "A lot of small islands and communities would rather set up their own governments if they feel they're not getting adequate services in return for the taxes they pay."

Frank nodded at Gloria's assessment. "Mark is the chair of the island's Board of Selectmen. They just authorized him to hire a law firm to research the legal implications and liabilities of secession. I fired off a proposal a few weeks ago, and the board chose to give their business to the law firm of Francis G. Murphy."

Watching my boss preen as his story unfolded, I couldn't think of a time when I had seen Frank so proud of a business coup. He was always thrilled with legal victories, but had little patience for the business of creating business. He believed a good reputation would keep clients coming in, and while that was generally true, he was obviously very pleased that his proposal had gone over so well.

"That's wonderful, Francis," Gloria exclaimed. "What exactly does it mean for the firm?"

"Well, it means a lot of work for our two friends here," Frank said, gesturing first to me, then Morgan where we sat at opposite sides of the table. "We need to research municipal law in general and secession issues in particular. Just off the top of my head, I can guess that it's going to involve looking into tax issues, leasing fire and police services, schooling, and insurance."

Slapping his hand down on the table, he laughed, "I'm glad you two are finally getting along. I see a lot of late nights together in all of our futures."

Fabulous.

It was going to be hard enough avoiding Morgan when his second year of law school ended in a few months and he began working at the office full time through the summer. Now we were both assigned to work together researching the same subject.

I dared a glance at Morgan, only to find him looking in my direction. Our eyes met for the briefest of moments before we both turned quickly, but it was long enough for me to see the same emotions I felt shimmering back at me – fear… shame… fear… regret… fear… sadness…

And did I mention, fear?

Tuning back into the sound of Frank's voice, I realized he had been waxing poetic about Lightship Island and summers spent there as a boy the entire time I had drifted off to obsess about how I was going to work with Morgan. The man was practically bouncing over this new assignment, and it was a known fact that Frank Murphy simply did not bounce.

There was no way I was going to burst his bubble.

An idea suddenly dawned on me. This could actually be a great opportunity. What better way to show Frank I was partner material than to take an important new assignment and bat it out of the park?

"So, what do you think, Sarah?"

Knowing the answer Frank was looking for, and feeling only slightly like a liar, "It sounds terrific, Frank. Where do we start?"

March

S-

YOU CAN'T IGNORE ME forever. I'll be in town Friday.
Grab a booth at the Beer and I'll meet you there at seven.
Invite Livvie. You can't kill me in front of a witness.

-D

Like hell I couldn't.

I crumpled David's e-mail back in my purse and took a sip from
my drink, waiting at our favorite bar, the Grizzly Beer, for both
Livvie and David to arrive. I was surprised at David – he should
know that one of Livvie's greatest traits was her loyalty. If I called
her any time of the day or night and told her I needed help disposing
of a body, her only question would be whether she should bring her
own shovel.

Thinking it over, once Livvie found out David had screwed up
my date with Morgan, it was actually my presence that might be
David's best chance for survival. That thought made me giggle to
myself as I sat watching the happy hour crowd mill around the bar.

From my vantage point near the back, I immediately noticed my
friend as she walked in the door. It was an unusually warm spring
day, and while my hair was frizzed and linen suit wrinkled, Livvie
was crisp and cool as always. She wore a flowing print dress topped
with an emerald green blazer that just matched the large polished
stone hanging from her neck. Spotting me waving from the corner,

she waved back and sauntered over, thoroughly oblivious to the admiring glances she received from some of our fellow patrons.

"Hey, Sarah." She scooted into the booth next to me. "Bitch of a week, huh? How are you doing?"

I shook my head. There was no way I'd consumed enough alcohol yet to begin reliving the Morgan debacle, but I knew Livvie was dying for details. All I had shared with her so far was that the date was a disaster, it was entirely my fault and I was considering which religious sect I should join that embraced both celibacy and cute shoes.

"Can my story wait?" I begged. "David should be here soon and I can't bear to tell it twice."

"Fine, but I expect full disclosure later. What do you want to talk about in the meantime?" Livvie asked, pausing briefly to order a cabernet from our waitress.

An easy question. "Tell me about Byron. Are you going to go out with him?"

Byron was the carpenter Livvie had hired to remodel her downstairs bathroom. He was divorced with no kids in his late forties and owned his own business. On paper he was perfect, but Livvie was still reluctant to accept his offer of dinner and a movie.

"I haven't decided yet. His background check came back clean, though."

I dropped the peanut I'd been about to shell back into the bowl in the middle of the table and turned my gaze to my friend. "I'm sorry...his what?"

Livvie had the good grace to look embarrassed, playing with the sugar packets on the table as she responded. "His background check."

I said nothing, but my raised eyebrows alone spurred her to continue. "Fine, go ahead and judge me, but I do a quick check on a few lists whenever I date someone new. Just the biggies. You know, the national sex offender registry, the Better Business Bureau..."

"No, I do not know. I don't investigate my dates."

My friend's silence was very suspicious, and she resumed her interest in lining up the pink sweet & low packets in orderly rows.

"Please tell me you didn't."

"Hey, I work for the District Attorney and see a lot of scary files paraded by my desk," Livvie replied. "People didn't just make up the whole, 'he was very quiet and kept to himself' thing, you know. It's not like serial killers wear neon signs announcing themselves to the world."

"So you do background checks on my dates as well as yours?" She smirked. "Well, given your dating history, it's not like it takes up a lot of my time."

"That's just cold." I returned my focus to the peanuts in front of me while Livvie sipped at her drink for a moment before finally breaking the palpable silence.

"You want to know, don't you?"

"No."

"Fine." Livvie picked up the menu. "Do you think an order of calamari is enough to get us started?"

I held out for all of twelve seconds before I called her bluff and ripped the menu from her hands. "Okay. You win. What did you find out about Morgan?"

"Oh, Sarah, I couldn't possibly tell you. I wouldn't want to compromise your high moral standards."

"Bite me."

"Temper, temper, dear." Taking an exaggerated sip of wine, Livvie finally said, "he's pretty clean. A few speeding tickets and one misdemeanor charge when he was a high school senior. Some kind of prank involving the cross-town team's school mascot. Probation and a fine."

"Was it by any chance a goat? Are you telling me I'm dating Greg Brady?"

My friend shrugged her shoulders. "Nope. You're not dating Greg Brady. You apparently screwed up and got dumped by Greg Brady."

"You're just a little ray of sunshine today aren't you?"

Livvie just laughed. "Hey, I can't help that I'm cranky. All you've told me is that you suck and you won't be dating Morgan again, but you won't tell me what happened."

I looked up as the problem walked through the door. "What happened is that I listened to David."

"Hi, ladies." David ignored my pronouncement, leaned over the booth and gave me a crushing hug.

"Don't try to make up with me." I complained, wriggling from his grasp. "I'm still mad at you."

"Okay, then, I'll hug Livvie," he said proceeding to do just that.

"You got here just in time, Thornton," Livvie replied returning the hug. "Sarah is blaming you for her dismal date."

David cocked his head to the side. "Yeah, well, she might have a point."

With that, Livvie's already limited patience had reached its end. "Okay, spill. What exactly happened between you and Morgan?"

I took a long swallow from my beer before I admitted, "I asked him if we were in a relationship. I asked him if I could be his girlfriend. I basically stopped just short of asking whether he wanted stuffed chicken or prime rib at the wedding reception dinner."

Yup.

From the look on Livvie's face, my mistake in judgment had been every bit as horrible as I thought it was.

Her mouth opened and closed a few moments before the words finally pushed themselves past her lips. "What. The. Fuck. Possessed you to ask that on a first date?"

I pointed at the guilty party. "Him. It was his fault. David suggested it."

Livvie's eyes narrowed as she regarded David. All six foot three inches of him began to shrink under her gaze. He shrunk even further at her icy tone. "Tell me David, exactly why would you suggest Sarah be so forward on her first date with Morgan?"

"Seemed like a good idea at the time?"

David's weak attempt at levity didn't score him any points.

"Well, it was bad advice. Incredibly bad advice."

"It was very bad advice." I agreed, smug in Livvie's condemnation of David's behavior.

My smirk disappeared pretty quickly as Livvie swung her attention my way.

"Oh, you're not off the hook here, Sarah. You're the moron who executed the plan. What were you thinking?"

Wow. Having earned Livvie's undivided wrath was kind of scary, and I decided my best plan for survival was diversion. "I was thinking that David is a guy and probably knew what guys wanted to hear. Ask David what he was thinking."

Before he could speak up, though, Livvie jumped in with, "Oh, I know what David was thinking."

Well that was cryptic. What was especially strange was that David didn't defend himself from Livvie's odd comment. He merely caught her eye and gazed down at the tabletop, clearly guilty of something.

"What did that mean?" I swiveled, posing my question between my friends. "What's going on between you two tonight?"

"Shit."

Well that wasn't the response I was expecting from Livvie. But, before I could question her, I noted she wasn't looking at me. She was looking toward the door of the bar where five young men and one woman had just entered.

One of the men was Morgan Donovan.

And the woman was Cory Latham.

"Shit," I agreed.

"What's going on?" David turned and spotted Cory. "Oh. I guess they'll serve anyone at this bar."

"That's not all." I informed him, feeling fresh nausea as the waitress placed a plate of calamari in front of us that I barely remembered ordering. "The guy in the blue button down and Dockers is the famous Morgan Donovan."

David whipped around again. "Huh. He's kind of short, don't you think?"

"To a giant like you, yes." Livvie rolled her eyes. "To mere mortals like us, he meets the minimum height requirement."

"It figures he's here with Cory," I muttered. "That really does sum up the way my life is going."

Livvie opened her mouth to either continue yelling at me or soothe my wounded heart, but wasn't able to do either as her cell phone chose that moment to ring.

"Bail? Who in their right mind authorized that?" She rolled her eyes at us and mouthed that she'd be just a moment as she left the table to unravel the evening's crisis.

"I've got an idea."

I considered David with some distrust given his recent track record. "What kind of idea?"

"An idea that will turn things around with Morgan and make him admit he's interested in you."

"And why should I trust you?"

"Come on, Bennett." David playfully smacked me on the shoulder. "I've been giving you advice for over two decades. You can't give up on me over one misstep."

That did sound reasonable. "What's your idea?"

"My brilliant idea is based on the premise that every man wants the one thing he can't have. If Morgan thinks he can't have you, then you will be the only thing he wants."

The lightbulb went off. "You want me to make Morgan jealous?"

David gestured toward the group at the bar. "When Morgan walked in with Cory, what were you feeling?"

The man had a point.

"Scoot over." I ordered before I had time to reconsider. But, as David put his arm around me and pulled my chair even closer, I wished that perhaps I did.

The gesture felt wrong, somehow, but in the time it took me to realize, David had grabbed a morsel from the plate of fried calamari in front of us.

"Mmmm, delicious! Sarah, you need to try this." The crispy sea creature was dangled above my mouth and I was forced to open my lips and eat from David's fingers while he turned his head slightly and gave me a quick kiss on the temple.

"You can stop the floorshow, kids. Morgan just walked out." Livvie announced with a clipped tone as she returned to the table.

"Did they notice?" I cringed, anticipating the answer.

"Notice what?" She replied, pushing the food as far away from her place setting as possible and downing her drink a little more quickly than usual. "The fact you were making asses out of yourselves?"

"Oh, Livvie, come on..." David started, but swallowed his words as Livvie's index finger came dangerously close to the tip of his nose.

"Do not even get me started on you, Thornton." Turning back my way, she sighed. "That was the stupidest thing I've ever seen. Do you even remember that Morgan was the one you flirted with at the singles party last month to get rid of Ryan?"

Um, no, actually. I hadn't.

"So, this time you were flirting with David to make Morgan jealous, but he didn't know that. He probably thought you were crawling all over David to make Morgan go away just like you crawled all over Morgan in an attempt to make Ryan go away. And by the looks of the way he bolted, it worked."

My heart stopped at Livvie's words. Driving Morgan even further away was the last thing on my mind. "I didn't mean…"

"Just don't. Okay, Sarah?" Livvie sighed, picked up her napkin and placed it back in her lap. "Let's just forget this little scene ever happened and have a nice quiet meal. In fact, let's make a pact not to mention Morgan, Cory…hell, anyone that isn't on the front cover of the National Enquirer."

David nodded, duly chastised and happy to be out from under Livvie's wrath. "Celebrity-only conversation. You've got it. The Emmy nominations are next week. Rooting for anyone in particular?"

I didn't really care about the Emmy nominations, but I tried to pay attention to the conversation and inject a little celebrity gossip when it was my turn. Unfortunately, though, my mind kept returning to the thought that instead of achieving goals before I was 30, I was actually losing ground and making stupid decisions.

I needed to regroup and regroup fast.

* * *

"You're an idiot."

I snapped my tape measure back into place and rose from my knees where I'd been measuring the width of the master bedroom wall. "I'm aware of that. Care to be more specific?"

Livvie opened the drapes to scrutinize the view of the backyard. "Sure. You were an idiot the other night at the Grizzly Beer. I can't believe you let David fall all over you in front of Morgan."

"What can I say?" I opened and closed the closet door to be certain of the tight fit. "I know. I'm an idiot. You've told me a hundred times in the last two days. I will apologize to Morgan and then flog myself in the town square. Can we just leave it at that and go look at the kitchen again?"

Apparently satisfied at my penance, she walked slowly through the two bedroom, one bath ranch my broker Eliot had taken us to visit. It was our fourteenth house of the day and we'd unbelievably worn even the energetic real estate agent to the point he was resting on the resin porch furniture waiting for Livvie and I to take one final tour of the place.

"The cabinets are a little outdated, but I think a change of hardware would make a huge difference. The doors themselves are in good shape."

"I thought the same thing," I agreed.

"It's a good neighborhood. Lyle Sampson grew up just around the corner."

I listened to the words, but as I touched my hand to the flecked Formica counter, I shook my head. "No. This just doesn't feel right. Let's see what else Eliot has to show us."

"Sarah. This house is exactly what you're looking for. The price is right and its fifteen minutes from the office. It's big enough to entertain, but small enough for one person to keep it clean. Tell me what's wrong with it."

I shrugged, unable to put my dissatisfaction into words. "I don't know. It just doesn't have the right vibe."

"Unacceptable. I don't care about vibes. Tell me objectively one thing that makes you not want to buy this house."

"Okay, fine. It's set on a slab foundation."

For not speaking, Livvie's expression clearly stated, "And?..."

"It has no basement. Where will I put the treadmill?"

Livvie pinched the bridge of her nose. "Sarah, my lunatic friend, you don't have a treadmill."

I nodded. "But if I had a basement, I'd buy one."

"You're hopeless." Livvie pulled out the notebook she'd been scribbling on all day and began reading from her notes. "The first house had poor water pressure. The second house had a pink bathtub. The third house was on Peach Lane and you're allergic to peaches. The fourth house..."

"What about the fourth house?"

Livvie closed her notebook and put it back in her purse. "The fourth house was that dive on Longfellow Street. I'm actually going to give you that one."

"What's your point? You didn't expect me to find a house on the first day of looking, did you?" I slumped against the counter.

"No." Livvie admitted. "I know it takes most people a long time to find a house. It's a huge commitment and you shouldn't make a snap decision."

"Why do I feel a 'but' coming?"

"*But*, most people actually want to buy a house when they go shopping for one. I just don't think your heart is in it. I think you want to buy a house because you wrote down on a piece of paper the fact that you think you should buy a house."

"It's not just written down. It's laminated." I reminded her.

"Seriously, Sarah, before your twenty-ninth birthday I hadn't heard you talking about buying a house in years. It wasn't even on your radar until that stupid list put it there."

"Maybe so, but it's on my radar now. Don't think of it as a new goal. Think of it as a goal I used to have and forgot about until my list reminded me."

"Maybe it's not your goal anymore, though. Have you thought of that? It's okay for a person's goals to change over the years."

"I know that."

I began to trace the pattern in the counter with my thumbnail, avoiding further eye contact. "I know that, but when I was 25, the items on that list were very important to me. I don't think my goals have changed since then. I think maybe I've just settled for less than what I truly want somewhere along the way."

Livvie pulled out one of the kitchen chairs and gestured for me to do the same. "Can I say something that's going to piss you off?"

"Oh, sure." I rolled my eyes. "That sounds promising."

"I don't think you ever wanted to buy a house. Not at 25, not at 29, and you still won't at thirty. I think you wanted to buy a house *with Ryan* at 25. Now that he's out of the picture, it really is alright to let go of the rest of it."

Livvie's words didn't piss me off. Quite the contrary – they made a lot of sense. I loved my apartment and as inconvenient as living over the diner could be from time to time, none of the houses we'd looked at so far had come even close to making me feel so cozy and warm as my little apartment did.

"Ryan, huh?"

"Ryan." Livvie confirmed. "And, before you even ask, you did the right thing by blowing him off at the party. From what I hear, he's already moved on to an associate in his firm. They might have been together already when he came to the diner that night."

Hurt, but not terrifically surprised by the news, I almost missed the fact that it had been delivered by someone who should have no more insight into Ryan's dating life than I did. "How do you know who Ryan is dating?"

"Oh." Livvie rose and placed the kitchen chair back to its place under the oak table. "Well, um, I had dinner with Donnie last week."

"You had dinner with Donnie? Were there drugs involved? Did he force you at knifepoint?"

"No, nothing like that." She walked toward the refrigerator and began arranging the letter magnet in alphabetical order. "His aunt Grace died last week, so when I read it in the paper and called to offer my sympathy, he asked me out to dinner. She was always very nice to me."

"Nicer than her nephew, probably."

"Probably." She grinned. "But this conversation is not about me. The point is, Ryan is out of the picture. You need to let go of him and let go of the things you wanted only because of him."

I considered my friend's words and slowly stood up, looking around a perfectly lovely home that I had absolutely no interest in purchasing. "I don't really want to buy a house, do I? I don't want to move from the diner."

"No, sweetie. I don't think you do."

"So what do I do now?"

"Well, eventually we have to go out and face Eliot to tell him we've wasted his day. For the moment, though, we could always go down the hall and snoop through the medicine cabinet to cheer you up."

I shook my head, appreciating Livvie's gesture but just not in the mood.

"We could peek in their bedroom dresser drawers," she suggested, poking me in the shoulder. "Come on. They had a leopard-skin bedspread. They've got to be hiding something good. You know you want to look."

I'd forgotten about the leopard skin bedspread.

Pushing my chair back under the table, I allowed my friend to gently push me down the hall. "Livvie, what about the rest of my list? It wasn't all about Ryan, you know."

"I know. We'll just reprint the list, Sarah. Leave off the item about buying a house. It's not that hard."

"The list is laminated, you know." I whined. Reprinting the list may not be physically difficult, but symbolically was another matter.

"It also has freezer burn. We'll re-laminate it." She steered me into the bedroom. "Just think how thrilled Jeremy will be to know you're not moving."

I nodded at her words and how right they were. I wasn't moving. Not at all. Not away from the diner and not toward anything that I had once considered important. My life, my weight, my relationships, they were all standing still. In fact, it seemed nothing around me was moving. Nothing except the days ticking ever more quickly toward my thirtieth birthday.

April

LIVVIE WAS RIGHT AS USUAL. My scene with David at the bar had gone a long way toward ratcheting my already shaky work environment to new levels of discomfort. Weeks passed with virtually no contact between Morgan and me due to well-orchestrated court and library visits on both of our parts.

When we were in the office at the same time, things had settled into what could only be described as hideously distressing. I stayed in my office as much as possible if only to avoid Morgan's startled deer-in-the-headlights look every time he saw me, followed by a crab-like scuttle back to his own office whenever I attempted actual contact.

Stockpiling my copy jobs so I would only need to visit Gloria's desk once, I realized things couldn't go on as they were. My future as a partner in Frank's office depended upon my ability to deal with personnel matters and I needed to try to get things back to pleasant with my co-worker.

If not pleasant, than at least bearable.

Unable to stand the environment for one more day, I waited until Frank left for court and Gloria went downstairs to sneak her daily cigarette, a habit she thought was much better hidden than it was, before squaring my shoulders and heading into the lion's den. I tapped at the frame outside Morgan's office door until he looked up.

"Oh, hey, Sarah." The look in his eye was on par with that poor squirrel I had seen on my last drive to Boston, an instant too late, just before he became part of the pavement on I-95. Morgan dropped his eyes again quickly, but it was at least progress that he hadn't shimmied open the window and risked the four story drop.

"Hi. Do you have a minute?"

"Sure. If you're looking for the Marrick brief, though, I haven't quite finished. I still need to investigate the..."

I closed the office door behind me with a quiet click, causing Morgan to stop talking, cut off all pretense that the two of us had a normal working relationship and look at me with alarm.

"Don't panic." I held my hand up. "I just wanted to say a few things in private."

"Okay, sure." His tone was wary, but since he appeared at least willing to hear me out, I ripped the band aid clean off.

"I want to apologize for a few things. I'm sorry about my performance at the bar the other night."

"You don't owe me an explanation." Morgan held up his hands. "I figured you and that Thornton guy had something going on. You know – between the flowers he sent you and the fact he was all over you."

"But we're not..." I stammered, trying and failing to find the right words.

"You're not?"

"No. You know my tendency to grab the closest guy in sight when I don't know how to deal with a situation. That was just me being stupid."

"Oh." Morgan blew out a breath and rubbed his hand through his close cropped hair. "I see. You used me as a shield against Ryan at the diner. I guess this time you felt you needed to be shielded from me and used your friend David."

Shit.

"No, wait. That's not it either. That was what Livvie was afraid you'd think. That wasn't what I was doing, I swear."

Morgan tilted his head in confusion. "It wasn't?"

"No."

"I'll bite, then. What was your intention?" Morgan made little air quotes as he said "intention".

I tried to ignore the fact that I usually hated people who made air quotes and decided to be honest. That's right; I was going to give honesty a try. Any port in a storm, right?

"I wasn't trying to get rid of you. I was trying to make you jealous."

"You were?" He didn't even try to hide the surprise in his voice. He shook his head murmuring to himself quietly, as if trying to make the pieces of some puzzle slip into place.

Not wanting to chicken out before I finished my story, I continued, "so, that's your first apology for petty, stupid behavior. Are you ready for seconds?"

"I get a second apology? I'm intrigued." With the small crooked smile I received, for just a moment, I felt the crackle of chemistry between us again.

"I want to apologize for our date a few weeks ago."

"Oh." And with that word, the electricity in the air went from crackle to pop to fizzle in the space of a heartbeat.

Morgan picked up his pen, dropped his eyes again and gestured to the papers in front of him. "No worries. Look, I really need to finish this up for Frank."

"I'm not apologizing for the date itself," I clarified. "I'm apologizing for freaking you out."

"You didn't freak me out."

"Yes, I did."

"No you didn't."

"Yes, I did, Morgan." I insisted, bringing my hand down hard on his desk.

"Fine!" Morgan threw down his pen and finally met my eyes. "You freaked me out. You freaked me out on our date and you freaked me out at the bar. If you want me to be entirely honest, you're kind of freaking me out now."

I stumbled back a step and clutched the door knob, almost ready to bolt from the room. Because, really, that was probably a little more honesty than I had been looking for.

"I have pretty crappy social skills," I blurted, staring at the ugly bamboo rug at my feet. "I like you and had fun when we went out, but I think I have a deep-seated self-destruct mechanism in my brain. If things seem like they're going well, I have a perverse need to screw them up."

Risking a peek, I saw that at least I had Morgan's full attention. "I think our date was going pretty well before I screwed it up."

He nodded in agreement, but remained silent.

"I just wanted to admit it was my fault. I came on too strong and made a royal mess of things that night. Then, at the bar when I saw you walk in with..." I shook my head, not quite ready for that amount of honesty. "When I saw you walk in, all I could think was how embarrassed I was by the way I acted. Instead of owning up to that, I decided to pretend that I didn't care at all what you thought of me. I latched onto David which made things about a hundred times worse. And, well..."

Morgan remained silent, waiting expectantly for my next words, but I was at the end of my monologue.

"That's it. I just...I know I'm a hopeless case, but I try to admit my faults when I see them, and I admit that my faults lately have been pretty apparent. Especially to you. Maybe I should come with a warning label. Something like, 'objects in the rear view mirror may be crazier than they appear'."

That line earned me a grin and reluctant chuckle, followed by a very serious question. "So where do we go from here, Sarah?"

At least it was a question that I knew how to answer. "Let's just forget the last several weeks altogether. Let's forget everything and go back to how things were when you first started working here last fall."

"I'm sorry, but I don't think I can do that."

"Oh. Well. Okay then." I nodded my head reluctantly. It appeared that I really had burned my bridges with Morgan. Not only was he not interested in dating me, but he wasn't going to be able to get past my erratic, psychotic behavior in order to be my co-worker, either. I opened the door and began to flee the room in search of a pint of Chunky Monkey when his voice stopped me.

"Sarah, wait!" I turned and found him rounding the desk anxiously. "What I meant was, I don't want to go back to the days when I just started working here. Things were lousy back then, too. You hated me and we barely spoke."

"Oh yeah. Good point." How soon we forget.

"Maybe we can move the timeline up a bit? Remember the truce you and I struck in the courthouse back in January? The beginning of a beautiful friendship?"

I nodded my head, remembering.

"Great, then. Let's go back to January when we were friends and co-workers. You know, before there were any messy complications."

His nervous smile was so endearing it almost soothed the bristle I felt at his words. 'Messy complications'? Going out with me had been a messy complication?

Oh well. I swallowed down the insult and decided to be satisfied that Morgan wasn't filing either a sexual harassment suit or false imprisonment charges against me for trapping him in his office.

"Deal." I held out my hand until Morgan grasped it with a smile. Full-wattage this time.

"Deal."

*   *   *

Feeling generally positive about my conversation – by shoving the 'messy complications' line into a dark, unused corner of my brain – and wanting to share my glory with someone, I dialed the number to Livvie's office.

A gratingly cheerful voice answered the phone. "Good morning. Olivia DiMarco's office."

Of all the people working for the District Attorney that could have picked up Livvie's line today, it figured it would have to be Cory Latham. I hoped against hope she wouldn't recognize my voice. "Could I please speak to Ms. DiMarco?"

"Sarah!" She giggled, apparently overflowing with joy to hear from me. "Is that you?"

Busted. "Yes, Cory, it's me. Could you please put Livvie on the phone?"

There was a slight pause before Cory spoke again, any trace of warmth swept away by a frosty chill. "You know Sarah, you could at least try to be pleasant to me. It's been years since we had our differences and I just don't see why you have to be so hostile every time we speak."

Since we had our differences? For the love of God! She was acting like we'd had a petty quarrel. I felt fairly secure that 4 out of 5 dentists would agree that holding a grudge against someone who knowingly slept with your boyfriend could not be considered 'petty'.

I did not have the patience to deal with Cory acting like a poor wounded doe while casting me in the role as the evil hunter standing over her with a crossbow.

Sorry, Bambi, but that attitude was not going to fly.

"I'm not acting hostile, Cory. I actually am hostile every time we speak. Please put Livvie on the phone."

"I can't. She's out of town until next Tuesday. As her best friend, I would think you'd know that," she sneered.

I slumped in my chair and gave myself the V-8 slap for forgetting. Of course I knew Livvie was spending a week with her parents biking and camping at the State Park. While I felt stupid for forgetting my friend's plans, the image of Livvie clomping around the woods in her Juicy Couture outerwear while trying not to break a nail cheered me almost to the point where I could cope with Cory.

"Never mind, then. I'll leave her a message at home."

I had the receiver nearly to the cradle when I heard Cory whine, "I just don't understand why you're so unwilling to make amends. I know I've made some mistakes, but I just want us to be friends."

And to think that the day had started out on such a positive note.

Unfortunately for the world at large, I had used up all of my grace, humility and compassion during my conversation with Morgan and I didn't have a drop in me for the rest of humanity.

Not that I considered Cory Latham human, but even so, I felt the elastic band that was my patience snap. "Look Cory, I have no idea why you want to be my friend, but let me assure you it is never going to happen. I have no desire to make amends with you. You slept with my boyfriend, you cow! Most people smarter than a speed bump would be able to figure that out."

"God, Sarah, I apologized for that a hundred years ago! Besides, it was just one of those drunken mistakes. It didn't mean a thing."

"It may not have meant a thing to you, but to me it meant the end of a two-year relationship. I thought Ryan and I were going to be together forever, and in one fell swoop the two of you…"

No. I was not going to give this vile woman the satisfaction of knowing how deeply she and Ryan had hurt me. My anger raged once again as I all but yelled, "I am not going to have this discussion with you. You, Cory Latham, are a boyfriend-stealing tramp and we are never going to be friends. Tell Livvie I called or don't. I really don't care."

With that, I slammed the phone back in its cradle and jumped up from my desk, adrenaline coursing through my body. Wow that felt really good.

It felt good for a moment, anyway. That was as long as it took for me to look up and see Morgan and Gloria standing outside my office door which I had carelessly neglected to shut before making my phone call. Morgan's wide eyes and stunned look showed that he had heard every word of my conversation. Gloria just looked mildly amused as she deadpanned, "I take it Livvie was out of the office?"

"Yes." I straightened up the post-it notes and other bits of papers scattered about my desk as I tried to regain my dignity. "I left a message, though."

"So, we heard." Gloria chuckled and went back to the reception area while Morgan remained in the doorway.

Morgan continued to just lean against my door frame. "So, um... the other night at the bar. When my friends and I walked in. You know, before your little freak out. Did you happen to see that Cory was with us?"

I tucked my hair nervously behind my ears. "Oh, was that her? Really? I thought it might have been."

"You thought it might have been?" Morgan repeated, again not moving from my door, although I thought I caught the hint of a smile in his eyes.

Finally, he stood upright and remarked, "Yeah, well, anyway. I'm glad we made up. You're kind of scary when you're mad."

With an unexpected wink he was gone and I sat down in my office chair with a thunk, adrenaline finally and suddenly zapped from my system.

Jesus. It wasn't even ten o'clock yet and it had been a hell of a morning.

* * *

"Meet me at the diner for breakfast."

I had left that message on Frank's voice mail and could only assume he would be in equal parts intrigued and annoyed. I'd done my homework and made sure he had no meetings or court appearances scheduled until much later in the day. According to my calculations, Frank had no idea that my first effort in regrouping my focus on my life's goals was to propose he make me a partner in his firm.

It had been just over a month since Frank dropped the announcement about the Lightship Island assignment, and I had spent that time working like a dog. It had turned out that while secession still occurred in some states, much of the published case law was over a hundred years old, forcing me to conduct most of my research in the oldest of the law library stacks. Many of my afternoons and every Saturday had been spent hunkered down at an old pine table, happily blowing the dust from the older volumes.

It dawned on me one day while happily scribbling notes into one of my many yellow legal pads that I was a geek when it came to research. I wasn't terribly disturbed by that fact, especially since the project I was working on brought such joy to my boss. Prior to this experience, I thought his happiness scale moved only from "wicked cranky" to "kinda cranky".

I was proven wrong, though, within the first few days after the announcement in the conference room. Frank was as happy as I'd ever seen him, running around calling his old cronies and pretending to pick their brains over various municipal law questions. Everyone in the office knew that the true purpose of Frank's calls was to gloat over his new client.

Given my boss' excitement over the project coupled with the massive amounts of helpful, detailed information and strategy I'd provided him, I knew it was the right time to pitch the idea of "Murphy & Bennett, Attorneys at Law".

I had decided to broach the subject of partnership at the diner since it was my turf and Frank couldn't brush me aside or be distracted by the papers and phone calls that surrounded him back at the office. Of most importance to me, a meeting at the diner would be far from Morgan's curious eyes. If things didn't go as planned, the last thing I wanted was to crash and burn in front of him.

That was why, at seven o'clock on the dot I went downstairs, kissed Uncle Jeremy hello and appropriated a booth, preparing to meet my future.

"Hey, Frank." I ushered him to the table marked as occupied by the presence of my coat and briefcase the moment he walked through the door. "What do you want for breakfast?"

"Just coffee is fine." He removed his expensive wool top coat and hung it on the wall hook near the table. He nodded in greeting to both Jeremy and David while I got up to pour two cups of coffee. From his vantage point, lying on the counter, David must have seen my hand shake slightly. He snagged my wrist and whispered quietly, "Just remember – he's lucky to have you. Anybody would be."

Squaring my shoulders, I returned to my table and handed Frank his coffee. "I appreciate you meeting me here."

"I assume Gloria knows what this is about?" He asked, and I confirmed with a nod of my head.

Gloria would have never approved such a radical departure in Frank's schedule if she hadn't known the reason. One of Gloria's greatest assets was her undivided loyalty to Frank. While she cared about me a great deal and would support me to the end of the earth, in her eyes the earth ended at the exact moment when my interests conflicted with Frank's.

I had only received Gloria's support for this out of office meeting by informing her of the subject matter, and bought her silence only by promising that I would fully disclose my wishes, plans and concerns without holding anything back.

"Did I ever tell you the story of how Gloria came to work for me?" Frank asked, apropos of nothing.

"No." Thrown by the direction of the conversation, I had to admit I was intrigued. Frank and Gloria finished each other's sentences and I wanted to know how their bond had come into being. Although it would prolong my own presentation, I gestured for Frank to continue.

"I've known her since I was a kid. She worked as my dad's secretary in his insurance office. When I started my practice, I was so engrossed with the legal issues that I slacked off on the business end." Frank slurped at his coffee. "I begged Gloria to take a leave of absence and help me out for a month or two. That was twelve years ago."

I opened my mouth to ask exactly how two months had turned into twelve years when a thought suddenly occurred to me. "Frank, are you stalling?"

"Of course I'm stalling. Stalling is an excellent legal tactic. It's almost as good as luring your adversary into meeting you in a location where he's at a disadvantage." He tried unsuccessfully to hide the slight smile behind his coffee mug. "When the opposing party gets the upper hand, I generally try to shake things up a bit. Throws them off their game."

I was both appalled and thoroughly impressed.

"Frank, I'm not your adversary or the opposing party. I'm your employee and your friend."

He tapped his finger impatiently on the table. "We'll see. Okay, Bennett, let's get down to it. What is this about? Did you miss a deadline? Lose a case?"

He leaned in with a conspiratorial whisper. "Did you finally kill Morgan? Because if you did, I'm still not doing criminal defense work – even for you."

"Frank!" I chuckled at his wild speculation. Next to his fears that I had brought shame and disgrace to his firm, my mere request to be his business partner might actually be looked upon favorably.

"I just want to talk to you about my career."

My boss leaned back and nodded. He took a measured sip of coffee before answering, "That sounds ominous."

"It doesn't have to be," I quickly assured him. 'I want to discuss where I'm going and what your plans are for me. I think I work hard and do a good job."

I pulled a folder out of my bag, and flipped it open as I said, "I'd like you to see some of the charts I've prepared that document the various..."

"Oh Jesus, Bennett, you've got charts?" He pulled back like a Native American who'd just been offered a smallpox infested blanket. "I don't need charts to know you do a good job. Are you angling for a raise? Because I think I was more than generous with your last annual review."

"No. This has absolutely nothing to do with money."

"Then what does it have to do with?" Frank looked impatiently at his watch. "Cut to the chase, Bennett."

Things were drifting widely off course. Frank hadn't even glanced at my charts and I could tell he had already mentally checked out of our conversation. Having nothing to lose, I blurted, "I made a list."

Clearly not expecting that answer, I at least got some of Frank's attention back. "You made a list? A list of what?"

"I made a list of things I want to accomplish before I hit thirty."

Frank nodded, mildly interested, but uncomprehending. "What exactly does your wish list have to do with me?"

"It's not a wish list, Frank. It's a list of serious goals I want to meet in both my personal and professional life."

I wisely did not mention Item #6 – boffing George Clooney.

"One of the items on my list is that I want to be a partner in a law firm and that's what I want to discuss with you today. You say I don't have to convince you of my worth, so I won't try, but I think I've worked hard and deserve being considered for a partnership role."

Frank said nothing, his blank facial expression making it impossible for me to decipher what he was thinking. After measuring my words for an uncomfortably long period, he took a long gulp of coffee. "You know I was a cop before I went to law school, right?"

Not sure why the conversation had taken this turn, but willing to see it through, I nodded. "Of course. That's where you met Uncle Jeremy."

"Right. Well, what you may not know is that I loved that job. It was hard – real hard some days – but I came home every night feeling like I accomplished something."

"Then why did you quit?"

"I loved the job, Bennett, but I hated the politics. I had a shift commander to answer to, a sergeant and the chief of police. I was responsible for my partner, had to keep internal affairs out of my hair and not piss off the guys at the union. Every two years a new police chief was voted in and all the players changed, not to mention the fact that you couldn't get a day off or even wipe your ass without seniority. I loved the job," he repeated, "but I couldn't stand all of the trappings that went with it."

Frank leaned in, glint in his eye as if he were about to share a state secret. "I don't know if you're aware of this, Bennett, but I'm not much of a team player. I need a job where I'm the boss and I answer to no one."

The police analogy clicked into place and I suddenly saw the handwriting on the wall.

"I'm sorry, Sarah. I really am. I know I don't say it enough, but you're right. You are a huge asset to my firm and I don't want to lose you."

Trying to inject levity I didn't feel, I said, "Why does this seem like the old 'it's not you, it's me' speech?"

My boss attempted a tight lipped smile, but the crinkles around his eyes remained decidedly flat. "If you want to talk about vacation days, more pro bono work, hell, even money, I'm willing to talk. But if you really want to be a partner in a law firm, that is not something I can offer you. I run a solo operation and that's never going to change."

I was stunned into silence. The funny part was that I had expected Frank to say no and turn me down. I had expected him to tell me I was inexperienced and flighty and not ready for partnership. I had expected Frank to say, "Not now, Bennett."

But I really hadn't expected Frank to say, "Never."

"Sarah?"

I looked up, but just couldn't form any words. I didn't quite know how to respond.

"Sarah, you have to say something. You couldn't have really thought you would come to me and demand a partnership because of some wish list." Frank demanded, his tone gruff, but nothing but concern showing on his face.

When all else fails, I decided to settle on telling the truth. "No. Of course I didn't expect you to say yes right away, but I guess I did expect you to consider it as a future possibility."

Frank remained silent, confirming that I had read him correctly and partnership was indeed not a future possibility.

"I don't want you to think this is all about a wish list," I blurted. Suddenly it was very important to me that Frank understand. "That list I made just reminded me of what I want out of life and prompted me to ask for things that I guess I'd forgotten I really, really wanted."

"I'm sorry, Sarah." From the tone in his voice and the rare use of my first name, I knew that he truly was sorry. But that didn't change the answer.

I was never going to be a partner in Frank's law firm.

"Come on, let's get to the office." I grabbed my coat and bag, desperate to get away from the diner and the conversation. I waved a quick goodbye to Jeremy and David who had to have known from our body language exactly how the conversation had ended.

I walked quietly in step with Frank toward the office, and kept coming back to the question of why never being made a partner was such a big deal. I mean, I made good money and enjoyed my job. I loved working with Frank and Gloria, but still…

There was such a finality reached that I found it difficult to take a deep breath. This was it. I knew exactly how far my career would go. If I continued to work at Frank's firm, I would probably hold the same job at 55 that I held at 25.

If I stayed with Frank, I would never make partner, and if I wanted to be a partner, I'd have to leave Frank's firm. Realizing with a shock the answer to my internal struggle, I decided that the first thing I would do upon arriving at the office would be to call my friend Claire and find out if there were any openings at the large law firm where she worked.

As much as I loved my job, I wasn't willing to close the door on my career at 29 years old.

"Are you okay, Bennett?" Frank asked, holding the door for me as we entered the building that housed his law office.

"Yeah, Frank. I'm going to be fine."

We smiled at each other and continued walking, both pretending to believe me.

May

FOLLOWING MY EMOTIONAL CONVERSATION with Morgan, the outburst with Cory and my devastating conversation with Frank, I somehow made it through the rest of the week on autopilot. I completed my work, kept up my end of conversations, ate and slept at the appropriate times. While my body went through the motions, though, my energy level registered below all units of measurement. I was a walking zombie, getting myself from Point A to Point B, but with very little emotion behind it.

I was so thrilled when the weekend rolled around that I even begged off an invitation from Eddie to meet him in Boston where he had a four hour layover on his way to Toronto. He ended up catching a cab to a local gallery which was hosting a new Andrew Wyeth exhibit while I spent the day in my pajamas watching my collection of DVDs from old 80s television shows and eating cold Chinese takeout.

Sunday I was forced to get out of bed and actually shower only because a waitress and prep cook had both called in sick and Jeremy needed help in the diner. I secretly wondered if he'd conspired with Eddie behind my back and given his employees the day off. He knew I wouldn't turn down a plea for help, which would allow him to keep an eye on me.

Jeremy needn't have worried, though. I wasn't depressed. I was just completely and utterly spent, and needed time alone to regroup. At 3pm the diner closed and I begged off another invitation from Uncle Jeremy, this time to watch the Red Sox. I went back to my apartment, got back in my pj's and – having worked my way up to the early 2000s – pulled out my Gilmore Girls DVD box set. Next to me on the couch was a 2-liter bottle of soda, new package of notebooks and fresh set of pens. Armed and ready, I spent the afternoon scribbling away. I had new plans to make.

When the next morning rolled around, I got out of bed, worked eight hours and dutifully made small talk with my co-workers. I certainly wasn't rude, but neither could I have been considered engaged. While my co-workers may have thought my behavior was odd, there was no mention of it to my face. I did catch a few concerned glances behind my back, but those I pointedly ignored, having no energy left for confrontation. Morgan even invited me to go to the courthouse with him to drop off a pleading. If I hadn't known better, I might have thought he was genuinely disappointed when I turned him down.

By Tuesday night I was halfway through Season Two of Gilmore Girls – the Rory and Dean years – and well into my second loose-leaf notebook when I heard a pounding at my apartment door.

"Bennett!" I leapt from the couch and looked down at my attire. I was wearing my rattiest pajamas – the ones with pictures of cocktails next to their respective recipes.

Luckily, I recognized the voice behind the insistent knocking. Knowing Livvie had seen me a lot worse, I got up off the couch and opened the door. "How did you get up here?" I asked, throwing the latch.

"Nice greeting. Your uncle's downstairs and he let me up." My friend looked around the messy living room. Papers were littered everywhere along with books, soda cans and a few empty take-out containers. "I love what you've done with the place."

"Funny." I picked up one of the piles of papers I'd been working on and shifted it to find a few empty places for us to sit. "I've been working through some things during the last few days. For instance, do you know we haven't been exercising in almost three weeks?"

I picked up another pile of papers and glanced at the sheet on top. "Also, last week I made that corned beef hash everyone liked, but according to my calorie count book, it had more than 800 calories per serving."

Livvie didn't even glance at my work. She just shook her head at me. "You've lost your mind. How sad."

"I haven't lost my mind. I've regained my focus. My perspective. I just needed a few days alone."

I grabbed my food plan and showed her. "Look, according to this chart, I can still fit into a size eight by my birthday. I just need to get back on track."

"Okay, crazy lady. Put down the charts and back away slowly. Let's talk about your real life. When I left on my uber-vacation with Mom and Dad, you were going to talk to Morgan about your breakdown at the Grizzly Beer. Did you?"

"Yes."

Livvie rolled her eyes. "Don't make me pull out the bamboo strips. How did it go?"

"About as well as you'd expect. He thinks I'm crazy, but he's willing to overlook that fact so we can work together. We've actually been getting along pretty well together since we talked."

"And speaking of working at Frank's office…"

"Speaking of working at Frank's office," I dutifully continued. "We met and he told me in no uncertain terms that I will never be his partner. Never going to happen. So I called Claire, and believe it or not, they're understaffed at her place. I have a meeting with the senior partner in her firm a week from Wednesday."

"That sounds serious." Livvie sat up straighter on the couch, surprised by my announcement.

"It is."

"I'm sorry it went so badly with Frank, but that wasn't entirely unexpected. Just because he won't make you partner doesn't mean you have to actually leave the firm, though."

"I disagree. I'm hoping Claire's boss will be open to the idea of offering me a partnership a few years down the road. I may not make it by age thirty, but at least I'll be in a place where partnership is possible."

"Wow. That's hard core." It wasn't very often that I could impress Livvie. "It sounds like you had a very, very busy week."

"I did."

"And are you, uh, leaving anything out by chance?"

"Let's see, I squared things with Morgan, met with Frank, talked with Claire and set up a job interview." I considered the past week, ticked off on my fingers all of the activities that had kept me busy, finally remembering the one item my friend and I hadn't yet discussed. "Oh, I know. I had an interesting phone call with Cory Latham."

"You don't say." Livvie commented in a soft, sing-song voice that indicated she already knew all about our interesting conversation.

Uh oh.

Stretching her arms across the back of the love seat, settling into her storytelling mode she began. "Since you haven't asked, let me tell you about my day. I got back to work this morning only to find that my trial was moved up from three o'clock to ten a.m., and no one knew where my witnesses were. Then, if that wasn't bad enough, I was called into a meeting in the human resources office this afternoon."

"Why?" I winced, already knowing the answer.

"It seems that one of the pool secretaries – one Cory Latham – filed a labor grievance against me for harassment." Livvie gave me a pointed look. "It seems she found your conversation very interesting as well."

"Oh, shit."

"Actually, it was more like 'oh, deep shit' thank you very much. I spent an hour and a half in a room with Cory, some middle manager type from H.R. and a union rep."

"Oh, Livvie, I am so sorry." I clapped my hand to my mouth, regretting every evil comment I made. Well, I didn't exactly regret making the comments per se, just the fact that they got Livvie into trouble.

"You better not be sorry," Livvie warned, wagging a finger in my direction. "If you said even half the things she accused you of, I owe you several large drinks downtown."

"What happened? Are you in any trouble?"

"Not hardly. Even the union rep knew it was a bogus grievance. It's not like I was even responsible for the supposed harassment. Besides, several people in the office at the time of the call heard Cory bragging about how you tried to hang up, but she refused to give you the last word."

"Bitch," I muttered reflexively.

"Agreed. The grievance was found to be without merit, but we did agree that I'd give you my inside line so you won't have to place calls through the reception area anymore."

"The Union rep was very understanding," she winked.

"Oh?"

"Let's just say he thought it would be for the best if he got the number to my private line, too."

"That sounds promising." I took a long gulp from the can of diet soda by my side.

Livvie just smiled. Not willing to jinx a potentially good thing, she deftly changed the subject by again gesturing toward the destruction that was my living room. "Okay, so explain the great paper blizzard."

"I'm back on track. I spent the weekend refocusing on my goals and the fact that I'm making progress on the job front, but weight is stalled and my hopes of a relationship are – if anything – in a downward spiral."

"And what have you learned from all of this planning and plotting?" Livvie asked, sorting through the papers closest to her and scanning their contents.

"Well, if I want to lose weight, I need to eat less and exercise more."

Livvie stopped her paper shuffling and gave me a pointed glare. "You needed to kill a tree to come up with that brilliant deduction?"

"What can I say? I'm a slow learner."

"Not telling me anything I don't know." Livvie leaned forward and pulled a stack of Sunday paper ads from under her chair. "What are these?"

"Oh, those. I was pricing a few stair machines to help train for Mt. Katahdin. I thought since I'm not saving for a down payment anymore, I could stand to spend some of my savings."

"Stair machines? Seriously?" Livvie slumped into the love seat in a manner I couldn't quite name, but one that lived somewhere near the corner of frustration and exasperation. Shaking her head, she asked, "Where is it? The list. The original. The one I gave you on your birthday."

"Over there." I pointed to the largest stack of papers on my desk.

Grabbing the paper and thrusting it in my face, she asked, "Look at this. Tell me what you see."

"The tangible proof of my shattered hopes and dreams."

Apparently the wrong answer as Livvie responded through gritted teeth, "Killing me, Bennett. Seriously, seriously killing me here."

Taking a breath, though, she rallied. "You know what? Never mind. I'll tell you what this is. This is a list of goals to accomplish. The thing is, that some of them are truly your goals and some of them aren't."

"What do you mean?"

"I mean, look at the items that are crossed off. Like number four." She pointed to my desire to see Bruce Springsteen in concert. "You love Springsteen. You wanted to see him, so you went online, got us those crappy tickets and we went. And look at number seven."

"Jimmy Stewart's star," I muttered, suddenly clueing in on my friend's point.

"Right again, Bennett. Do you really think Eddie and David would have taken a full day out of their vacation to stand on a street corner and gaze at a piece of granite? No. You wanted it. You made it happen."

"I guess so."

"You guess, my ass. You made it happen." Livvie scanned my list and pointed at yet another item. "Look at this one. You finally manned up and decided you wanted to be partner in a law firm. So what happens? I'm gone for one week and you've already met with your boss, rejected what he had to say and set up a job interview with another firm."

I took a moment to digest my friend's words, but the taste was really quite pleasant. Still, I had to ask. "Since when did you become a fan of my list?"

"I'm not a fan of the list, you dope. I'm a fan of Sarah Bennett. I'm just trying to decipher which parts of this list belong to her and which parts belong to the life she thinks she should have."

"We already pitched the idea of buying a new house. I don't want to cut the list down too far."

"We won't. But Sarah, do you really want to climb a mountain?"

"Um, sure."

"Way to be convincing." Livvie walked into the kitchen, retrieved a can of soda for herself, silently judging my hostessing skills and resumed her perch. "Here's a different question for you. When we started exercising last fall, why did you choose the paved Boulevard route? There are tons of hiking trails around Portland."

"You know I like walking the Boulevard. It's clear, flat, near the city. We get dirty and dusty hiking on the trails. All kinds of critters and bugs out there, too," I shuddered at the thought. "Yuck.".

Livvie leaned back, the smug look on her face confirming that Perry Mason had once again coerced a confession on the witness stand.

"Oh, shut up."

"I didn't say anything."

"Yeah, well, you said it pretty damn loud."

Holding my list up once more and giving it a slight shake, she asked, "So, Mt. Katahdin?"

"Go ahead and scratch it," I replied, throwing a Sharpie at my friend, none too gently. "But you're not touching the items about losing weight and finding a relationship. Those are all mine. Besides I have new strategies to put into play."

"Strategies? Like eat less and exercise more?"

"Exactly."

"Fine. That's your strategy for weight loss." Livvie placed the pen and list on my coffee table. "So, what inspiring strategies did you reach about men and relationships?"

"Well, I know Morgan and I are barely speaking. He's out of the running. I think I'm back to your plan of meeting men outside of my current circle."

"You're probably right. The date with Morgan was a fiasco." Livvie agreed. "I don't know why you keep ruling David out, though. I'm pissed about his behavior at the bar and sabotaging your date, but he's a good guy. Why won't you give him a shot?"

It was a good question.

And it deserved an honest answer.

"I just can't do it, Livvie. I just can't date David."

"Why not?"

I collapsed bonelessly into my desk chair and faced my friend. "Let's say for the sake of argument that David is interested in me romantically."

"Yes, let's just pretend that's a possibility." Livvie leaned forward to keep from dripping her sarcasm all over my couch.

"David and Jeremy and Eddie are my family." I searched for the right words to explain the delicate balance that was my life. "My mom and dad are gone. The Thorntons are all I have. Since my first memory, we've been this weirdly meshed, completely dysfunctional and fantastically happy family unit. I love him, but in the exact same way I love Eddie and Jeremy. There's just nothing else there. If I try to force something, it's just not going to work and when I screw things up with David, I don't just lose him. I lose my entire family."

Livvie must have realized we were about to walk down a morose road. Showing exactly why she was my best friend, she merely gave my hand a hard squeeze and took a sharp conversational u-turn, deftly avoiding the potential emotion-fest. "Okay, then. David's out and Morgan's out. We're back to where we were a few months ago. You need to meet new men."

We took a few moments to quietly consider, and in turn reject, ideas before Livvie broke the silence. "You know my friend Alice from work?"

At my nod, Livvie continued, "She has this book club she wants us to join."

A book club sounded promising. At the very least, my potential boyfriend would be literate.

"Are there any men in this book club?"

"Yes." Livvie answered, her eyes not quite meeting mine. You had to love lawyers who answered only the direct questions asked of them.

"Are they single men?"

"Well, no. But married men have single friends."

"No they don't. That's a myth." I wasn't sure whether married men didn't like reminders of their single days, wives didn't like their husbands hanging out with the boys, or if once the first member of a pack found his mate, the others just fell into line, but I knew it was the truth.

Regardless of the message propagated by television sitcoms, married men did not vicariously enjoy the exploits of their randy, single friends. Married men hung out with other married men.

"Are there any single women in the book club?" I asked. Unlike married men, single women could be a great source for meeting single men. Much like a sale at Filene's basement, women often rejected men with no inherent flaws, but because they just weren't the right fit. Most secure, mature women were willing to share castoffs.

Unfortunately, Livvie dashed my hopes on that front, too. "No. I think the women in the club are married, too."

I gifted my friend with what I hoped was my most withering look. "Great plan, thanks. Next idea?"

Livvie tapped at her lip for a moment before straightening with a bright smile. "World Cup soccer."

"You want me to play World Cup soccer?"

"No, you idiot. One of the bars downtown is having a special broadcast next Saturday with half price drink specials. Men like soccer and they like cheap beer even better."

I tried to find a flaw with the new plan, but failed. I hated to admit it sounded like a good idea. "I suppose that might work."

"It's a couple of hours sitting in front of a big screen TV drinking beer." Livvie curled her feet underneath her, leaning back into the cushions. "I mean, how bad could it be?"

*   *   *

"How bad could it be?"

I found that the answer to Livvie's question was that it wasn't that bad. It was, however, mind-numbingly boring.

I did, though, reach a profound conclusion as I sat in Gladiator's Sports Pub, sipping the afternoon tap special.

I didn't like soccer.

I watched the fans in the crowd half a world away; the players running back and forth in the lush green field; and then thought about the countless riots and stampedes at which people had lost their lives due to the crazy fervor for the game. All I could think was...

"Eh."

Livvie, who had pushed me out of the nest and made me attend the event alone to look more 'available' hadn't been wrong, though. The room was filled with men. Unfortunately, most of them were actually boys who looked barely old enough to drink and were by far too young for me to be involved with any way short of offering to baby-sit them.

At the other end of the spectrum was a table full of lecherous – probably married – men in their late fifties who took turns individually coming over and asking me to join them. I smiled politely, but gripped onto my bar stool for dear life.

To be fair, there was a table occupied by mixed gender fans rooting for Italy. They were friendly, seemed normal enough and had also asked me to join them. I considered it briefly before noticing the ratio of men to women was exactly 1-to-1 and the women were shooting me death glares. Heeding the unspoken Code of Women, I chatted briefly, but in the end returned to my perch.

As it turned out, the most action I got during the game was the friendly chatter from the bartender, Tim, but knowing he was an old "friend" of Eddie's, I couldn't even work that angle.

After an hour, a beer, and a generous tip for Tim, I left the bar, shading my eyes against the day which had turned out much sunnier than the forecast had called for. At loose ends with what to do with myself and only a few blocks from the office, I decided to put in a few hours' worth of work.

Not knowing what my future work life would look like, I'd been spending numerous hours recently cleaning up old, back-burnered matters and paying closer attention than usual to my filing and documentation. I knew leaving Frank's office would be hard, and my boss was nothing if not unpredictable. When I finally mustered my courage to resign, he could just toss me out, seeing my action as disloyalty to our personal relationship.

Even knowing this could be his reaction, I couldn't leave his clients in the lurch or his files in disarray just because Frank had a temper.

Unlocking the office door, I reached to enter the alarm code on the pad near the door, not entirely surprised that it was not engaged. It was a gorgeous, bright Saturday. I should have known Frank would be working. Dropping my purse on Gloria's desk, I walked into my boss' office and plopped into the visitor's chair.

"What are you doing here?"

Frank looked up, equally unsurprised by my presence. "I could ask the same."

"I work for an incredibly unreasonable man who keeps ridiculous hours."

"Sounds like my kind of guy." My boss' eyes crinkled. "I went to the deli at lunch. There's half a sandwich in the fridge out back. It's yours if you want it."

Sadly, factoring in my failure at the bar, Frank's offer was the most appealing one I'd gotten all day. Rising to claim my newly acquired lunch, I was surprised to find Frank and I were not alone.

"Hey, Frank..." Morgan burst into the office, stopping short and obviously every bit as surprised to see me as I was him. "Oh, hi Sarah."

Crap. He was dressed in his "Casual Ken" attire which I hated to admit I still found unreasonably attractive. What was wrong with me? I saw this guy in an expensive shirt and jacket almost every day and had steeled myself against most inappropriate reactions. I saw the guy in a 2004 Springsteen World Tour t-shirt and jeans, though, and turned into a babbling 14 year old.

"Hey," I managed to reply. I sidled past Morgan, still standing by the open office door and retrieved my purse from Gloria's desk. Once I had distanced myself a step or two from whatever kryptonite-like hold Morgan held over me, I stopped long enough to feel the old workplace jealousy course through my veins. Morgan Donovan was still a law student for crying out loud. Why was he here, making points with Frank on the weekend?

"What are you doing here?" I blasted at him the moment he left Frank's office.

"Working. What are you doing here?" Morgan shot back, not giving an inch or backing away from my obvious confrontation.

I had to admit his attitude was pretty impressive.

And more than a little hot.

It was also just snippy enough to throw cold water on my less than friendly behavior. "Point taken. I was downtown watching the World Cup and bored off my ass. I decided to clean up my desk a little."

"You left a bar full of people and a sporting event to come to work?" Morgan perched on the end of Gloria's desk, casual stance matching the clothes.

I shrugged. "It's not like the Sox were playing. What's your excuse?"

"I had plans to go hiking with my best friend, but he got sick. Didn't feel like going alone."

I nodded, understanding and knowing I would have done the same. "Sounds like we're both losers."

"Sounds like it." The conversation stalled for a moment, but neither of us moved away.

"So, Sarah, do you ever hike? I mean, would that be something you'd be interested in doing some time?"

"Nope." How funny that Livvie and I had just crossed mountain climbing off my list. Otherwise I might be interested in Morgan's friendly invitation. "I'm not really interested in hiking."

Before he could respond, my cell phone started buzzing. I looked down at the familiar number and flipped it open.

"Hey, Uncle Jeremy. What's up?"

"Hey, kiddo. Gloria is over here now, and we were thinking about putting a few burgers on the grill for dinner. Want one?"

"That sounds good, thanks," I checked my watch. "I'd like to get some work done first, though. When are you planning to eat?"

"Around five. Are you at the office now?"

"Yup."

"Hold on." Jeremy instructed and I heard a muffled discussion take place before Gloria's voice came on the line.

"Is Frank there?"

"Of course.

"Good. Tell him he's to join us. Don't take no for an answer."

With an abrupt click, the line disconnected. Chuckling to myself that only Gloria could get away with ordering Frank Murphy to do anything, I threw my cell phone back in my purse, turned and found myself again facing Morgan.

Huh. I forgot about him for a moment.

I chewed on my lip as I contemplated my next move. It would be kind of rude to invite Frank to dinner in front of Morgan, without extending the offer to him as well. I knew Gloria and Jeremy would welcome one more guest, and theoretically we were all supposed to be friends. Friends invite friends over for friendly barbecues, right?

Right?

What the hell. I turned to Morgan, "Hey, would you like to come over for a barbecue later?"

"A barbecue?"

I was pleased to see he didn't refuse me out of hand. If anything, the fact that he took a step closer appeared like he might even be mildly interested in the invitation.

I chalked it up to hunger, and tried to quickly erase any lingering doubts that I was offering anything more than friendship. "That was my Uncle Jeremy. Gloria is at his place and they're planning a barbecue. She told me to invite Frank. I thought you might like to come, too."

"Oh, um...I don't know." I was surprised when Morgan's initial interest seemed to wane and he stepped back to his former position.

Realizing that this was going to be trickier that I originally thought, I wracked my brains trying to remember the tactics Marlin Perkins used to employ when cornering a scared, wild animal. I cast my eyes downward, kept my hands in sight at all times and spoke in calm, even tone as I reminded him, "You said you have nothing better to do today."

"I know, but..."

While Morgan didn't finish his sentence, I tried to imagine what the unspoken "buts" could mean.

"...but I don't want to socialize with you outside of work..."

"...but this sounds suspiciously like a date and that didn't work out well the last time..."

"...but you're a complete and utter fruitcake and I left my ninja throwing stars at home...."

"It's just burgers on a grill. Even I can be well behaved and conduct myself in a socially acceptable manner for one afternoon. Especially in front of my uncle and my boss."

"I don't want to intrude."

"You're not intruding. Look, if you don't want to come, that's fine. No harm no foul. But, I wouldn't have invited you if you weren't welcome."

Finally I got a nod in return. "Sounds good."

I wrote down Jeremy's address and handed it to him. "Here. Show up at five with your favorite beer. We'll take care of the rest."

Having accomplished the hard part, I walked back in the corner office. "Frank!"

"What?"

"You've got two hours then you're shutting down your computer. Jeremy's having a barbecue and you're invited."

"I'm in the middle of something here, Bennett. I can't just pick up and…"

I held up my hand and took out the big guns. "Gloria told Jeremy to invite you. She said in no uncertain terms you are to show up."

"Oh. Okay, then." Matter settled, Frank put his head back down and I turned back to the reception area to finally get some work done when I was called back with a shout.

"Bennett!"

"What?"

"Why is Gloria inviting me to Jeremy's house?"

Oh, this was just delicious.

I turned on my full wattage smile and gestured for Morgan to follow me into Frank's office. This was going to be too fun not to share with someone.

I sat down and smoothed my skirt over my legs with slow, deliberate motions. "You mean you don't know?"

"Know what?"

"Jeremy and Gloria are dating. It's a full-fledged romance as a matter of fact."

I waited a beat. Two. Three. Finally, Frank regained the power of speech and spluttered, "My Gloria?"

"No, Frank." I smiled sweetly. "Apparently she's Jeremy's Gloria."

"But, but…when did this happen?"

"I've known for a few months, but I think they were dating secretly for a while before that."

"This is a law office. This shouldn't be…" I'd never seen my boss so seriously unhinged that he was unable to express a thought. "A law office should be filled with serious professionals."

"Did you know about this?" Frank turned his attention to Morgan who looked both amused and just a little afraid.

"Are you kidding?" He held up his hands in supplication.

Taking pity, I tried to explain in simple terms. "Gloria is a serious professional, Frank. She's also dating my uncle. People are allowed to have lives."

I got nothing in return but a blank look. Reminded that life outside of work did not register as a known quantity in Frank's world, I tried again. "You love Gloria and you're also very fond of Jeremy. They're good people."

"Of course they are," He bristled. "Didn't say they weren't."

"This is a good thing, then."

He looked at me with mistrust, but still as if a small part of him wanted to believe. "It's a good thing?"

"Yes, it is," putting as much conviction as possible into my voice.

"How can this be a good thing? People need focus and I want my employees to focus on their jobs, not their lives."

"That's a lovely sentiment, Frank. Thank you for that."

I really wanted to be partners with this man?

"Seriously, though," I continued. "People focus better on their jobs when they are happy in their lives outside of work. This is a good thing."

Frank's eyes narrowed. "This is a good thing?"

"Yes, Frank."

"Well, it better be. It things don't work out with Gloria and Jeremy and her productivity suffers, I am holding you personally responsible."

"You're holding me personally responsible?"

"Yes."

"Frank, I can barely hold together my own life. You can't hold me personally responsible for the well-being of two consenting adults."

"You said it was a good thing." Frank pointed a menacing finger in my direction.

"You did say that." I turned to find Morgan nodding, with innocent, yet utterly insincere eyes baling down at me.

When had I become outnumbered?

"Fine." I knew when I was sunk. "I am personally responsible. If something goes wrong between Gloria and Jeremy, you can dock my pay. Does that make you feel better?"

"Much." Frank said with a predatory smile, insanely happy that he now had someone to blame and the possibility of monetary compensation for punitive damages. "Now get out of my office. I have work to do."

Morgan and I walked through the reception area, neither of us quite sure what we'd witnessed, but I did know one thing. "You know, one good thing about working here is that on the emotional evolutionary ladder, I feel very secure I'll always have a few rungs up on Frank."

"One or two maybe." Morgan said with a mock seriousness, lightened slightly by his light bump of our shoulders and wink to take away the sting of his words. "One or two."

June

"IT IS NOT A STUPID LIST." I argued on the phone with Livvie for what must have been the millionth time, and quite honestly the refrain was getting old, even to me. I wasn't sure what had set my friend on her most recent tear. I had merely mentioned that I was grocery shopping after work for the ingredients needed to start my new cabbage soup diet. I was in a bit of a slump since realizing my brilliant idea of 'eat less, exercise more' only worked if a person did, in fact, eat less and exercise more. Since I hadn't worked very hard at either activity, I was ready for a more drastic alternative.

"It is a stupid list if it's going to lead you to existing on nothing more than hot water for three days."

"Hot water and cabbage."

Looking up from the chair in my office where this inane conversation was taking place, I was surprised to see Morgan lurking in my doorway. "Sorry, Liv. I've got to go do actual work."

Disconnecting the call, I waved Morgan all the way through the door and gestured toward my visitor chair. "Come on in. What do you need?"

"Was that Livvie? What were you two talking about?"

"Nothing. It's stupid."

Morgan smirked his reply. "That's funny. I thought I heard you adamantly defending the fact that something was not stupid. Did I hear something about a list?"

I remained silent in an attempt to hold onto my dignity when Morgan's next words brought me up short. "I thought we were supposed to be friends."

Now that was a low blow.

"Fine." Most of my other friends knew about my list already. It shouldn't be that different to share the information with Morgan, should it? "A few years ago, I wrote up a list of things I'd like to accomplish by the time I turn thirty. A deadline which is rapidly approaching."

"What kind of things?"

"Oh, you know. New Year's resolution kind of things. I want to lose weight, have a certain measure of success in my career and with my personal relationships. It's just a list of random goals."

"Personal relationships?" He parroted back at me. "Like maybe having a boyfriend?"

Like driving a car that hits a patch of ice at a stop sign, I could see where this was going with absolutely no control over the outcome. "Well, yes. I suppose finding a boyfriend might be on my list."

Morgan stood up, the tone of his visit suddenly and undeniably less friendly than it had begun. "Is that the reason you went out with me? Because you needed to check an item off a list?"

"No." I rushed to assure him. "Well, not really. I guess kind of. But only in a roundabout way. Maybe."

"Well that's as clear as mud." Morgan quirked an eyebrow, a minute, but important, shift from annoyed to intrigued.

"I went out with you because I wanted to. I didn't know I wanted to until you asked me. You asked me because of the singles party and the party was thrown so that I could meet a new man that might turn into a relationship. So, I guess I did go out with you because of my list, but only in a roundabout way."

Morgan sat heavily back into the chair. "You are one of the most confusing women I've ever met. Just for the record, though, I didn't ask you out because of the singles party. It just presented me with an opportunity."

That was news. I had figured the scene with Ryan and forcing Morgan to pretend to be my date had planted the seed, and never considered Morgan might have wanted to date me out of his own free will. I was so busy mulling over that new piece of information that I had to ask my co-worker to repeat his next words.

"I just asked if your questions in the car at the end of our date – about wanting to be my girlfriend – were because you have a deadline to be someone's girlfriend by the time you're thirty. Anyone's girlfriend."

Yikes. Stated in black and white terms, that sounded pretty pathetic. Perhaps because it was pathetic. I dropped my head to my desk, my words probably muffled by my arms which had come up to cover my head. "Can we please drop this conversation? I'm sick of being embarrassed every time I talk to you."

"I'm not trying to embarrass you. I'm just trying to figure some things out."

"Well, figure it out on your own time, okay?" I replied, getting a little cranky. After all, I had already apologized and paid my penance. "Besides, it wasn't entirely my fault. I took some very bad advice that night."

"What do you mean?"

"Nothing." I sighed, diverting the conversation. "Let's just change the subject. Did you have fun at Jeremy's barbecue?"

Lucky for me, the fish decided to take the bait, but with a long pause that showed me he was fully aware he was being reeled in. "Yes, I did. Thanks again for inviting me. It was cool to see Frank and Gloria in a social setting, and Jeremy is a terrific guy."

At his words, Morgan stood again and began wandering around my office. One wall was the huge bookcase which housed most of the firm's research library which he had seen many times before. Directly behind my desk was a window that looked out on the courthouse, and a small bulletin board to my left housed the only personal effects in what was otherwise a very professional space. Morgan zoomed immediately on the board looking at random snapshots of me, Livvie and the Thornton boys, a ticket stub from the last Red Sox game I'd attended and a small floral card.

Pulling the card from behind the ribbon that held it secure, he asked, "Is this the card that went with the tulips you got right after our date?"

I nodded, not sure where the interest in these flowers came from.

"You know," Morgan tapped the card to his chin, "you never did mention what your friend David was apologizing for."

"No, I didn't."

"You must be a bitch to come up against in court." Morgan laughed at my simple response, his open admiration softening his words. Clearing his throat, he stood tall, clasped his hands behind his back and launched into full-on lawyer mode. "So, counselor, in the interest of full disclosure, and the fact that we are now supposedly friends, would you please describe for the court exactly what your friend David was apologizing for?"

"Fine." I sighed, worn down, and not sure anymore why I was protecting David in the first place. "It was David's idea that I tell you I wanted to be your girlfriend. It was his idea that I tell you I was looking for a relationship. He thought you'd appreciate my honesty and assertiveness."

"Honesty and assertiveness? Really? David suggested that you lay all that on a guy on the first date."

I nodded.

"This friend of yours," Morgan continued, "he's actually been on a date with a woman, himself, and isn't like mentally challenged or anything?"

"Yes, of course."

Morgan nodded slowly and again tapped the card, this time against his lips. Turning to me he smiled, "I agree. I think your friend David is very, very smart indeed."

Walking toward the door, I expected Morgan to exit and was therefore very surprised when he instead shut my office door, flopped once again in the visitor chair and announced, "Cory Latham is dating my friend Larry."

"Excuse me?"

"That night at the bar. Cory was there with my group because Larry brought her. He's starting his third year with me this fall and is interning with Branson, Higby & MacLean. They met at the courthouse a few months ago." He leaned forward, hands on the edge of my desk and shrugged. "I just thought you might want to know."

I might want to know that Cory had her sights set for someone other than Morgan? Yes, I really did want to know that. I felt a momentary twinge of sympathy for poor dumb Larry, but that disappeared in moments.

"So, are you almost done here?" Morgan asked, gesturing to the work still scattered across my desk.

"Just about."

"Great. Let's get a bite to eat."

My mind froze, unable to fully comprehend the meaning behind the words just spoken. Did Morgan want to grab a bite to eat as friends and co-workers at the end of a long day or was there a larger purpose behind this request? If there was a larger purpose at work, what was it? And what did it have to do with all the questions about David and his random revelation about Cory? Above all, if Morgan truly was asking me out socially, how would I keep myself from once again screwing it up?

I was torn from the cluttered thoughts in my head by a bark of laughter. "Stop, Sarah."

"Stop what?"

"Stop doing whatever you're doing or thinking. Whatever you're thinking that is responsible for the pained look on your face." Morgan plucked my coat from its perch on the hook behind my door and held it out to me. "Let's go get some dinner."

"I don't look pained." I hotly denied, although I had a very strong feeling that I was probably lying. The truth was that I felt pained, and had every reason to believe that feeling was easily viewed by others.

Plunging in before my brain could stop my mouth, I questioned, "Is this a date?"

I hated to ask, hated to ruin the moment. Morgan was smiling and I had that warm fuzzy feeling in my stomach that usually followed consuming a warm apple cobbler, but I had to know.

"Always with the questions." Morgan remarked, shaking his head in a manner I could only describe as fondly. "Yes this is a date. I think our last outing was purposely sabotaged and I call a do-over. This whole 'friends' thing isn't working out for me. I think we should give dating another try. Tonight. Dinner. Possibly a movie. Definitely a good night kiss."

"A do-over?" Could someone actually call a do-over on a first date? Weren't there rules against such a thing? I debated this while tabling the other words Morgan had spoken. I didn't have the brain power necessary to contemplate the possibility that David had actually sabotaged my date on purpose. If I went down that road, I would have to try to determine why he would do such a thing, and I wasn't ready to face the answer that I probably already knew.

"But what about what happened last time?"

"Yes, about that…Here's the deal, Sarah…" Morgan cupped the back of his neck and squinted, a pained expression of his own coming across his face. "I don't know if I want a relationship right now and I don't know if I'm ready for a girlfriend. If that's what you need – to fulfill some wish list, then you shouldn't go out with me. I'm a full time student with a part time job who can't work up the courage to tell his father what he really wants to do for a living. I'm not in any shape to bring another human being along for that ride right now. But, if you like me and you had as much fun as I did the last time we went out, then I think we should give it another shot."

"I wanted to ask you upstairs." I blurted, apropos of nothing except that the belief that one heartfelt speech deserved another.

"Huh?"

"That night. After our date I wanted to ask you upstairs, but I was afraid of what you would think it meant. So, I started to get all worked up in my head, which you probably notice I tend to do, and ended up ruining the whole evening."

Morgan seemed to consider my words for a moment before he said, "Just so you know, when a girl I like invites me upstairs, I generally don't think anything beyond 'yay'."

That was good information to file away for later. Perhaps even later tonight. I was almost ready to accept Morgan's offer until I looked down at my wool plaid suit and ribbed beige turtleneck. It was my least attractive outfit, pulled out only at the end of a week when I hadn't visited the drycleaner during the prior weekend.

"I can't go out with you tonight. I'm not dressed for a date," I whined.

Morgan looked me over with a critical eye. "No. You're right. I couldn't possibly be seen with you in public."

As he turned to hang my coat back behind the door, I leapt up in outrage. "You're seriously going to take back your invitation and cancel our date because of what I'm wearing?"

"Oh, so it's a date now? See, I thought you were trying to get out of it and using your clothes as an excuse. And, that's a shame, really, because I think you look just fine." Morgan replied with an expression that could only be called a leer.

I was never one to underestimate the power of a good leer.

This was especially true if the said expression was worn by a very attractive man on a day I had previously felt like I resembled Jack Lemmon in drag.

"So, it's a date?" He asked again.

"You're not giving me any time to think."

"I know. No time to think, no time for your friends to plant bad advice. Nothing but you and me and maybe a nice bottle of Cabernet. What do you say?" He held out my coat like a challenge.

Briefly infused with the bravery of a matador I grabbed at my rustling cape and accepted. "It's a date."

* * *

"So, did you sleep with him?"

"No!" I exclaimed, stealing a French fry from Livvie's plate since none came with the cottage cheese and fruit platter I had ordered.

"But he came upstairs?'

"Yup." My coy smile unintentionally revealing some details to my friend.

"Oh, come on. You have to give me something to go on."

"A lady doesn't kiss and tell."

"First of all, I know you much too well for you to pull the lady card." Livvie laughed. "And second, if that's your answer, it means there was at least some kissing involved."

I ducked my head at my friend's shrewd deductive skills and could feel the blush burning my cheeks. Throwing her a bone, I admitted, "Yes. There was some kissing."

"Oh, just take them already." Livvie pushed the fries toward me, an amused grin on her face. "So, can I only assume that the second date was better than the first?"

It was odd. I was dressed all wrong, didn't have time to prepare what I was going to order or what we were going to talk about and still the evening had gone amazingly well. Ready to share a few details, I looked up at my friend surprised to find her chewing on her perfectly lined and glossed lips. It was Livvie's nervous tell, a very rare sight, indeed. I looked at her plate and realized her burger had been barely touched and the only fries missing were the ones I'd consumed.

"Hey, how come you aren't eating?"

Livvie continued to chew on her lip. "I have to tell you something and I think you're going to get mad."

"That sounds promising."

"I've been keeping a secret from you."

"How big?" I asked, trying to lighten the tone and not let on just how freaked out I was to be faced with an uncharacteristically timid Livvie. "Did you steal twenty bucks from my purse while I was in the ladies' room or were you actually born a man?"

"Somewhere in between." My friend smiled, a little of the tension broken.

"Come on, then, spill."

"Well, I've been kind of seeing someone for the last few weeks."

"That's great!" I exclaimed, not sure why Livvie would have kept this information a secret. I supposed she would have considered it poor form to tell me she'd met someone special while I was still looking. But still, that wouldn't have been a reason for me to get mad. Upset, despondent and in search of a pint of Chunky Monkey, perhaps, but not mad. "So, who's the lucky guy? Tell me about him."

"Here's where I think you're going to get mad." Livvie said, shredding a paper straw wrapper, yet another atypical show of nerves. "You already know him."

My heart stopped as I considered the worst case scenario. "Tell me you're not dating Ryan."

"It's not Ryan." Livvie admitted, but with her eyes downcast in a manner that made me believe the worst case scenario was probably not far from correct. I considered who I hated most in the world.

"Cory Latham?"

"God, no!" Livvie's eyes leapt from the table to meet mine, thoroughly exasperated. "Jesus, Bennett. Even if I did swing that way, I'd have way better taste than to date Cory Latham."

"Well, I know you're not dating Eddie and you're too loyal to go after a guy I like, so that leaves Morgan out."

"It's not Morgan. It's Donnie."

"Donnie? Donnie DiMarco? You're dating your ex-husband?"

"Well, not so much dating him as sleeping with him." Burden of her secret lifted, Livvie pulled back her plate of fries and began munching away with gusto. It was just as well, as I'd suddenly lost my appetite.

"Donnie is arrogant and thoughtless."

"I know."

"He broke your heart," I reminded her.

"I know."

"I've never had a conversation with the man where he looked me in the eye instead of the chest."

"I know." She dragged a fry through a puddle of ketchup. "We're working on that."

I tossed my napkin from my lap into my plate. "So you admit Donnie is horrible, and you're voluntarily sleeping with him anyway?"

My friend just shrugged. "He's comfortable. As bad as Donnie can be, he can also be very sweet, and that's the side I've been seeing lately. He's also very smart and funny and for some reason, we just work together. I don't know if it's a permanent thing. I mean, we haven't talked about being exclusive, but for now it seems to be working."

About to launch into the list of reasons why Donnie wasn't good enough for my friend, I was interrupted by the insistent buzzing of my cell phone. Checking the number, I turned to Livvie. "It's Eddie. I can let it go to voice mail."

"Go ahead and take it," she waved. "Besides, he already knows."

"He knows?" I answered the call. "You know?"

The younger Thornton brother laughed at my greeting. "I know a lot of things. What are you talking about specifically?"

"Livvie and Donnie. You knew about that and didn't tell me?"

"Sorry, but I was sworn to secrecy. Livvie was afraid you'd kill her for dating the evil ex and called me for advice in keeping you on a leash."

"Nice. I'm glad my friends are conspiring behind my back."

"Everyone needs a hobby." Eddie dismissed, entirely undisturbed by his behavior. "I suppose this is an incredibly bad time for me to ask you for a favor, then?'

"Yes, but that's not going to stop you. What do you want?"

"I need you to get something out of Dad's safety deposit box for me."

"You want me to break into Jeremy's safety deposit box and steal for you?" I repeated, entirely for the purpose of piquing Livvie's interest and drawing her into the conversation. It worked as my friend leaned over the table, waiting for further details.

"Oh, jeez," Eddie groaned. "It's nothing like that. I need a copy of my high school transcript and diploma. All I want are papers that already belong to me. I just don't want dad to know I need them yet. Since Dad rented the box with Uncle Ed when they opened the diner, I know you have the other key."

"Why do you need that stuff? And why can't you just call Portland High for a new copy?"

Eddie sighed. "I knew you were going to make a big thing about this. You remember Carl Harris, right? Well, I can't call the high school because Carl works in the Registrar's office and I think we both know that's not a good idea."

I did have to agree with my friend. When it came to failed romances and relationships that had gone down in flames, my dating history didn't come close to rivaling Eddie's. "But that doesn't explain why you need the papers in the first place."

"If you must know, those are the last pieces I need to submit to collect my Associate's Degree in business marketing."

"Are you serious? That's terrific, Eddie! Why are you keeping it a secret?"

"It won't be a secret much longer. I just want to show Dad an actual diploma when I tell him and I need to prove I graduated from high school to get it processed."

"He's going to be thrilled." My uncle's belief in the value of a higher education was unmatched. Eddie's lack of interest in such things bothered his father, and the knowledge that this one rift in the otherwise ideal Thornton family was about to be healed filled me with immeasurable joy.

"Yeah, I think he's going to be pretty stoked." I heard a sheepish pride in my friend's reply. "I mean, it's only a two year program and it took me six years to get through, but it is an honest to God degree from an accredited university. Real sheepskin and everything."

"I'll FedEx the papers to you tomorrow," I assured my friend. "But why didn't you tell me?"

"I know how you hate keeping secrets from my dad, and you've already got my back with kind of a really big one. I just didn't want to add to the list."

I laughed at the truth of the statement.

"I'll be up next month and I should have the diploma by them. I worked out the plans with David last night. I'm flying into New York to pick him up and we're going to drive north for a big family dinner and unveiling. Big brother has to go to that annual conference in London, so he got his flight out of Portland the next day."

"Sounds perfect." I could barely stand the thought of waiting a month to see the look on Jeremy's face.

"Hey, Sarah. There is one more thing."

"Sure. Anything."

"In case you haven't noticed, Livvie's really happy. I want you to go easy on her."

I said my goodbyes and turned back to Livvie with a critical eye, realizing that Eddie might very well be right.

"You're happy?"

"Yeah. I think I really am."

"Alright." I went to grab one final fry but was disappointed to find they were already gone. Attacking my diet soda with much less enthusiasm, I continued. "But I want you to be careful and keep your eyes open. If Donnie hurts you, I'm going to pull a Fried Green Tomatoes and have Jeremy serve him as Wednesday's meatloaf special."

Livvie smiled, bright and sincere for the first time since we sat down. "I would expect nothing less."

We ate in silence for a moment before she asked, "So, Eddie has checked in for the week. Have you heard from the elder Thornton brother lately?"

"I talked to David yesterday to update him on the job interview at Claire's law firm."

"Did you tell him you kicked ass?"

I laughed at the description only a loyal friend would provide. "I told him it went well and I'm guardedly optimistic that I might be called back for a second interview in the next few weeks."

"Did you happen to mention your date with Morgan?"

I stabbed at a grape with a little more vigor than was absolutely necessary. "Didn't come up."

"Really? That's just shocking. David didn't ask out of the blue whether you went on a date with a man that he still thinks you're not talking to? I can't imagine why it didn't come up."

"I'll tell him eventually." I asserted my eyes to study the overripe melon slices and under-ripe strawberries still tinged with yellow which decorated my plate. "I just have a feeling telling David about Morgan is going to lead to some other conversations."

"Do you think?" Livvie's sarcastic edge could not be missed. The problem was, she was right. I had been hiding my head in the sand for so long that the only course left was a confrontation of epic proportions.

I knew it. Livvie knew it. And I was afraid that sooner, rather than later, David would know it.

July

I SIGNED MY NAME TO THE LETTER in my hand, blew gently on the ink until I was certain it was dry and returned the heavy fountain pen to its rightful place in my desk drawer. The expensive pen had been my college graduation gift from my father, and was used on infrequent occasions to sign documents that deserved an extra flair of formality. This pen had seen my law school application, my first Superior Court Complaint, and now it had witnessed my letter of resignation from Frank's firm.

It had been a long and difficult few months as I discussed career options with other attorneys in town and engaged in several rigorous interviews. After our talk in the diner, I had weighed Frank's words heavily and finally decided that while I loved working with him – and I truly did – he couldn't offer me what I had come to realize was important to me. My career was not going to progress any further while working at his firm. At the end of the day, 29 was just too young an age to settle.

I carefully folded the letter in thirds, placed it in a heavy bond envelope I'd brought in from home and walked down the hall to my boss' office. I had waited until late afternoon to make sure we would be able to talk uninterrupted, and turning to meet Gloria's eye, I confirmed he was finally free.

"Yes, dear, you can go on in."

I knocked and turned the knob to let myself in at the same time. "Hi, Frank."

"Now isn't a good time, Bennett." He grumbled without looking up from his work. "I'm very busy."

"That's funny, because Gloria said you were available." I smiled, allowing a moment of nostalgia as I realized I would miss this daily banter. Frank could put on his belligerent act all he wanted, but I knew inside lurked the heart of a bunny rabbit.

"Well, she was wrong. I'm busy. What do you want?"

Okay, maybe he wasn't a bunny rabbit. More like a grumpy teddy bear.

"I'm serious, Bennett." Frank glared at me over the top of his glasses. "What the hell do you want?"

Maybe I wouldn't miss the belligerent act all that much.

Ignoring the tone, I sat in his visitor's chair, surprised to see that it was clear of papers for once. "I'll get right to the point. I've been thinking about our talk a few months ago when I told you that I wanted to be a partner. The thing is, I've realized that being a partner in a law firm is very important to me."

Frank sighed and pushed his chair away from his desk. "Is this about that stupid list you made? Because, Bennett, I've got to tell you…"

"It's not about the stupid list!" I blurted. Realizing I had just insulted my own self-improvement plan, I sighed deeply and tried again. "I mean, it's not about the list. Which isn't stupid. But, it's not about that anyway. The list. Stupid or not, I mean. It's not about that."

Oh, god. I had apparently lost the ability to speak in well-constructed sentences. I listened to myself talk while a small part of my brain screamed, "Would you shut up already!?"

After an eternity, the latter side of my brain finally seemed to take control and my mouth stopped moving. Unfortunately, it wasn't soon enough because Frank was looking at me as if I'd lost my mind.

I sighed and decided to just cut to the chase and end the torture for the both of us. I handed him the envelope and said, "It doesn't matter how or why I made this decision, but I have. Making partner means more to me than just checking an item off a list. It means helping to manage the firm and the direction it takes. I want to feel a real sense of ownership in its accomplishments and its failures."

I was surprised to find that finally – perhaps for the first time since I'd begun working for him – I had this imposing man's full attention. He was holding my letter, but all of his focus was on me and my words. "Frank, you became a lawyer because you needed the autonomy that being a cop couldn't offer you. I understand that, so I want you to understand this. I need to know that my career is on a course that I am helping to steer. I don't want to just be along for the ride for the next fifty years."

Frank waited a moment, perhaps to make sure I was done before he stated. "Well then, since I've already told you I don't want a partner, I guess we're at an impasse."

"No, we're not."

I took a deep breath and plunged in. "I spoke with Norman Clark at Richardson, Clark and Carbasco. My friend Claire works there and it turns out they are looking for an experienced attorney. Norman offered me a position as a senior associate. He's willing to take my time working here into consideration which means I'll be up for partner in two years."

Frank nodded, the look on his face unreadable. He gestured to the envelope he still held. "So then, this is…?"

"My letter of resignation."

A silent beat passed between us before I continued, "I told Norman that I wanted to give you a month's notice. I'll tie up all of the loose ends on my cases and stay around to help you interview my replacement. Morgan has been putting in full-time hours since he graduated last month and I know you're planning to offer him a permanent job as soon as he takes the bar exam. That should take some of the pressure off in the short run."

Frank tapped the letter thoughtfully against his desk. "That's all very interesting information, Bennett, but I have to remind you that the first rule of poker is don't bet more than you can afford to lose. That goes for job negotiations, too. Don't make an idle threat that you're not willing to back up."

If I hadn't been expecting that response, it might have hurt my feelings. Instead, I was prepared for Frank to perceive that the entire conversation was a bluff – an attempt to force him into making me a partner. I knew it would be his reaction, because I also knew it was the play Frank would have made in my place.

"This isn't a threat or a negotiation. You told me what you could offer me and after a great deal of thoughtful consideration I decided it wasn't enough."

My boss just tapped the letter against the desk.

I waited, but still he said nothing. Unable to bear the silence any longer, I rushed in to fill it with pointless babble. "Look, Frank. I'm never going to be able to thank you enough for everything you've taught me. This job has given me the most amazing experience, and I can't tell you how much it has meant to me. I can't begin to tell you how much you have meant to me."

Then, to my shock and absolute horror, I felt my eyes begin to well with tears.

It was the threat of tears that finally broke through Frank's stoic exterior. He reached to the credenza behind him and threw a box of Kleenex at me. "Oh, will you stop that before you embarrass yourself? You're not going anywhere."

Before I could even process his words, Frank ripped my letter of resignation in half, then again into quarters for good measure before tossing it unceremoniously into the trash.

"What are you doing?" I asked, stunned by his behavior. "I told you I'm not making a threat. I am seriously quitting."

"I know you're serious." Frank leaned forward, his hands clasped together on the surface of the desk. "I knew you were serious when I got the call from Norman Clark asking for a reference."

"Norman called you?" My first reaction was anger at my future boss' lack of discretion. I had told him Frank wasn't yet aware of my job search and I was a little ticked that Norman had gone behind my back asking for a reference. But before I could begin to boil over on that point, I realized something.

"You knew? You knew I was looking for another job?"

"I knew. When I got that call, I could see that you were serious about wanting to be a partner. It wasn't a lark or because of a stupid list. It was something you wanted badly enough to go somewhere else to find."

The last few words trailed off as Frank leaned over, rummaging through the bottom drawer of his desk, obviously looking for something specific. With a triumphant grunt, he raised his head and looked me square in the eye as he continued, "That's why I asked Gloria to run a sheet through the printer just to see how it would look."

Grinning in a very un-Frank like manner, he flipped over the pale cream piece of slightly crumpled stationery. At the top, just above the office address, phone and fax number were the words that made my heart skip a beat.

Murphy & Bennett
Attorneys at Law

"Frank." There were a million questions in my head, but I couldn't seem to find the ability to form one into actual words. I took the paper between my nerveless fingers.

"I would have done this years ago if I'd known this would be your reaction." Frank joked, but there was little humor in his voice. My silence was clearly unnerving him.

"What does this mean?" I finally asked.

"It means that Norman Clark is an idiot and I'm not about to let him benefit from everything I've taught you over the last five years." He took the paper into his own grip, looked at it again and nodded in approval at the words he read. "It also means that if you've really got your heart set on this partnership thing, you might as well stay here."

Part of me warned that I shouldn't press my luck. Instead, I should take the letterhead and run. But, unable to let well enough alone, I had to ask. "You told me you didn't want a partner. What changed?"

"It's called a negotiation, Bennett." My boss replied, disgust evident in his voice. Before I could probe further, though, he held his hand up to still my question. "The thing is, I guess I broke my own rule."

"What rule did you break?"

"I bet with more than I could afford to lose."

I couldn't help it. My eyes began to well up again, and before I could stop myself or think better of it, I rose and walked toward Frank, my intentions clear.

"What are you doing?" He rolled away from his desk as far as the credenza at his back would allow.

"Frank..." I put as much of a warning into that one syllable as was possible and held out my arms.

"No. Partners do not hug! There are rules about these things."

I raised my eyebrows and wiggled the ends of my fingers until Frank slumped further in his chair, obviously defeated.

"Fine. One hug, but that's it and we never speak of this again."

"Agreed." I solemnly vowed before leaning over and hugging the stuffing out of my new partner. And as much as he may deny it to his dying day, Frank Murphy reached out and hugged me back.

I practically bounced out of Frank's office and stopped at Gloria's desk where we shared a knowing smile.

"Did your meeting go well dear?"

"Why, yes. As a matter of fact it did." I tried – unsuccessfully – to keep the shit-eating grin off my face. "Frank showed me a very interesting printing job that you helped him with."

Gloria smiled, showing the deep dimple in her left cheek. "Did you like it?"

I rushed behind the desk and this time didn't find even token resistance as I enveloped her in a hug. "It was the best damned piece of paper I ever saw."

"Did I miss something?"

We both looked up to see Morgan walk out of the conference room, clearly puzzled by the unusual public display.

"Hi." I straightened up and walked toward him, still unable to wipe away my silly smile.

"Everything okay here?" he asked, clearly happy to see me in such a good mood.

I was struck by the fact that my mood should be nothing less than spectacular. I had just made partner in a law firm, and while I was not in an official "relationship", Morgan and I had been out several times since our breakthrough second date, and each outing had been more successful than the last.

He was smart, funny and rooted for the Red Sox. I mean, really, what more did a woman look for in a man?

If these attributes weren't enough, it seemed I was adding more to the list every time he and I spent time together. Morgan's favorite actor was Jimmy Stewart, he could recite the full text of the

Gettysburg Address, and – whether he admitted it or not – he actually cried at the end of the movie The Color Purple. His very best trait, though, was his ability to foresee and subsequently prevent my crazy moments. Like a dog trained to warn an epileptic of an upcoming seizure, Morgan must have catalogued the symptoms that meant I was retreating in my head for a little psychotic adventure. Not taking these episodes personally, he would identify one and pull me back into the bright light of day before I got too far down a dark road.

"Everything is very okay." I replied, pulling him into an embrace. Almost instantly, I realized my serious error in judgment. Morgan and I had been trying to keep our dating a secret in the office for fear of Frank's inevitable outburst.

I began to back away awkwardly when Morgan drew me tighter into his arms and I felt, as much as heard, the warm chuckle at my ear. "I forgot it was national Hug-Your-Co-Worker-Day. Thanks for reminding me, Sarah!"

Letting me go, he moved toward Gloria and held out his arms. "Care to celebrate?"

An amused, but mildly disapproving smile crossed Gloria's lips. "No, thank you. And if you know what's good for you, you won't let Frank catch you 'celebrating' in the office."

I caught both Gloria's eye and her meaning. She knew exactly what was going on between Morgan and me, but would adopt a 'don't ask, don't tell' motto as long as we didn't force her hand. "No more celebrating," I vowed.

Morgan nudged my shoulder with his. "So, care to tell me why you're in such a good mood?"

I wanted nothing more than to share my news with Morgan, but didn't think it was the right time. Gloria was watching us like hawks for inappropriate office behavior and Frank could have burst from his inner sanctum at any moment. I decided instead that privacy and better planning were needed before I was ready to tell Morgan he was dating the boss. "I'd love to, but I have to tell some other folks first if that's okay."

Gloria's smile erupted into a deep laugh. "If you don't tell Jeremy your news right now, then I will. I've been half crazy keeping this from him."

"You've got it." I grabbed my coat and paused at the door, calling back, "Hey, Morgan?"

"Yeah?"

"'I'll probably spend tonight with my family, but if you're not doing anything tomorrow...?"

"I'd love to." He said with a wink that made me bow my head, suddenly very interested in the pattern of the carpet.

I made a hasty retreat from the office, head spinning from the events of the day. I was a partner in a law firm and had a date with a man I was becoming increasingly very fond of. If I could just cut back on the Ring Dings and fit into those size 10 jeans, I could just maybe conquer the world.

*   *   *

I skidded across town in record time, anxious to share the news of my partnership, and beyond the moon that David and Eddie were both still in town. There was going to be even more celebrating at the Thornton/Bennett household tonight.

The boys had arrived mid-afternoon the previous day for the whirlwind Portland tour. Everyone except Jeremy knew that all the elaborate travel plans had been made with only one purpose in mind – to unveil Eddie's brand new diploma.

The evening had gone without a hitch. David made reservations at our favorite Italian restaurant and the four of us feasted on wine, garlic bread, pasta and sauces galore and finally the most amazing tiramisu this side of Napoli.

Uncle Jeremy – tough ex-cop that he was – had actually misted over when he saw that his youngest son had achieved a degree – his fondest wish. While David was exceptionally supportive of all his brother's choices, himself, I knew it made him uncomfortable to be held up by his father as the shining example of success for Eddie to aspire to. To see that rift soothed between father and brother lifted his heart.

Somewhat.

For as happy and engaged as David appeared at dinner for his brother's sake, I knew there was something amiss, and I further knew what had caused it. Just as the wine was poured, Jeremy had innocently turned to me to ask how things were going with that 'nice boy' Morgan.

"Morgan? You've met Morgan?" David had demanded of his father.

"Sure. He came over for a barbecue several weeks ago." My uncle had answered, oblivious. "He and Sarah are quite an item, it seems."

"They are?" David spun in his chair, focus entirely on me as I began to pick at my lasagna.

"We've been out a few times." I admitted reluctantly, and then in a cowardly move, raised my glass. "But this isn't about me. It's Eddie's night. Let's toast the graduate." We raised our glasses as one, and from that moment on, David had turned his attention back to his brother, but still something was just not quite right. Luckily, though, I now had yet another topic to distract David from my current social life.

He had been very interested in my job interviews, and had even helped me edit the letter I wrote to Frank. Knowing that I wrote the letter with a heavy and conflicted heart, he would undoubtedly consider my promotion nothing less than the perfect outcome it was.

We had a few short hours before my friend had to leave for the airport for his trip to London. We could spend that time celebrating as a family, and then I could only hope things would sort themselves out by e-mail and phone before we saw each other again.

"Anybody home?" I yelled, letting myself into Jeremy's house with my key.

"Uncle Jeremy? David? Eddie?"

Disappointed that the boys weren't sitting at home waiting to hear about my career achievements, I considered rounding them up by cell phone, but couldn't think of a non-emergency related excuse that would bring them home. Since I really wanted to see their faces when I shared my news, I decided to just settle in and wait for someone to return.

Moving into the kitchen I was annoyed to find my bread maker sitting on Jeremy's counter. Eddie must have grabbed it from my place to make the disgusting low-carb rosemary bread he favored. I looked at the dried, flaky residue inside and cursed my friend for not even bothering to clean it. Rather than transport it home while dirty, I filled the sink with soapy water and had just finished my task when I heard the jingle of keys in the back door.

"Sarah?" David's deep baritone called out to me. He must have seen my car parked in front of the house.

"Hey! I'm back here."

David smiled as he turned the corner into the kitchen. "I see you're cleaning up after my baby brother."

I nodded. "I stopped letting him borrow my things, so now he just steals them. I would really expect more from a college graduate."

Drying my hands and apparently not cured of my desire to randomly hug everyone I came into contact with, I rushed to my friend. "I have some fabulous news for you!"

Expecting one of David's usual bone-jarring embraces, I was surprised to receive instead a perfunctory pat on the back.

"So, what's up?" He asked, unable to hide his obvious disinterest.

"Geez, Thornton. What's with the attitude?" I backed away, no longer interested in sharing my partnership news.

"I don't have an attitude."

"Sure you don't. That's why you're standing there, stiff as a board, treating me like someone who just rang the doorbell and wants to talk you into questioning your religious affiliation."

David met my eyes defiantly and replied, "I don't know what you're talking about."

The last thing I'd wanted was a confrontation, but looking at my situation as an outsider, I realized it wasn't like things could get worse between us. "Look, David, you've been upset with me since last night. Don't tell me you haven't been."

David neither confirmed nor denied my charge, but he didn't move to stop my words, either.

Flopping into one of the hard, ladder-back kitchen chairs, I continued, "You know more than anyone how much I like to ignore my problems, David. I'd stick my head firmly in the sand if I could, but I can't do that anymore. Something is wrong between us and if you leave for London tonight before we fix it, I'm worried that we won't ever be able to."

David nodded slowly, a small acknowledgement of my words, but still he said nothing. It took all of my reserves of strength to stop myself from filling in the silence with mindless babble, but I know that only by keeping quiet would I draw out my friend.

My patience was rewarded, but instead of an explanation, I only got a statement delivered in a flat monotone. "You're seeing Morgan."

"I am." I admitted, frightened by the monsters that might be lurking for us behind the door we had just irrevocably opened.

"You didn't tell me."

"No, I didn't. I should have, but I didn't. For that I am sorry, but I don't understand why you're so angry about it."

Again, I was met only by silence, but I could sense a difference from before. David was not planning to answer this charge without further prompting, so I dove into the deep end. "Did you purposely sabotage my first date with Morgan?"

"Sabotage is such an ugly word." He blew out a breath, stooping his shoulders in a defeated posture. "I suppose it was possible that telling Morgan you wanted to be his girlfriend might not have been such a great idea."

"Why would you do that?"

David walked toward me, "You know why, Sarah." With those words, David leaned down and kissed me, his lips gentle and soft as his right hand brushed the hair away from my face.

It was a lovely kiss.

And I couldn't wait for it to be over.

The moment David's lips met mine, I wanted to flinch away. The skin on my arms began to itch like I was wearing a scratchy wool sweater without a cotton t-shirt underneath and I could feel my fingers fidget at my side not knowing where they should land.

While Morgan's kisses had made my heart race in anticipation as he eliminated the space between us, David instead caused my heart to thunder uncomfortably in my chest as I waited for him to step back and out of my personal space.

I loved this man dearly, but my physical reaction to this intimacy left no doubt that my love was platonic.

"Nothing, huh?" He asked, his cheeks beginning to flush as he walked to the refrigerator and pulled out a bottle of water. "I was afraid of that."

"David..." I began, not really sure what to say, but knowing I had to at least make an attempt. I had just been confronted with everything I'd been afraid of and hiding from for the past year.

He held up his hand. "Don't, Sarah. Look, Eddie should be back any minute to take me to the airport. I'm just going to wait for him outside."

I grabbed his arm to keep him from walking away from me. "David, wait. We need to talk."

"All we ever do is talk." He shook his arm from my grasp. "You want to talk? Well, then, let's talk about this. I'm in love with you, Sarah!"

I felt his words like a punch to the chest.

David stood where he was, the stricken look on my face probably responsible for the softening his tone. "I've been in love with you since we were children. Since I knew what the word meant, I've associated it with you and only you."

"David..."

He blew past my words as if he didn't hear them. "You treat me like your girlfriend. You confide in me about your love life and the men you're interested in, but every time you do it kills me a little bit because every passing year I know with more certainty that I will never be the man for you."

David closed his eyes and let out a deep breath, easing the tension in his shoulders somewhat. "I keep listening to you, though, and coming back for more. I guess I kind of snapped last night when I found out you didn't tell me you're seeing Morgan. It's kind of sick really. It hurts so much to know, but kills me even more not to."

The magnitude of what he was telling me finally hit home. All of these years. All of the hurt that I'd caused. "I'm so sorry, David. I never knew."

A slight smile crossed his features as he approached me and rubbed his thumb gently across my cheek, drying a tear I hadn't noticed had fallen. "Oh, Sarah. Of course you did."

And in that moment, I knew he was right. As much as I tried to ignore David's feelings for me, or minimize them as a harmless crush, I'd known all along that they were there. Caught up in my world of self-recrimination, I barely noticed when David started speaking again.

"It's not like I've been wasting my life pining for you. I mean, I date other women. I even get laid on a regular basis." He smiled without humor and continued, "It's just that I have never met a woman that can make me feel as good standing next to her as you can from six hundred miles away."

"Hey, Dave – sorry I'm late. You better get your ass in gear!" Eddie flew into the kitchen, and stopped dead in his tracks at the sight before him. My face was blotchy with tears, and David's jaw clenched with tension.

"My suitcase is in the hall, bro. Take it to the car? I'll be out in a minute."

"Yeah, sure." Eddie said, uncharacteristically doing what he was asked without protest. He hesitated for a moment as he reached the door. "Everything okay here?"

David nodded. "Wait outside for me."

Even after Eddie left, we just stood and stared at one another for a long moment.

"Where do we go from here?" I asked, terrified of the answer.

"We're family. Nothing will ever change that."

Thank God. My heart once more resumed at sinus rhythm until David began speaking again. "I do think I need a break for a while, though. I obviously need to get over this and I can't if we're calling and e-mailing every ten minutes. I need some time to get past this. Past you."

I nodded. If I couldn't give David my heart, the least I could give him was the space he needed. But, before he left, my friend needed to know one thing. Just as he reached the door, I yelled out, "I do love you, David. You have to know that."

He stopped in his tracks, then turned, hand up as if to ward off any further words from being spoken. Finally collecting himself, he smiled at me and asked, "Hey, Bennett, what was that Molly Ringwald movie you and Eddie used to watch all the time when we were growing up?"

"*Sixteen Candles?*" I answered, confused by the question.

"No. The other one. You know – with Andrew McCarthy."

"Pretty in Pink."

"That's the one. It's funny, but I always thought that movie ended wrong. I always thought Ducky was supposed to win the girl in the end." David shrugged then opened the door. "Guess I was wrong."

With that, David Thornton walked out of my life.

I waited until I was sure that the car was safely backed out of the driveway and halfway down the street before I slid down the wall and started a bout of hysterical crying I didn't think would ever stop.

August

"YOU'LL HAVE TO EXPLAIN TO ME just who this 'Ducky' fellow is." Gloria said, eyeing me with concern as she sipped her tea.

Exhausted from the emotionally draining afternoon, and lacking the energy to discuss the issue further, I waved my hand at Livvie, silently asking her to respond.

"Jon Cryer played a guy named Ducky in the movie Pretty in Pink." She began, facing Gloria from her lotus position on the floor. "It was one of those John Hughes movies that were big in the mid-eighties."

"I don't think I've seen that one, dear. What does a movie have to do with David and Sarah?"

I dug my spoon into the pint of Chunky Monkey that had almost completely frozen a hole in my hand, and listened as Livvie tried to explain the plot of a brat-pack movie to a woman who hadn't been to the theater since John Wayne switched from war movies to westerns.

Livvie took a quick sip from her soda can, placing it next to her on the floor. "The no-frills version is this: Molly Ringwald plays our heroine Andie – plucky girl from the wrong side of the tracks who falls in love with rich boy Blaine played by Andrew McCarthy. On their road to happiness the couple runs into a number of stumbling blocks. The one that's relevant to us is that Andie's quirky but loyal friend Ducky is also in love with her."

"Oh dear," Gloria clucked her tongue. "I think I'm beginning to see the problem. What happens to Ducky?"

"After the requisite ninety-eight minutes of heartache and misunderstandings, Ducky gallantly stepped aside so Andie and Blaine can end up together."

"They don't end up together," I clarified. "They only ended up at the prom together."

Livvie reached up to pat me on the leg. "It's a movie set in a high school sweetie. Going to the prom is the same as riding off into the sunset."

Gloria nodded, taking in Livvie's shotgun synopsis. "Well, that certainly explains David's comment as he left the house."

I nodded, not quite trusting my voice, and dug deeper into the pint of ice cream Livvie tossed to me when she walked into my living room half an hour ago. When Eddie sent out his distress calls to Livvie and Gloria, God love him for remembering to mention the need for junk food.

As much as I got annoyed with the youngest Thornton man on a regular basis, he always came through when I needed him. I assumed David told his brother about our confrontation – or at least provided the highlights – so that Eddie wasn't surprised to come home from the airport and find me still curled in a sobbing ball in the kitchen.

He hauled me up and out the door, deposited me in the passenger seat of the truck he was borrowing while in town and asked suspiciously few questions while throwing concerned glances my way as often as the traffic pattern would safely allow. On the way to my apartment he made two very brief calls on his cell phone – one to Livvie and one to Gloria – telling each to meet me at my apartment as soon as possible, and to stop for ice cream on the way.

After hanging up the second time, he looked at me with a face that was almost comically earnest. "Women really do eat junk food when they're depressed, right? It's not just an urban legend is it?"

I nodded my head and blinked my swollen eyes at him, somehow conveying that he had done exactly the right thing. The next ten minutes of the drive were spent with him pretending not to check on me, and me trying to get the last of my snuffles under control.

Eddie was still strangely quiet when he walked me up the back stairs and into my apartment, a trait I found disconcerting in my normally boisterous friend. I wondered whether his reluctance to ask questions was out of kindness toward my hyper-emotional state, or because he already knew the answers.

"Sit." He ordered, pointing toward the couch as he fetched my box of Kleenex from the bathroom. He even brought back a wet facecloth for my blotched, tear-streaked face. Eddie wasn't one to take care of others very often, but when he did, he was remarkably good at it. I was feeling almost human by the time he brought me a cup of my favorite tea, sweetened just the way I liked with a teaspoon of sugar and splash of milk.

"What did David tell you?" I asked, needing to know whether Eddie was being kind of his own free will, or at the behest of his older brother.

Eddie picked up my comb from where he found it on the coffee table and began smoothing his hair into a ponytail holder fished from his side pocket. "Well, he mentioned that you two had a talk about your feelings for each other. He said you were pretty upset, and asked me to make sure you got home okay."

"Whose idea was it to call Livvie and Gloria?"

Eddie cocked his head to the side, and gave me his best self-deprecating grin. "It was mine, actually. I decided to call in the cavalry."

We sat quietly for another moment, Eddie rubbing small circles on my shoulder as I finished wiping the tears from my eyes. "How is he?"

Eddie paused for a moment before speaking. I knew him well enough to understand that he was taking a moment to phrase his words. He wanted to offer me reassurances, but was afraid of crossing the line by breaking his brother's sacred confidence. "Let's just say he was a little bruised, but not broken. He'll be okay."

I shook my head, unable to believe the day's odd turn of events. I would have sworn I was closer to David Thornton than any other person on earth, and here I was checking in with his brother to make sure he was going to be okay. The worst part was the knowledge that if David wasn't okay, it was my own fault.

"Will you?"

Eddie's words broke into my thoughts, and I had to shake my head to clear them enough to ask, "Will I what?"

"Will you be okay?"

It was a good question. I had been asking it myself for about an hour.

"The only funny thing about this entire night is that I don't really have anything to be upset about." I laughed, albeit a bit more high-pitched than usual. "An hour ago I had a great guy serve himself to me on a silver platter. I turned him away and hurt one of my best friends. I have no right to cry about it now."

Eddie gave me a rueful smile as he reached over to pull the afghan off the back of my couch and cover me with it. "Don't even start with me about what you are supposed to want. Trust me when I tell you that most people – me included – usually don't want what they should."

"You don't always want what you should. Is that the flip side to, 'You can't always get what you want'?" I asked, sipping my tea, comforted by the weight of the blanket around me, even if it's warmth was a little much for an early August evening.

"But you get what you need." Eddie smiled, glad to see I had begun talking, and my sniffles had calmed to merely intermittent.

"You and David both seem to be re-writing pop culture tonight." I smiled, and repeated the Pretty in Pink reference.

"My poor, dumb, romantic brother." Eddie groaned, then seeing my distress, tried to joke. "It's a lousy comparison, anyway. Ducky was always way cooler than David."

"Did you have a secret crush on Jon Cryer?"

"Nah. I was always a James Spader man, myself. His character was a total closet case who wanted Andrew McCarthy for himself. It was so obvious."

Hearing a car door slam in the street, Eddie rose to look out the window. "Livvie's here and it looks like she brought some Ben & Jerry's with her."

"The good stuff. She must know it's going to be a bad night."

My friend scooched in front of me until we were eye to eye. "Do you think it would be okay if I left now? I won't leave if you need me, but I think it would be kind of weird if I stay."

I was ready for a little alone time with Livvie and Gloria. As dear as Eddie was, he was still a man and therefore clueless in so many ways. He was also David's brother. "You've done your duty. I understand that your loyalty is to David."

"Hey." Eddie tapped my nose with his finger. "My loyalty is to my family, and last I looked, you still qualified. Take care."

He kissed me on the cheek and slipped out the front door of my apartment just as Livvie burst in the back door, which Eddie had thoughtfully left unlocked. She took one look at me and rushed over.

"What the hell happened? You look like shit."

"Thanks."

"Eddie told me to bring ice cream, so I assume Morgan broke your heart. Did he dump you?"

I laughed realizing that for the first time in a very long time, I had spent several hours without a single thought of Morgan. "Believe it or not, this has nothing to do with Morgan."

Livvie sighed and went into the living room where she retrieved two spoons. "It's David, then?"

"How do you know it's about David?"

"Eddie told me to bring ice cream. Ice cream means heartache. If it's not about Morgan, it's got to be about David. Those are the only two men I know with the power to make you look like such crap."

I shoved a good-sized portion of the sinful goodness into my mouth and mumbled, "You know, you can stop telling me how lousy I look any time now."

She looked at me with concern. "So, what is going on?"

"Gloria's on her way. Let's wait a few minutes, because I can only get through this story once."

So we waited, ate ice cream and steeped more tea. When Gloria finally arrived, I had evolved from emotional basket case to merely morbidly depressed. I relayed the events of the day, stopping to wipe away the occasional tears. Once Gloria understood who Ducky was, and the role Jon Cryer played in my own personal drama, I sat back and waited for their empathy and advice.

Livvie's comments were quick and to the point. "I hate to break it to you, Bennett, but you didn't do anything wrong."

"I agree with Olivia," Gloria concurred. "You were honest with David, and while you're clearly upset that you hurt his feelings, you had no other recourse."

Somehow, I was hoping for something a little more prophetic from my friends. "Tell me why," I demanded of them.

The two women glanced at one another, unsure of what I was asking. Livvie voiced the question on both their minds. "Why what?"

"Why didn't I have any other recourse? Why couldn't I tell David that I loved him, too?"

Again my friends looked perplexed, and Gloria asked, "You don't love David, do you?"

"No! Of course I don't! But why don't I?" I yelled, imploring my friends to furnish me with an answer. "David is everything I should want in a man. Am I so completely damaged that I can't reach out to a good thing when it's offered?"

"You are not damaged, Sarah, but I want you to brace yourself for a newsflash." Livvie waited until I met her eyes before she continued. "You just don't love David. You told me yourself a few months ago."

"If you love anyone at all right now, I think it might be Morgan," Gloria finished.

"I love Morgan? Well that's just great. Let's not forget he told me he may not want a relationship and now that I'm a partner, he's technically my employee." I pulled the afghan up to cover my face. "God – I am so messed up."

"No more than anyone else trying to negotiate through the world today," Gloria soothed, leaning over to pat me on the knee.

I took a deep breath, throwing my legs over the side of the couch. "Let's just look at this rationally for a minute."

"Look at love rationally?" Livvie mocked. "Oh, yeah. That'll work."

"David told me he was in love with me, and I let him walk away. He is one of the most important people in my life – he's sweet and kind, and makes me feel safe. What do I think I'm going to find – with Morgan or with anyone – that's better than what I already have with David?"

"David is a wonderful man, and I won't take that away from him," Livvie responded, taking the ice cream from my hand and digging her spoon to the bottom. "The thing is, 'safe' is very nice and all, but the goal in the game of love is to find a man that makes your toes tingle. Don't even try telling me you feel the same spark with David that you feel when you're around Morgan."

I ignored the question, not willing to divulge the answer. "You don't understand. David toddled into the hospital the day I was born. He's been there for every important moment in my life. He and Jeremy and Eddie are the only family I have. He's my rock."

I turned to Gloria, hoping she might better understand what I was trying to say. "Isn't all of that more important than a few tingling toes?"

Gloria's kind, but condescending smile threw me. "Sarah, dear, if there is one thing I've learned during my many years on this Earth, it's that there is nothing in this world more important than tingling toes."

I picked at the threads of my afghan, letting my friends' words seep in. I didn't love David, and it would have been cruel to let him think I did. "I did the right thing, didn't I?" I asked softly, still not looking up.

"You did the right thing," Livvie reassured, moving to sit next to me on the couch.

"What am I going to do without David to talk to every day?" I asked, aiming the question at myself more than either woman beside me. "I never even had a chance to tell him about my promotion. Who do I go crying to when Morgan does dump me or Cory lures him away? Who am I going to call in the middle of the night when I get freaked out about life in general?"

I lifted my head in time to see a meaningful glance pass between my friends.

"Do you want to tell her or should I?" Gloria asked.

"I think it will sound better coming from you."

Gloria took the challenge, reached over and grasped my hand. "Sarah, dear, without David around to lean on, you'll have to take care of yourself."

"We'll still be here for the things you can't handle," Livvie jumped in, trying to help. "But some of the things you relied on David for, you could always do yourself, anyway."

That wasn't the answer I was looking for.

"I'm scared."

Livvie nodded, not surprised at my confession. "I get scared every single day, Bennett. It's part of the initiation rite to adulthood. Congratulations, you're now a grown-up."

"Being a grown-up is hard."

"Yes, it is, but you're not alone, Sarah," Gloria said. "You always have your family, and I include David in that grouping. It's just that you need to allow him a little time on his own, during which you both will have the opportunity to grow."

"Besides," Livvie winked. "It's the hard that makes it great."

I groaned. "Tom Hanks. *A League of their Own.* Can we please get through the rest of the night without any more movie references?"

Livvie threw a pillow my way, which started me on a giggling fit, then finally into full-fledged laughter. Granted, it was a little giddier than normal, but I was amazed to find that it was still there.

*   *   *

Four nights later I heard someone rap softly on the back door of my apartment. Knowing that door could be reached only from the diner, it could be only one person.

"Come on in," I called. "It's open."

"I thought I told you to keep the door locked when you're in here alone," Uncle Jeremy admonished.

"I just unlocked it. I'm expecting Livvie to drop by with a movie later, and didn't want to have to stop what I was doing to rush to the door."

He looked at the plate of whoopee pies I'd just finished making and sniffed appreciatively. "So, I suppose these are all for Livvie, then?"

"Help yourself." I walked to the refrigerator and poured a large glass of milk. Turning away from my uncle gave me a moment to steady my nerves and my slightly trembling hands.

I had been on pins and needles waiting for Jeremy since my confrontation with David. I'd called Jeremy the next day to tell him about my promotion, but I'd steered the conversation clear of his sons and had successfully avoided a face-to-face meeting until now.

"These are very good, kiddo. We should put them on the menu downstairs." He reached for the milk and washed down half a pie in one bite. He looked up, but instead of opening his mouth to speak, became involved with my dessert tray once more. He took several long minutes selecting another treat and chomping into it.

Okay. Jeremy clearly wasn't about to start the conversation, so it was up to me to say something or risk losing my entire night's work to his nerve-induced appetite. "I'm sorry." I managed, my eyes downcast at my task, focused on keeping the cream filling on its target.

"What for?"

"Are you serious?" I squeezed the pastry bag a little too tight, and it went oozing onto the counter as I stammered, "I mean, I assumed Eddie told you. David and I..."

I must have made a pathetic picture, because Jeremy immediately took pity on me by coming around the counter to wrap his arms around me. "Shush. I know what happened with David. I just don't know why you're sorry."

"You're not mad at me?" I asked, needing to hear the actual words.

Jeremy sighed and stepped backward a bit so I could see his face. "If I live to be a hundred, I will never understand women. Why on earth do you think I'd be angry with you?"

"I hurt David."

Jeremy and I both flinched at my simple answer, but he did not remove his hand from my arm.

"Yes. Yes, I imagine you did. But if he's hurt, it's only because you told him the truth. I respect that, and so will David."

I gave him a hesitant smile before I returned to my baking. For the next few minutes we exchanged harmless small talk about the tropical storm brewing off Bermuda, the fishing lure he'd picked up and whether the Yankees' loss last night was enough to keep the Sox alive. The easy banter wasn't enough, though, to keep Jeremy from picking up on my unease.

"Is there something else on your mind, kiddo?"

I took a beat, trying to decide whether I should pretend I didn't hear him. Finally working up the nerve, I whispered, "I guess I was just scared."

That caught Jeremy's attention. His head bobbed up from his plate, and his face suddenly became very stern. None of his kids were allowed to be frightened on his watch. "Who has you scared? Of what?"

"You, David and Eddie. You're all the family I have, and I thought I might have screwed it up. I won't be able to stand it if I lose you all."

"Why would you lose us?" Jeremy was clearly puzzled now.

"Come on, Jeremy. David told me he needed to back out of my life for a while. That has to impact my relationship with you. David is your son. I know you love me, but I'm not your blood."

Instead of the empathetic, gentle expression I was used to seeing, I was surprised when an emotion I didn't expect – was it anger? – shimmered briefly across Jeremy's features. "You just put that nonsense out of your head right now."

"I was being silly, I know." I gave a wan smile, trying to convince my uncle that I was sure of my place in the Thornton family. I must has failed, because he shoved the final piece of his second pastry in his mouth, placed the fork on the side of his plate and motioned for me to take the counter seat next to him.

"If that education of yours taught you anything, Sarah, I would have thought that you had figured out that blood is not a factor when it comes to being a member of a family."

I pulled my chair closer, trying to draw from the larger man's strength. "I wish I felt differently, Jeremy. I hate knowing that I've been hurting David for such a long time."

"Oh, Sarah." The flash of anger was gone, as Jeremy's features instead expressed the pain of a man who would do anything to take away the hurt his child was feeling. "You stay right here next to your Uncle Jeremy while he tells you a little bedtime story."

I smiled indulgently, leaned my elbow on the counter and asked, "Are you going to tell me a fairy tale about a beautiful princess to take my mind off my troubles?"

"You know I don't tell fairy tales." Jeremy smiled, then after having thought about it further said, "Well, maybe I do, actually.

You see, I'm going to tell you the story about how I fell in love with your Aunt Connie. Do you know where I met her?"

I shook my head. "No."

"I met Connie – her maiden name was LaChance – at the 1962 Policeman's Ball in Baltimore, Maryland. You know that your daddy and I were partners in Baltimore for a few years before we ended up in Portland, right?"

I nodded, remembering bits and pieces of how Jeremy and my father had met in Baltimore, worked together, and then somehow both transferred to Portland, Maine. Since my mom was born and raised here, I assumed she was somehow a key in their relocation, but I had never been told the exact chronology.

"Well, Connie was at the ball on the arm of another officer. Your daddy was her date that night."

"Aunt Connie was out on a date with dad?" I exclaimed, mildly scandalized. "How did that happen?"

"The dance was their first date. She was a nurse on the pediatric ward of Baltimore General, and a friend of your dad's was a doctor there. He set it up."

"So what happened? Did you glance at each other across the crowded room, fall into each other's arms and dance the night away?"

Jeremy smiled wistfully. "That would have been nice, but that's not quite what happened. You see, she and your father hit it off right from the start. I stole one dance with her when your father went to get us all some punch, but that was it."

"What do you mean 'that was it'?" I nudged at his arm. "When did you realize you were in love with her?"

"Oh, I knew instantly," he responded. "One dance and I was a goner. But, you see, she was there with your father. He was just as crazy about her as I was, so I couldn't say anything."

"For how long?"

Jeremy raised his chin and studied the ceiling as he thought about the answer. "I'd say the two of them ended up dating for nearly a year."

"A year!"

"A little less, maybe." Jeremy backtracked, surprised by my astonishment. "I'd tag along as often as I could just to be near her. The three of us were inseparable. Your daddy, God bless him, never complained, but I always felt like a third wheel."

"Why didn't you say anything?" I demanded. Although I knew the end of the story – that my father would eventually meet and marry my mother – it was alarming to realize how things could have gone in a drastically different direction.

"I couldn't. Your father was my best friend, and he was in love with Connie, too. He was saving up to buy a ring, you know. Getting ready to pop the question."

"My dad and Aunt Connie?" I had completely forgotten the food I was cooking, and was instead enthralled by the tale my uncle was weaving. "Jeremy, you are seriously freaking me out!"

"Do you want me to stop?"

"God, no!" I needed to hear this story out to its conclusion.

Jeremy nodded, seeming to understand. "One day there was a riot down on the waterfront. It was the early sixties, and Maryland had some particularly ugly times back then. So on this day – for some reason I remember it was a Thursday – two Baltimore officers were shot.

"As soon as the situation was contained, every spare cop in town turned up at the hospital to check on their condition. I'm still not sure exactly how it happened – I guess Connie heard that an officer was down, but didn't know who it was."

"You're not sure exactly how what happened?" I prompted.

"Your father and I were in the waiting room of the emergency division when I looked down the corridor and saw Connie fly around the corner toward us. She had this enormous look of relief on her face as she saw your father and me standing there. She must have been terribly worried." Jeremy broke off, lost in his memories.

"And?"

"Well, when Connie finally came running into the Emergency Room, she didn't have time to think about what she was doing. She ran past your father and fell into my arms, instead."

Whoa.

I bit on my lip, experiencing a phantom pain on my father's behalf for a heartache that was now more than thirty years old.

"I swear I had no idea how she felt about me until I held her in my arms that day. She was horrified when she realized what she'd done. We talked to your father, explained that neither of us had meant for this to happen, and begged him to forgive us."

"Obviously he did." I responded, trying to get over my misplaced feeling of betrayal. Certainly if my father had forgiven the couple, there was no need for me to hold a grudge based on an event born five years before me.

"You know your father. He said he forgave us, but we could see the hurt that we'd caused. But, we were young and in love, and I'm ashamed to say it didn't mean as much to us as it should. Connie and I decided we'd already wasted enough time apart, and decided to marry within the month."

"March 22." I chimed, knowing the date of Jeremy's anniversary by heart. It was ironic that a date that had once promised such happiness was now circled on my calendar to remind me to pick up a memorial wreath on the way to the cemetery.

"Your father Edmund was my best man, of course. He was a true friend to stand beside me in church, then to make a toast at our reception." Jeremy rose and went to the refrigerator to pour a second glass of milk. "You know, I thought I knew the meaning of courage, but I never really saw it until your father raised his glass to me and my new wife in a room full of our friends."

"What happened? How did you all get past it and get to be friends again?" I hoped Jeremy's story ended with a life lesson that would give me hope for my future relationship with David.

"There was a point when I didn't think it was possible," Jeremy admitted. "Connie and I got back from our honeymoon and your father was gone. He'd quit the force, and left me a note saying he couldn't be around us for a while. Asked us both to forgive him and said I shouldn't try to find him."

I rubbed my eyes with the heels of my hands, frustrated beyond all measure. "Why have I never heard this story before? I can't imagine Daddy running away from anything. Did you go find him? What happened?"

"I did the exact opposite of what he asked, of course. I contacted my friends in the police unions up and down the coast until I found out he had gotten a job in Portland, Maine. Once I knew he was safe, I did what he asked and waited. We didn't hear from him for more than two years."

"Two years?"

"Yup. Two years later, the doorbell rang, and a man in a blue uniform handed me an envelope." Jeremy pulled his cracked leather wallet from his back pocket and pulled out a faded piece of yellow paper. He unfolded it and handed it to me, pointing to the "Western Union" label on the top, and the date, September 23, 1966.

GETTING MARRIED SATURDAY STOP NEED A BEST MAN AND HIS BEST GIRL STOP MISS YOU BOTH STOP PLEASE COME

I ran my finger lovingly over the keepsake Jeremy had kept close to him for so many years. Touching the memento of my parents' history, the animosity I'd felt toward my father's best friend since this story had begun, vanished instantly.

"Long story short, we caught the next train to Portland and just never left. Connie and your mama got on like a house afire. Meanwhile, your daddy and I picked up where we left off without missing a beat."

I handed the telegram back to Jeremy and watched him line up the creases perfectly to prevent more from appearing. "What happened to your lives in Baltimore?"

"Baltimore was just a place," Jeremy shrugged. "Portland was a home. Connie had already quit her job when she found out she was expecting David. She was six months along when we came for the wedding, and before our return trip she started cramping. There were some complications, and she was told she shouldn't travel. Back in those days the Police unions were like big fraternities and made up of some good men. I got an emergency leave and transferred to Portland. Your daddy's partner stepped aside and we worked together like nothing had ever happened. The rest, as they say, is history."

I shook my head in disbelief. "I think I'm in shock."

"I didn't mean to shock you, Sarah. I just wanted to explain that I truly believe people don't have the ability to choose who they love. Things would be very simple, and life would go a lot more smoothly if they could, but it just doesn't happen that way."

Since his story had apparently rendered me mute, he continued, "Connie should have fallen in love with your father. He was smart, handsome, funny and a few years younger than his broken-down old partner. More than that, he was just crazy about her."

"So were you," I reminded him.

"That's true, but I never would have acted on it. Loving Connie was the hardest and most selfish thing I've ever done, before or since. Your father was able to understand that I didn't have a choice, and I don't know how, but he forgave us both."

"Did my mother know this story?" I asked, wondering what she thought about my father's history with Aunt Connie.

"Your mother knew everything about everything, kiddo." Jeremy winked at me. "And I know what you're really asking. Let me assure you that your mama had absolute faith in exactly three things: the love of her husband and child, her Irish heritage and God. In that order. I remember that Mandy used to say that the first person you loved earned a place in your heart, but the last person you loved earned a place in your soul."

"What else did she say, Jeremy?" I said, eyes filling as they always did when I heard stories of my mother.

"Well, I remember how she used to slip me an extra piece of pie sometimes when Edmund wasn't looking. She said it was payment for stealing Connie away and giving your daddy the chance to find the woman he was meant to love all along." My uncle walked behind me and took me in his arms. "All we can do now is sit back and hope the same miracle happens for David."

"I want that more than anything," I whispered.

"Me, too, kiddo. Me, too."

September

I SCRAPED MY FORK around the inside of the cake pan, looking to consume the final remnants of frosting. It was funny how the same action had felt bitter and desperate only a year ago. Today, despite the fact I had turned the corner into true adulthood and was now the dreaded age of thirty, the only feeling I could readily put a finger on was that of contentment.

Sensing my contemplative mood, Livvie asked, "So, how are you doing with the big 3-0, anyway?"

"Believe it or not, I'm okay. Of course, a big party in my honor didn't exactly hurt." I smiled, then admonished, "I told you not to make a fuss."

"Eh. You didn't really mean it. Everyone wants a fuss made on their birthday."

Livvie was probably right. As much as I had complained that I didn't want a party, there was nothing worse than having a birthday ignored outright. Besides, I couldn't pretend that I didn't feel a small rush of joy when I walked into the darkened diner only to have friends and family jump out and wish me a happy birthday.

Livvie – with help from her band of merry men – had done an amazing job transforming the space from a diner into a fall wonderland of twinkle lights, balloons, flowers and harvest decorations. I had no idea how Jeremy was going to get the place in shape for the morning crowd, but he, Eddie and Morgan had pushed me upstairs after the party was over and wouldn't even consider letting me help straighten up. Instead, Livvie had grabbed my leftover cake and presents and corralled me upstairs to keep out of the way of the cleaning crew.

"Maybe you're right and I did want a little bit of a fuss," I admitted. "But you went above and beyond. It was almost perfect."

I hoped my friend would take no offense at my statement that the event was slightly less than ideal. The place, atmosphere and music were spot on. It wasn't even the attendees that were a problem. Livvie had outdone herself on the invitation list and ensured that my birthday party found me surrounded by friends from high school, college and law school as well as our neighbors and regulars from the diner. To my delight, even Trenton had made a brief appearance. Despite this large group, though, there was a huge void in the room.

"I wish David had come," I sighed, finally putting a voice to the mild melancholy I'd felt all night.

"I know, Sarah. I guess it was still just a little soon for him"

I nodded, agreeing with the words, but failing to find much comfort in them.

"And don't forget, it's not like he blew off your birthday altogether."

Livvie was right in that point. I had received the unexpected birthday gift of a phone call from my friend. It was the first contact we'd had since the breakdown in Jeremy's kitchen, and while the conversation had been more than a little strained, it was tangible proof that David Thornton was not completely out of my life.

"It's a start." I agreed. Then trying to change the subject to something more pleasant, I remarked, "Hey, were you as surprised as I was that Frank actually showed up?"

"Are you kidding? Frank Murphy at a party? It must be some kind of sign of the apocalypse."

"Thanks for inviting him."

Livvie punched me lightly on the arm. "Only for you, Bennett. I want you to know how much it killed me to call that man and politely invite him to attend your party as my guest. I still shudder at the memory. I've got freaking PTSD on account of you."

"Well, I do appreciate it. It meant a lot that he showed up, especially since he's still so pissed off with me."

"Is he still blaming you for the fact Morgan quit the firm?" At my confirming nod, Livvie shook her head in disgust. "You said it was Morgan's dream to switch to public defense law. I mean, the fact you made partner just spurred him along. It's not like the only reason he quit was because he wanted to sexually harass his boss."

"Thank you for that very classy summary." I blushed furiously at the nugget of truth in Livvie's statement, remembering the day after my promotion when I had finally crawled out of my bed of depression over David, called Morgan and asked if we could meet for dinner. I had desperately needed some cheering up and hoped that the news of my partnership would be something he could help me celebrate. We met at my favorite burger place and found a booth tucked far in the back where we ordered beers and (with a slight nod to a certain purple suede skirt), I stuck to a vegetarian burger, no bun.

"So what's up?" Morgan asked after our meals had been delivered and small talk exhausted. Wrapping his mouth around a greasy bacon burger that made my mouth water, he continued, "You were on top of the world yesterday at the office but today you seem a little down."

I gave points to Morgan's powers of perception. "I guess I am. I had a fight with David yesterday and it ended pretty badly."

"Do you want to talk about it?"

"Not really. I appreciate it, but I want to talk to you about why I was so happy yesterday. I've been talking to Frank for a few months about the possibility of becoming a partner in the firm. Yesterday he made an official offer. You are looking at the new junior partner at the firm of Murphy and Bennett!"

I was practically buzzing with anticipation, waiting to see Morgan's reaction, but either he was the most low-key celebrator I'd ever seen, or I had completely overestimated his reaction. Waiting out the silence as long as I could – which, knowing my tolerance wasn't really all that long at all. I deflated over my plate of zucchini fries at Morgan's lack of response. "Great. You think Frank is making a mistake, don't you? You think I can't handle the responsibility and I'm going to be the ruin of his firm."

"No! Not at all." I took Morgan's startled denial as a good sign. While his enthusiasm for my partnership was underwhelming, at least his belief in my talents as an attorney did not seem faked. "I think Frank would be an idiot not to promote you to partner. I'm sorry I'm not as excited as you thought I would be. I guess I just never considered the possibility that you could become my boss."

In some dusty back corner of my brain I'd been afraid that Morgan would not be jumping up and down with the news of my new title, but had chosen to ignore the possibility until forced to confront it. "Does that bother you?"

"Bother me? No." I searched his eyes and found only the truth. "It does complicate things a bit, though. Like with Frank. I mean, does he even know we're dating?"

I shook my head and stole an onion ring from Morgan's plate. "Not unless you told him after I left the office yesterday. You saw his reaction when he found out his secretary had a personal life. Frank doesn't believe in personal lives."

"What do you think he's going to do when he finds out he promoted you to partner – that you're technically now my boss – and that we've been seeing each other behind his back for the last several weeks?"

"Frank is going to lose his shit," I answered. In reality, I'd hoped to wait until I was sure of my relationship with Morgan before we went public with my boss, but now that I was partner at the firm, I knew I owed Frank my complete loyalty. We were going to have to come clean and soon.

"Yup." Morgan considered that thought for a moment, then took a large bite out of his burger. His mouth more than half full, he remarked, "Well, then, I guess there's only one thing to be done."

I nodded, feeling worse than I had felt the day before if that was possible. If I'd realized earlier that this date with Morgan would be my last, I definitely would have ordered the onion rings. Hoping it wouldn't hurt quite so much if I was the one to say it, I straightened my shoulders, "We have to stop seeing each other."

"We do?" His eyes popped open, surprised as they searched mine. "I was going to say that I have to quit."

"Quit?"

"Well, yeah. I mean, I told you before that Frank doesn't take on the kind of cases that really interest me. I want to do criminal defense work and if I'm going to pursue it, now is as good a time as any. I can't work for you and still date you, and I still want to date you."

It took me a moment to realize Morgan had stopped talking as I replayed the last few moments of my life. Morgan wanted to keep seeing me. I meant enough to him that he was willing to quit his job.

Talk about an unexpected turn in the conversation.

"Sarah."

I looked up, startled to find Moran gazing at me intently if not a bit nervously. "Huh?"

"Just so you know, now might be a good time to say you want to keep dating me, too."

No wonder he looked nervous. Morgan's declaration of his feelings had been met with only silence. He actually thought I might reject him. "Oh, yes. I'm sorry. Absolutely, yes. I got a little drifty there for a minute, but I do want to keep seeing you. Definitely."

"Okay, then. It's settled. Tomorrow morning I'll go to Frank and give him my notice."

Not wanting to jinx the moment, but needing to be sure Morgan understood the consequences of his actions, I asked, "What about your dad? Wasn't he less than thrilled with the idea of you doing criminal defense?"

His soft laughter at my question was not entirely based on humor. "Yeah. I thought about that, too. The fact is, I don't want to spend my life practicing a certain type of law just because my father finds it more respectable than the law I want to practice."

Polishing off his meal with a shrug, Morgan continued. "I'm 28 years old. If I can't stand up to my father about my choice of careers now, I might as well just cut them off, hand them over to Dad now and be done with it."

I wasn't sure how to respond to such vivid imagery. "If those are your only two choices, I'd like to put in my vote that quitting is definitely the best one."

"Yeah, me too." Morgan picked up his last onion ring and became quite consumed with using it to paint paths through the ketchup pile remaining on his plate. "So, now that we have that settled, I guess we only have one more thing to discuss."

Morgan's tone was serious, and from the nervous way he was playing with his food, I assumed the subject matter would be uncomfortable. I made a brave attempt not to prematurely freak out.

"Do you remember the conversation we had on our first date? In the car?"

Did I remember? Was he kidding? I managed a nod.

"Yeah, well, your timing was lousy, but the topic was a good one and I'm ready to talk about it now." Morgan sighed and pushed back his plate before raising his eyes to mine. "I'd really like it if you agreed not to see other people."

"I don't want to see other people." I rushed out in a single breath, glad we weren't playing poker, as I had apparently lost any ability to bluff while simultaneously pushing my chips all in. "What about you?"

"I don't want to date anyone else, either."

"Well, then..." I was shockingly at a loss for words, especially when he took my hand and began softly rubbing the inside of my left wrist with his thumb. "I guess that settles that, then?"

"I guess so. Although," Morgan chuckled to himself, "I feel kind of sorry for you."

"In what way?"

"Well, I'm dating a hotshot attorney who is partner at her law firm. You're dating a soon-to-be unemployed law student. I totally got the better end of this deal."

"I guess it is a lucky thing that you're so pretty, then." I moved my free hand to cover his. "Never underestimate the power of a little eye candy."

"Oh, so I'm eye candy, am I?" Morgan challenged, his grin showing he was in on the joke.

"Yup." To prove my point I grabbed the check the waiter had set down moments ago and put down my AmEx as payment. "Of course, if you think you have skills or talents I'm unaware of, I'd be happy to hear you out."

"I think I'd like a chance to defend my honor, Miss Bennett. I mean, I'd hate to think you were only after my looks. Perhaps we should take this discussion somewhere more private."

I agreed, feeling lighter and happier than I had in months. And just for the record…that night Morgan proved he was more than just a piece of eye candy.

The next day, we walked together the few blocks from my apartment to the office and caught Frank in his office early to confess our sins.

As expected, Frank lost his shit.

Unexpectedly, he was less concerned by the fact Morgan and I were dating than by Morgan's resignation. Oh, the dating bothered him, of course. Frank was angry and amazed that we'd shown the gall to allow our personal lives to invade his law practice, but after half an hour of huffing and puffing, he finally calmed to the point that he was ready to hear Morgan's big news.

At that point the ranting began again in earnest. It turned out that what really bothered my new partner was the fact Morgan could possibly be interested in practicing a type of law that Frank didn't personally endorse. Entirely dismissive of our relationship, he focused concern on Morgan's career and future legal prospects, alone.

I tried not to take it personally.

I was incredibly proud of Morgan's reaction in the face of Frank's childlike tantrum. He deftly countered each argument and at the end of their heated discussion, while not exactly supportive, Frank at least respected his protégée's decision that it was time to move on.

As I knew would be the case, and without any basis in logic, Frank blamed me entirely. Luckily, forcing me to bear the burden of the hiring process as we set about replacing Morgan amused Frank to no end and served to fulfill my penance.

"Just the fact that he came to my party tonight shows that he's started to forgive me." I remarked to Livvie while ghosting a finger across the screen of my shiny new iPad, the overly extravagant gift from my friend. "As soon as I hire a new intern for him to torture, we'll be back to normal."

"Speaking of interns…" Livvie pointed to my apartment door being opened at that very moment by the newest intern at a mid-size Portland law firm that just happened to specialize in criminal defense.

"Hey there." As I crossed the room for a quick kiss from my boyfriend, I wondered briefly what the shelf life was on the blissful early stages of love. I hoped it fell somewhere on the continuum near Spam. Morgan caught what must have been an odd expression on my face and gave me a bemused grin in return. "What are you thinking about?"

"Spam," I admitted, sheepishly. "I'm thinking that Spam has a pretty long shelf life."

Livvie and Morgan shared a look undecipherable by me, but one which caused Livvie to rise from her stool and grab at her coat. "And on that note, I'm turning the birthday girl over to her night warden. Day shift is over."

Morgan held out Livvie's coat for her. "I'm sorry to see you go, but you should probably get home. Donnie called the diner twice wondering if you'd left yet."

"Speaking of Donnie..." I turned to my friend. "Your ex was on his best behavior tonight. He bought me a lovely gift and chatted up Uncle Jeremy for nearly an hour. He didn't even try to look down my blouse. Not once!"

Livvie ducked her head, grinning slightly. "I know. I really don't know what's come over him. Ever since I told him I'm not interested in a relationship, it's like he turned over a new leaf."

"Maybe he's trying to woo you," Morgan laughed.

"Maybe," she agreed. "I don't know what it is, but I know I like it. He's attentive and sweet and generous, but he's still just snarky enough for me to know it's still my Donnie."

I was worried for my friend, concerned that her ex-husband was intrigued by Livvie's refusal to commit, and that if she ever ended the chase and allowed Donnie to catch her, he would again move on to other pastures. Even so, I couldn't ignore the fact that the man had been incredibly well-behaved as of late.

"Tell Donnie thank you again for me." I hugged my friend at the door and said goodbye. "And don't forget to remind him I will kill him if he hurts you again."

"Done," she replied happily, closing the door behind her.

"Are you turning in?" Morgan asked, walking toward the bedroom, obviously tired from the post-party clean up.

"Not yet. Go ahead and I'll be there in a while."

"Don't stay up too late, birthday girl." He kissed the tip of my nose before heading to bed.

Birthday girl.

I was a 30 year old birthday girl.

I sat heavily on the couch, amazed that an entire year had passed since the last time I'd blown out candles. So much had occurred in such a short time. I had a wonderful relationship and was partner in a law firm. Of course, the year hadn't exactly gone smoothly. I mean, I missed David like crazy and although I had accomplished a lot, there were still a number of items I hadn't accomplished from my original list.

Lightning struck suddenly as I rushed to grab a pen and piece of scrap paper. I was only thirty years old! Everyone knew that thirty was the new twenty. Well, everyone who worked at Cosmopolitan magazine, anyway.

I needed a new list –a list of things I would accomplish by the time I hit 35. By then, I would certainly be married. If nothing else, I could drag my purple suede dreams out of mothballs and trim down to a size six within five years.

Excitedly committing my plans to paper, I decided that if my weight loss regime included hiking, I could put Mt. Katahdin back on my list.

"Sarah?"

I looked up and saw an adorably sleep-rumpled Morgan stagger out from the bedroom in mid-stretch. "What are you doing?"

"Nothing." I lied unconvincingly. Stepping behind the couch to read over my shoulders, Morgan took in the partial list I'd written and sighed deeply. "Okay, Sarah. Put down the pen and back away slowly."

"But…"

"Sarah."

"But, Morgan," I protested weakly as he forcibly removed the pen from my clutches and pulled me away from the living room.

I hesitated briefly as I considered my options. On the one hand I had a black sharpie marker, crumpled sheet of notebook paper and dreams of thinner thighs.

Behind door number two was a smart, beautiful, real-live boy trying to lead me to my bedroom.

Yeah. Pretty much no contest.

With a wicked smile, I fell into step behind Morgan.

Besides, I could always finish the list tomorrow.

The End

MORE GREAT READS FROM BOOKTROPE

One Week **by Nikki Van De Car** (Coming-of-age novel) Celebutant Bee wants nothing to do with fame, so she takes off from LA to find her own identity. Little does she know that one week can change everything.

Grace Unexpected **by Gale Martin** (Contemporary Romance) When her longtime boyfriend dumps her instead of proposing, Grace avows the sexless Shaker ways. She appears to be on the fast track to a marriage proposal… until secrets revealed deliver a death rattle to the Shaker Plan.

Riversong **by Tess Hardwick** (Contemporary Romance) Sometimes we must face our deepest fears to find hope again. A redemptive story of forgiveness and friendship.

Thank You For Flying Air Zoe **by Erik Atwell** (Contemporary Women's Fiction) Realizing she needs to awaken her life's tired refrains, Zoe vows to recapture the one chapter of her life that truly mattered—her days as drummer for an all-girl garage band. Will Zoe bring the band back together and give The Flip-Flops a second chance at stardom?

Lark Eden **by Natalie Symons** (General Fiction) A play chronicling the friendship of three Southern women over seventy-five years. At once a deeply moving and darkly comic look at the fingerprints that we unknowingly leave on the hearts of those we love.

…and many more!

Sample our books at:
www.booktrope.com

Learn more about our new approach to publishing at:
www.booktropepublishing.com

CPSIA information can be obtained at www.ICGtesting.com
Printed in the USA
BVOW011340061112

304742BV00001B/23/P

9 781935 961727